THE SEVENTH CALLER

A NOVEL

JOHNNA HOWELL

This book is a work of fiction. Names, characters, places and incidents either are products of the author's imagination, or are used fictitiously. Any resemblance to actual events or locales or persons living or dead is entirely coincidental.

ISBN: 10:1456402897
ISBN-13:978-1456402891

DEDICATION

To Donna Littrell Treat
My sister—My friend
1948-2009

And to the Lord Almighty; the Only Wise God;
who Was, and Is, and Is To Come

If my people, who are called by my name, will humble themselves and pray
and seek my face and turn from their wicked ways, then will I hear from
heaven and will forgive their sin and will heal their land.
II Chronicles 7:14

.

ACKNOWLEDGMENTS

A number of people have contributed greatly to the completion of this book. They have my sincere gratitude and thanks.

The first, and most important, my husband, Jerry Howell, my soul mate and spouse for over three decades. The Lord couldn't have blessed me with a better life partner.

Reviewers: These individuals took time out of their busy lives to read the manuscript in its rawest forms: several even volunteered their services multiple times. Bless them. They have provided invaluable insights that have enhanced the end product substantially: Christine Faria, Tracey Turner, Dianna Littrell, Melissa and Julia Chamberlain, Susie Thorkelson Garcia, Susan Hasekamp, Vivian Valentine, Jennifer Upp, and Laura Nelson.

To my son, Jeff Turner and son-in-law Darlino Faria a special thanks for supporting me by supporting their wives as they helped with editing and re-write reviews.

Editorial Services: Judy Bodmer, a long time friend, fellow author, professional editor, and new grandmother, provided her most excellent insights, guidance, and teaching. Because of her, the characters are richer and the story more thrilling.

Last, but not least, my wonderful grandchildren, who light up my life on a daily basis; Manuel, Mikayla, Jeremy, Lauren, and Reagan.

PROLOGUE

The warm afternoon sun flickered through the giant California redwoods that surrounded the campfire circle where twelve-year-old Megyn Buckman straddled a log. This was her fourth year to attend the High Sierra Christian Camp, and she desperately missed her best friends Jenny and Penny, twin sisters from the Sunday school class she sometimes attended at her grandparents' church.

She pushed the forest debris around with her dusty white tennis shoes. Her mind was on her disastrous morning. She had sat next to the bus window, her legs extended across the seat to save two places. She watched as each car dropped off eager campers. Her anxiety had increased as the minutes ticked closer to their departure time. Then the bus driver started the engine and closed the doors. The Camp Director unhooked the microphone from the dashboard. "Jenny and Penny will not be able to join us. Their grandfather in New Jersey has fallen ill and the girls left this morning with their mom and brother to take care of him. They won't be returning."

Now Megyn sat alone with six long days stretching ahead. She didn't make new friends easily and loneliness overwhelmed her heart.

"Here it is," said a petite girl entering the arena from the path to Megyn's right. "This is the campfire circle. Every night we sit on these logs and roast marshmallows, sing songs, pray, and share. It's the best part of camp."

The three girls took in the area, and together they noticed Megyn. The leader pushed her long brown hair away from her face

1

revealing huge hazel eyes. "I'm Rosey and this is Sarah and Rachel. It's their first time to come to camp and I'm showing them around. Aren't you the girl that usually hangs out with the twins?"

Megyn made an effort to straighten her drooping shoulders. "They couldn't come."

"Want to hang with us?" asked Rachel. "We're headed back to the cabin to play a game before dinner."

Megyn shrugged. "Sure."

Rosey led the way up the narrow winding path. She jabbered about places and events along the way. They stopped at the third cabin. "We're in here, Megyn. Where are you?"

"I'm in Dogwood, just over there."

"Would you like to stay with us? We have an extra bed."

Megyn brightened. "I'll go get my stuff."

"While you're doing that we'll get the game ready," said Rosey.

~

Megyn watched as Sarah and Rosey set the Ouija board between them on their knees. Rachel read from the directions, "Place the planchette in the center and rest your fingertips lightly on either side. That's the plastic triangle." She checked the instructions once again. "Now invite the spirits to join you."

The girls did as they were instructed and then Sarah closed her eyes and whispered softly. "Is anyone there that would like to talk with us?"

Nothing happened.

She asked again.

Nothing.

"Can I try?" Rachel said.

She swapped places with Rosey, closed her eyes, and asked the question once more. This time the planchette moved slowly to the word "Yes" and stopped.

Megyn felt her stomach tighten.

Sarah took the lead. "What is your name?"

Again nothing happened.

"My name is Sarah. What's yours?"

The plastic triangle proceeded around the board stopping on the D and the S.

"Who are you DS?" asked Sarah.

"A-N-G-E-L," spelled the triangle.

"A good angel or a bad one?"

Megyn stared as the planchette glided to the corner and stopped on the word, "Good-bye."

Sarah prodded, but the pointer remained motionless.

Megyn was offered a turn with the suggestion that a different partner might bring renewed action. She positioned herself in front of Sarah, placed her fingertips on the triangle, and held her breath while Sarah gave the summons. It didn't respond. Megyn released the air from her lungs and relaxed her tense shoulders.

After that, no matter how they paired up, the pointer refused to budge. The dinner bell rang and they agreed to try again later. Megyn was grateful when the week finished with no further opportunities.

~

Megyn stood on Rosey's front porch holding the birthday and slumber party invitation in one hand and a present in the other. Her suitcase and sleeping bag were at her feet. Her grandmother waited in the car until the door opened, and waved good-bye when Megyn stepped into the Sanchez's living room.

This was her first sleep over. It had been a month since she'd seen her friends and was excited to stay up all night, watch movies, play games, tell stories, and eat lots of junk food. The birthday party went by fast, the guests left, and Rosey's family went to bed.

A half hour later Megyn, Rosey, Sarah, and Rachel sat on their sleeping bags in the basement game room slurping red hot jaw breakers and reminiscing about the great times they shared at camp. They then watched a scary movie and at one in the morning Sarah pulled out her Ouija board, placed one side on her knees and extended the other to Rosey.

"You first, Rosey, since you're the birthday girl."

Rosey laughed. "It didn't work with me last time. Play with Megyn. Her turn was cut short at camp."

Sarah pivoted toward Megyn. "Okay. Let's try again."

Megyn didn't like this game. She felt uneasy and wasn't sure why. Reluctantly she placed her fingertips on the edge of the plastic triangle.

"Is anyone there that would like to talk with us?" Sarah whispered.

The pointer remained in place.

"This is Sarah. Is anyone there?"

3

Again, no answer.

Megyn adjusted herself and giggled nervously. "I don't think it likes me. It worked with you and Rachel before. Maybe that's the best combination." She scooted over and motioned for Rachel to take her place.

Rachel eased forward and barely got her fingertips on the pointer when it began to whirl across the board pulling both girls' hands with it. Everyone was caught off guard and surprised at the speed in which it communicated. Rosey ran to the desk drawer, grabbed a pen and paper and wrote as fast as she could while Megyn called out the letters.

"W-H-E-R-E-H-A-V-E-Y-O-U-B-E-E-N-W-H-E-R-E-H-A-V-E-Y-O-U-B-E-E-N-W-H-E-R-E-H-A-V-E-Y-O-U-B-E-E-N."

Then, abruptly, it stopped.

Megyn leaned over to examine the hastily scribbled letters. "What does it say?"

Rosey held the pad up.

"It looks like 'Where have you been,'" said Megyn. "Maybe it wants to know why we haven't contacted it since camp."

"Okay, Rachel. Let's try again," Sarah said, her voice rising with excitement. "Are you DS?"

"W-H-E-R-E-H-A-V-E-Y-O-U-B-E-E-N?"

"We haven't been together and couldn't contact you until now. Would you like to talk?"

"A-B-O U-T-W-H-A-T?"

"Are you DS?" Sarah asked.

The planchette moved to the word "Yes" at the bottom of the board.

"What does DS stand for?"

"D-E-M-O-N S-P-I-R-I-T."

"You said you are an angel. Are you, or are you a demon?"

"Yes."

Megyn glanced around and spoke for the others who also looked confused. "We learned at camp that the devil is an angel who once followed God but turned against him and took other angels with him in his rebellion. Are you an angel that rejects God?"

"A-N-G-E-L."

"Can you prove you're real and not a figment of our subconscious minds?" said Sarah.

"L-O-O-K I-N C-L-O-S-E-T C-L-O-S-E D-O-O-R S-I-T O-N S-T-A-I-R-S F-I-V-E M-I-N-U-T-E-S."

Megyn rolled her eyes, shrugged, and opened the closet door. Rosey's mom was a meticulous housekeeper and everything was neat and organized. She followed her friends to the stairs, took a seat, and listened to the others nervously joke about what fools they were to follow instructions given by a board.

Five minutes later they checked the closet. Clothes were all over the place. Coats were turned inside out, shoes were balanced on hangers and sweaters were everywhere.

Megyn was shaking. "Put that thing away."

Sarah grabbed the box and shoved the board and pointer inside.

"Let's play one of the Christian CDs I bought at camp," said Rosey.

~

Megyn's phone rang.

"Guess what?" said Rosey. "Sarah invited Rachel to use the Ouija board again. They've communicated with DS at least ten more times in the last three months."

"You're kidding. That thing is dangerous."

Rosey's voice trembled. "They thought they could control him, but DS started to swear and curse every time they contacted him. He scratched Sarah's arm to prove his presence. And once he wrote something on a piece of paper when they were out of the room. Another time he made suggestive comments and when they told him they weren't going to contact him again, he threatened to hurt them and their families. Rachel blames Sarah and doesn't want to see her again. Sarah cried and said it was all her fault. They've been playing with the thing in her bedroom and now she's afraid to sleep in there. I don't know what to do. We've all been friends since we were toddlers. Now no one wants to talk to each other." She paused. "Megyn, I don't know what to do."

Megyn was silent. She didn't know either.

CHAPTER ONE

Turlock, California

Twenty-two year old Megyn Buckman examined her bank account for the hundredth time. One semester of graduate school remained, and she had no idea how she could earn the money to finish in May. She lived a frugal lifestyle, but most work schedules that would accommodate her heavy academic requirements didn't pay enough to cover books and tuition. The small inheritance she'd received from her grandparents was depleted two semesters ago, and her parents' substantial wealth disqualified her for student loans. Besides, they hadn't spoken in over three years, and contacting them for money was not an option.

She slumped forward, closed her eyes, and massaged her temples. She could see her grandparents seated together at the breakfast table; their heads bowed and hands clasped. Megyn remembered the peace she always experienced in their home. They said it was because they knew Jesus, and in her youth she'd believed them. But the opposite had been true in her house. Her life had been surrounded with her mother's alcoholism and her father's high control, and in her teen years, Megyn found it increasingly harder to believe in God. He had turned his back on her, so she turned her back on him.

In the background, the radio played "He's Got the Whole World in His Hands." She thought of her childhood once more. *If only that were true.* After the song ended, the announcer invited single listeners between the ages of eighteen and thirty to call in and win ten thousand dollars. "All you have to do is be the seventh caller and provide the name of the song I just played." The number was given and Megyn reached for her cell. *This must be a new contest. Oh, please, please. Let me be the seventh caller.* Her heart beat faster as she punched in the digits and got a busy signal. She paced the kitchen floor while pushing redial. On the fourth try she heard the phone ring and the host's voice tell her she was the seventh caller.

"What's your name?"

"Megyn."

"Okay Megyn, you're our seventh caller. Can you identify the song?"

She identified the tune, received hearty congratulations, and was handed off to the call screener who provided instructions on how to claim the money. "Be downtown at 6:00 tonight. Here's the address. You'll be given a briefing; sign papers, and receive your ten thousand dollar check. Bring proof of age and photo ID."

Megyn's head was spinning. She couldn't believe how her life had just changed so suddenly. Now she could finish school without money worries. She scooped her books into her backpack, hefted it onto her shoulder, and hurried to her final class of the day.

~

At 5:45 p.m. Megyn arrived at the hotel and located the penthouse suite. She rotated her shoulders and wiggled her fingers. *In and out quickly*, she told herself. *Get the money and finish school without their help.*

She was greeted by a warm, trim, gray-haired woman named Maria who shook her hand and offered her a seat. "Would you like a drink?" She pointed to the counter. "I've got sodas, bottled water, decaf coffee, and hot tea."

Megyn chose a bottled water and took the seat across from Maria. "Thank you. I was thirsty."

Maria smiled. "Everyone's a little nervous when we have these orientations. Let me tell you about our program."

Megyn stiffened. *What orientation. What program?*

"You're the seventh contestant in a group referred to as the Callers," Maria said. "You've been given this title because each of you randomly called into various pop radio stations across the nation and

7

named the correct tune. We varied the songs and stations, thus ensuring a totally random selection of winners."

Megyn licked her dry mouth. "I didn't know any of this. Why didn't the host explain?"

"I'm not sure. We provide a script. I can't imagine he didn't follow it." Maria searched her stack of papers. "Here it is."

Megyn looked it over. "I guess I missed the first part of his introduction. I was busy with other things and just caught the last couple of sentences."

Maria switched on her lap-top. "Watch this video and then let's talk."

Megyn's breath caught as images of her favorite TV show flashed across the screen. The Vanguard of Volunteer Voices, or V³, was the most popular program in history. Now in its third year, Megyn was to be a part of a movement targeted at the mobilization of young people throughout the world. Teenagers and twenty-somethings, students and non-students, were encouraged to work together to make the world a better place. No idea was too small, or too large. She thought of the houses, cars, food and money that had been given out over the last two seasons. She remembered the environmental efforts made by this group to restore waterways, and vegetation, as well as, the impact of their recycling achievements.

The voice from the video explained how the coalition had been launched through the reality show bearing its name. Technology allowed for global participation. Media-based communications were used to share ideas, post results, and promote the call to action.

The promo ended and Maria turned to Megyn. "As a Caller, you'll be one of seven iconic youth leaders to facilitate and drive global change." She leaned forward. "Megyn, this is a huge commitment. In just four months, you will be required to leave your current life behind for the next year and work nonstop for the Vanguard."

Megyn couldn't believe her luck. No interview or test was required. She simply made a phone call, and now her lifelong dream to make a difference was coming true. She felt excited and hesitant at the same time. She slowly nodded her head.

A schedule of required pre-work was placed in front of her. She would receive a call in the next week to coordinate times for her part in supporting the show's promotional needs. Photo shoots, a video profile, and interviews with the Associated Cable Network's staff would take place before her final move to Los Angeles. Megyn sat back and took a deep breath. Her hands started to tremble.

Maria touched her arm. "I know it's a bit overwhelming, but you'll find the ACN staff quite supportive. We will stay by you every step of the way."

Megyn smiled tentatively. "Okay. I'm placing my life in your hands."

Forms were filled out, papers signed, housing discussed, and her ten thousand dollar check handed over. To Megyn's surprise, she was also given the latest in high-tech communication devices. Maria demonstrated each one and explained they were prototypes not yet in the public marketplace. Her personal contact list was already transferred and key Caller and staff information she would need over the next year had been added.

Megyn thanked Maria and headed for home. She'd been excited about her upcoming internship with Fredrick and Wright, a premiere marketing agency in Northern California. Their campaigns targeting environmental issues were known throughout the world. Now, that opportunity seemed trivial. She would call them in the morning and resign.

She smiled and envisioned her parents' astonished expressions when they learned she was front and center in the most popular youth movement and television show ever. She knew her father would be furious he couldn't claim credit for her success. She was completing her education without his help and had managed to become involved in a chance of a lifetime, a chance to change the world for the better. She'd made it on her own and was finally free of his control.

~

A little before 3:00 in the morning, Megyn woke up. Her heart was pounding. *What have I gotten myself into?*

CHAPTER TWO

Four Months Later – Los Angeles, California

Ethan Strong and Mary Evans sat at the executive conference table surrounded by eight wealthy V³ Oversight Board members from around the world. While the video presented the profiles on the seven Callers, Mary scrolled through her lap-top for Ethan's follow-up discussion.

Ethan pointed his laser beam across the pictures. "As you know, these people were obtained randomly. Because of this, we have followed up with extensive background investigations, and our research has surfaced much more than these promotional materials tell us. Fortunately, our new Callers are all decent picks, and one in particular, is a real find. Let me quickly go through them again and provide you with additional information. Based on our prior conversation with the Board, Mary and I have devised a plan to best utilize each person."

Mary scrolled through the candid photographs as Ethan talked. "All are single, ages eighteen to thirty. We established these criteria so the new leaders would be available for extensive travel and relocation, and not require parental oversight."

"A couple of our Callers have a history of volunteering with canned food and clothing drives. One has served holiday meals at a homeless shelter, and another tutored Spanish speaking kids in math. To our delight, we also discovered that between them, Spanish,

Portuguese, and French are spoken. These abilities will be utilized with our global Vanguarders. Hobbies vary and include car repair, spelunking, poetry, photography, cooking, reading, and backpacking.

One of the board members chuckled. "Spelunking? Who's our cave explorer?"

"Believe it or not, that would be Tawny," Ethan said. "You would never have guessed it with her thin physique and soft spoken demeanor.

"The last two Callers carry the most promise. We plan to use them to lead large youth rallies. Bret Steward is twenty-seven and from Arlington, Texas. He has a Master of Divinity and is the worship leader of a Christian church of about five thousand. He plays the guitar, sings, and speaks at Christian high school and college-age gatherings throughout the United States and a few other countries. Apparently, he is fairly well-known in Christian circles. We don't want to single out specific religious groups, but Mary and I believe he has the potential to attract millions of youth across the globe."

A middle-aged red head with a tight bun and no makeup cleared her throat. "I would like to caution you; we also need to leverage other spiritual groups. It is imperative we stay focused on our goals and not allow ourselves to become entangled in disputes about religion."

"Mary and I agree completely," Ethan said. "In fact, we've already contacted other key faith-based leaders and assure you we're actively pursuing diverse involvement."

Ethan grinned up at the last picture. "As you know, our seventh Caller is Megyn Buckman. She's twenty-two and recently completed a master's degree in marketing. According to her professors, she is quiet and thoughtful. She finished with honors and chose to miss her graduation ceremony to be with us. Her teachers also told us that she stays pretty much to herself, but, when she does open up and voice her opinions, others follow." He smiled and winked at the group. "She's not bad to look at either."

Several board members squirmed.

Ethan hurried on. "The point is; her good looks, education, and natural leadership abilities, will enable us to attract many thousands of volunteers. Girls will want to be like her, and guys will want to spend time with her.

"In addition, she is the only child of billionaire businessman Arthur Buckman, of Buckman Medical Instruments, or BMI. As you know, this relationship has already proven to be quite valuable to our efforts."

Ethan looked at his PDA. "It's 11:30, and unless there are questions, we should probably move over to the large conference room and greet our new comers."

Chairs scooted back and the member closest to Ethan commented, "Good job."

Several nods and mumbles of thanks were also voiced as the group exited the room.

A tall, silver-haired board member advanced toward Ethan. He was slender and distinguished, with a navy, pin-striped, custom-made suit, indigo shirt, and matching tie. His accent was British. He placed his fingertips on the table and peered down at Ethan's large grin. "This is not a game. Make sure you keep me posted."

Ethan's expression turned serious. He knew the stakes, and the people he worked for. Failure was not an option. The Callers were props in an overall plan to change the world. But not in the way everyone expected. "Of course," he said.

CHAPTER THREE

Los Angeles, California

It was almost noon when Megyn found the parking area described in her orientation packet. The meeting was to start at twelve sharp and already there were several cars in the row of designated Caller slots.

Posted at the front of the seventh space was a sign that read MEGAN BUCKMAN. She licked her dry mouth, parked her made in America, 2004 Ford Mustang, checked herself in the mirror, grabbed her purse, and opened the door.

The one-story brownstone building faced away from the street and toward a golf course. Tinted windows completely covered one side. The bright sun cast shadows across the green knolls and the smell of freshly cut grass filled the air.

In the lobby she found two waiting areas with azure and chrome accented furniture on either side of an imposing reception desk. Entertainment magazines lay across coffee tables, and soft music played in the background. Her neck muscles stiffened. She rolled her shoulders, rotated her body, and tried to slow her breathing. *This is it. Time to step up and do what I've always wanted to do. Time to show my parents I've made it on my own.*

Maria moved from behind the counter and extended her hand. "Welcome to our executive conference center. Here's your nametag. Please put it on. It'll help everyone get to know each other faster."

Megyn saw Maria checking her over. She looked down at herself and wondered if she was dressed appropriately.

"How was your drive?" Maria said.

"Long. About five to six hours."

"Well, you look great. If you're ready, I'll take you back."

Megyn gulped and followed her down the hall.

A tall, slender woman with rich, dark skin stood at the conference room door. She wore a golden blazer with black pants and looked to be in her mid forties. She took Megyn's hand and pulled her forward.

"Megyn, we're so pleased you're able to join us. I'm Trianna Newberry." She pointed to the back of the room. "And, my wonderful husband, and partner, Jason is talking with one of our board members. This is our third year as Executive Producers for the Vanguard of Volunteer Voices. Our team looks forward to working with you. Introductions will be made later, right now feel free to help yourself to the buffet. Seating has been assigned and the Callers are close to the front. I believe you're next to Ethan, our show's host."

Trianna turned as new people entered the room. "Here he is now."

Ethan eased his way forward, took Megyn's hand in both of his, and fixed his eyes on hers. "I've looked forward to meeting you."

Megyn felt warm all over. His hair was sunny blond, his eyes light blue, his smile broad and white, and he had a perfectly muscled six-foot frame. She could see where he got his reputation as a lady's man. He was much more handsome in person than on TV.

He released one hand, unlocked his gaze, and pointed to the seat assignment nameplates. I believe we're over here. I've also made arrangements for us to meet later for coffee and a talk."

Megyn blushed. *Is he asking me on a date?*

Ethan ushered her to the buffet table. "Let's see what's for lunch."

Megyn assembled a turkey sandwich, munched a few select vegetables, and looked around. In the center of the room was a large oval pecan table with ergonomic chairs designed to adjust to each person's specific needs. Windows overlooked the green rolling landscape. The opposite wall was wood paneled and held a library of media relating to the entertainment industry. Signed pictures of various on- and off-screen moguls occupied the entire back wall, and directly in front, a giant, flat screen panel filled the area.

Ethan asked about her drive down and impressions so far. As new people arrived, he introduced her to Board members and Associated Cable Network staff. She listened and watched the room fill with people. Warm greetings and laughter raised the noise level, along with her excitement over the next two hours. *These people are changing the world for the better. Not like my industrialist father.*

At noon Trianna moved to the front of the table. "The desire to create a world where everyone is treated fairly and equally, where we give back much of what luck and hard work have afforded us, and where we can make a tangible difference, is not new. Books are written about these ideas, talk show hosts make their bread and butter from them, and politicians try to convince us they are the ones to help us live to our highest potential. But, none of these leaders have delivered on their ideas and promises." She paused and examined the people in the room. "It's time for new voices. It's time for the Vanguard of Volunteer Voices."

The room erupted into applause.

She turned and nodded. "I think you all know Ethan Strong, our show's host."

Ethan stood and smiled down on the seven Callers.

All eyes turned toward the newcomers.

Megyn's stomach lurched and her face flushed red. She hadn't yet met the other Callers but felt like she already knew them from watching the video profiles Maria had posted on their shared computer drive.

"We're excited you've joined us," Ethan said, "and are delighted in the breadth and depth of the skills and abilities you possess. Let's take a quick minute so you can introduce yourselves. Give us your Caller number, your name, your age, and where you're from. Once this is done we'll transition into the promotional video."

Megyn's breathing increased and her mouth felt dry. She sipped her water and tried to think of how she should present herself.

The introductions proceeded quickly and the film began. The background of the Vanguard of Volunteer Voices was explained and visual examples of activities and methods for working together to make positive changes flowed across the screen. Clips of young people participating in rebuilding homes in Guatemala after an earthquake, setting up Earth Day rallies, and handing out supplies after a monsoon in South America, presented visual ideas and created excitement and purpose.

One at a time, five Callers were highlighted on the screen. Each talked about his or her volunteer experiences, hobbies, family, work or school, and other interests. These new profiles showcased the participants at their best. The viewers were drawn into their stories and momentum built along the way. Ethan watched the faces as audience members noticed a common hand gesture used by several Callers. "Looks like we've got ourselves a new visual for the show." he said. Callers had spontaneously used the same two-fingered V for victory, and immediately followed it with three fingers spreading out and pointing straight up—V to the 3rd.

Bret's profile was next and created a new round of positive comments. He was shown speaking to large groups of young people, playing his guitar, singing, and leading thousands in worship services.

Megyn's profile was last. She talked about her plans to spend time with the elderly, read books to children, feed the hungry, and help the homeless. She would use her new degree in marketing to influence positive social change and continue to influence the world for the better even after her year commitment was over; and she couldn't wait to get started.

She was glad the lights were dimmed. She could feel her face heat up from the attention focused upon her and was relieved when her clip was over.

Then her mom and dad appeared in the video. They were smiling their big smiles and her dad was telling the camera how proud they were of her as his massive headquarter building and corporate sign loomed behind him as he spoke.

Megyn's shoulders stiffened and she fought to block the tears from escaping her eyes. She couldn't believe ACN staff had contacted them. She had specifically asked them not to involve her parents.

She wrapped her arms around herself and stared at the glass of water in front of her. She remembered the day she left home. Her father was furious with her choice of college and career. He'd struggled through life as a self-made man and told her he didn't want his daughter to face the same trials he'd endured. He insisted she attend an Ivy League university and eventually take over the business. She argued big corporations were evil. They became rich on the backs of their employees, polluted the environment, and took advantage of their customers. She told him she wanted to do something important with her life. He reminded her of the thousands of jobs he supplied and the numerous life-saving medical devices his corporation created. It was a familiar argument that ended with an ultimatum. "If you don't do as I say, I'll cut you off. No money. Do you hear me? No money."

At that moment her mother had entered the room in her usual alcoholic condition. She sided with Megyn's father, and Megyn packed her things and moved out.

Now she looked straight ahead and tried to fade into her chair. The video ended with each Caller excitedly giving the V^3 hand signal. The lights were turned up and Trianna stood again as a pleased audience cheered and applauded. "Thank you Ethan, Callers, and ACN staff.

"Next, I'd like to introduce Michael Moran," Trianna continued. He's handling the finances for V^3. I've asked him to update us on the money situation. Michael?"

He stood next to his chair, straight and serious. "We have excellent news about the budget. The show has been so successful that sponsors are competing for the opportunity to participate in this venture. We will be selective in our choices, and each will be required to operate in a way that is consistent with the show's values. We are flush with cash and can dream bigger and accomplish more than we had originally anticipated."

Trianna took the lead again. "We will offer large prize money, utilize multiple media outlets, and have plenty of funds to deliver high quality communications. Thank you, Michael. Now I would like to introduce our V^3 Oversight Board. They will provide global expertise, contacts, and resources. We look forward to working with them."

Eight members were introduced and Megyn could tell by the attendees' reactions most were familiar. Trianna looked around the room. "And now, we have a surprise for you. We have added a ninth Board member. Maria, will you please bring him in?"

Trianna smiled at Megyn, and then the V^3 team. "Please welcome Arthur Buckman, CEO of Buckman Medical Instruments."

Megyn gasped.

"Once Megyn's father found out about our efforts, and her involvement in them," Trianna said, "he insisted on becoming a sponsor and offered the full backing of BMI resources. Let's give him a warm welcome."

Megyn observed her father. He was tall and slim, with the same dark hair and violet eyes as hers. His temples had turned gray and his clothes were still expensive. *Why doesn't he do something good with his money, not always spend it on himself and his image?* He clasped his hands, rocked on his heels and exhibited a broad smile, while the audience clapped their approval. *If they only knew how driven and controlling he is, they would never let him be a part of something like this.* He then pinpointed Megyn's location and eased his way toward her with his arms outstretched.

Megyn grimaced, and patted him lightly on the shoulder when he leaned down for a hug. Her jaw tightened and her body went rigid. She didn't want to make a scene and vowed to confront the issue at a later time; when her emotions wouldn't control her words. The remainder of the meeting was a blur.

CHAPTER FOUR

The conference ended and Megyn made her way to the nearest exit. She heard her father call her name, and then Ethan introducing himself as the door closed behind her.

She hoped no one else had noticed her hasty retreat, or even worse, would try to stop her. She barely rounded the corner of the building before her anger spilled out. *They betrayed me. I can't do this. I can't live through the drama again.* Tears filled her eyes and within seconds sobs broke from deep within her soul. *This was my chance to do something significant on my own. Now the ACN staff has taken that away from me.*

Megyn walked faster. She allowed her anger to flow freely now that she was away from the others. She wondered why he always did this, why everything was always about him.

She continued to walk the empty golf course paths for over an hour before the stress of the day began to subside along with her anger. She considered resigning but was conflicted. She had already signed a contract for one year, and turned down her marketing internship. Her apartment was no longer available and her belongings were stored. She was eager to do good things in a big way and the V^3 provided the perfect opportunity. She argued with herself about what to do until hunger pains finally took over.

She had barely eaten her lunch and the sun was about to set. The thought of food and shelter now became her primary goal. Her luggage had been taken to her room by ACN staff when she first arrived, and the prominently placed campus map revealed her new home to be nearby.

She opened the massive front door and entered a spacious common room reminiscent of an exclusive mountain lodge. There was a high-beamed ceiling with a rustic sort of look. A couple of seating areas with overstuffed chairs and lighted nooks for reading created a peaceful environment. Books and magazines were conveniently laid out. A large stone fireplace covered one wall. On the far side was an opening where the sound of voices and laughter could be heard from another room. She assumed this was her fellow Callers and decided to sit a minute to regain her composure before joining them.

She eaves-dropped on the conversation. She'd seen their videotaped personal profiles more than once and could easily recognize each voice. The conversation sounded friendly and fun. Tawny told about her spelunking adventures and Sami compared her experiences in backpacking. As each told her story, the three of them frequently burst into spontaneous laughter. Bret jumped in with a tale about a day hike to a hidden lake with a group of high school students. He told how he'd gotten them lost, and after several hours, began to look for shelter for the night. He ended with a return to civilization, where a couple of the students vomited from the altitude and stress of the day. His tone was self-deprecating and he made himself out to be the fool so everyone laughed along with him.

They sounded nice and Megyn smiled to herself. She was about to join the group when Bret entered the room and welcomed her to the house. "I've brewed a pot of tea. Would you like some?"

Megyn stretched in an effort to appear relaxed. "I was about to do the same thing."

"There're a couple of sandwiches left from the meeting today too. Can I get you one?"

"You read my mind. Turkey, if you have it. If not, whatever looks good."

Bret exited through the opening and soon returned with sandwiches, a pot of tea, cups, and napkins. "No turkey, but we've got beef and ham. I brought both. Also, the brew is Jasmine, green tea. Hope that's all right"

Megyn watched Bret as he poured her drink. He was about five foot, eleven inches, sandy brown hair, freckles, and deep green eyes. His teeth stuck out a little in the front. She probably wouldn't have taken a second look at him if they'd passed on the street. But there was something about his manner. He was comfortable. Not boring comfortable, but nice comfortable, like a brother.

He settled into the chair next to hers. "How're you doing? I noticed you left immediately after the meeting."

Megyn opened her sandwich and picked at an edge of dried cheese while she debated whether or not to tell him the whole truth. "The drive from Turlock this morning was long, and I felt like I needed fresh air and a walk."

"You looked genuinely surprised to see your dad. I got the impression you weren't too pleased."

Megyn stiffened. "I don't want to talk about this. You couldn't possibly understand."

Bret handed her the cup and looked her straight in the eyes. "I'm not trying to upset you. I've been in the ministry several years now and have grown up around mega-churches. I've known several kids who've been raised in the shadow of fathers who run multi-million dollar, all consuming, businesses. My comment was meant as an offer of understanding."

Megyn's gaze switched to her shoes. She knew his background and was afraid the conversation would turn religious. "It's complicated. I wish it was that simple."

"Don't worry. I'm not going to press you to talk. Instead, I'll tell you about our new home while you eat, and give you the royal tour when you're finished."

Megyn was thankful she had been spared a sermon. She thought about her empty room but wasn't ready to go there just yet. I'm meeting someone at 8:00, but I'm all yours until then."

Bret told her about the daily housekeeping service, trash day, and the grocery list, while she finished her sandwich.

He then stood and waved his arms around the area. "This— living room."

Megyn laughed at his overdone words and movements. She could feel herself relaxing.

He refilled her cup and took her dishes. "Follow me. I'll show you parts of the house you haven't seen yet."

She tagged along through an opening where he extended his arms again. "This—kitchen. As you can see, it is multi-purposed. It can be a great party room with several areas for food preparation and service, or, it can be used as we are doing, for family-style dining."

He seated himself at the breakfast bar and gestured. "There are wood cabinets and granite countertops. We have a stove surrounded by this bar where seven plush stools are comfortably lined up around the edges." He stood and opened the refrigerator and several cabinet doors. "Food. Dishes," he proclaimed.

Megyn chuckled as he escorted her into another large space. Bret continued to brandish his arms pointing out the pool table, juke box, dartboard, and game table. He then showed her the impressive media set up. Broadly waving he said. "Overstuffed recliners with drink holders, game chairs with private sound systems, popcorn machine, large flat screen, computers, DVD players, speaker system, and everything else you can imagine. No need to worry about working all this. Everything comes with handheld controllers and cheat sheets."

Megyn giggled. "Thanks for pointing out the obvious."

Bret smiled and glanced at the digits on his cell. "Your room is down the hall. I have sisters and I know how girls are, so I'll leave you a few minutes to get ready for your 8:00, and see you in the morning."

Megyn smiled shyly. Much of the tension was gone and she felt more relaxed. "I appreciate your time. This was nice, and, exactly what I needed right now. See you tomorrow."

She headed to her room feeling better about things, but still not sure if she would stay.

~

The size of her private quarters reminded her of the small apartment she had left behind in Turlock. The space was laid out like an upscale hotel suite. She had a private bedroom and bath, with a modest living room attached. There were two TVs, a small coffee maker, microwave, refrigerator, comfy sofa, chair, and writing desk with Wi-Fi and telephone. It was perfect.

Her mind turned to the evening ahead. She hadn't dated much and was nervous. Everyone knew from the tabloids that Ethan was one of the most eligible bachelors in the world and he had invited her to spend the evening with him.

Her cell rang. "Hi, it's Ethan. I have a change of plans. We'll still meet for coffee at eight, but I have someone important I'd like you to meet. She's put together a small cocktail party and we're to be the guests of honor. It starts at 9:00."

CHAPTER FIVE

A t 8:00 sharp Bret dialed the number that allowed him to join the tail end of the weekly leadership meeting. He was careful to use the phone the church board had provided him the morning he left.

Pastor Sharpe received the call and opened the communication line. He welcomed Bret and invited him to share.

Bret was aware of the two-hour time difference from California to Texas and kept his comments brief. "Thus far, things have gone well. I've met my fellow Callers and attended the welcome luncheon. Our agendas are highly guarded so I'm not sure what tomorrow holds."

"All ten of us are here and we've just finished praying," Pastor Sharpe said. "We are still united in our belief that God has called you to participate in this movement. Since the contract doesn't allow you to share your faith unless you're specifically asked, your road will not be easy. We are confident he will use you powerfully when the time comes. Be strong and courageous. God is with you."

~

The coffee shop was filled with busy young professionals, and Megyn found Ethan in the back absorbed in a conversation on his hand held communicator. She watched the intentness of his actions and marveled at how he was the ideal person to be the face of the Vanguard of Volunteer Voices. He had looks and personality, and according to his profile, extensive professional work credentials and education from a prestigious university.

She pulled out a chair and sat down while he finished his business. "Hi," she whispered.

He signed off, leaned back, and she blushed as his eyes slowly examined her body from head to foot. "I know you like soy lattes," he said, "so I ordered one."

Megyn blushed.

He caught the eye of the server, signaled that they were ready for their drinks, and turned his gaze back to Megyn. "What did you think of the meeting?"

"It was great to connect with everyone and learn more about the show. I'm still in the dark about my role. I'm hoping I'll get additional information tomorrow."

"Isn't it wonderful about your dad?" Ethan said.

"About my dad . . . ." Megyn shuffled in her chair trying to think of the best way to approach the topic. "I was disappointed to see him. We haven't spoken in over three years and I had specifically requested he not be included in this."

The server delivered the drinks.

Ethan gave her a roguish smile. "It just happened, Megyn. One of the ACN people told me that apparently, someone on your father's staff heard you on the radio. He contacted us. We didn't contact him. Besides, your paths shouldn't cross except at the information sharing meetings, like the one we had this afternoon. These are held once a quarter. Board meetings are separate from our Caller working sessions. You don't have to interact with him at all if you don't want to."

Megyn exhaled. "You underestimate my dad."

Ethan gently touched her arm. "You can trust me. He won't be around."

His touch sent a current of emotion throughout her body, and she could feel her heart rate quicken. She sipped her fresh latte and tried to control the intensity of her feelings.

"Now, would you like to know why I've invited you here?"
She smiled. "Why?"

"The leadership team requested I talk with you and Bret before tomorrow's activities. I met with him earlier today, and am with you tonight."

She felt like a fool for thinking someone like Ethan would be interested in her. "Oh," she said, her voice dropping to a whisper.

"We would like to use the two of you in a broader way than the other Callers. You both have knowledge and skills that can help us motivate the youth of the world to get involved. You're natural leaders. We see you in the majority of up-front roles."

Megyn placed her latte on the table and pushed her chair back. "Whoa. You've got the wrong person. Bret's led numerous groups, speaks before large crowds, and has been on radio and in front of cameras. My speaking experience is minimal, and I'm not a leader. I would feel much more comfortable in a supporting role."

"Don't sell yourself short." Ethan placed his hand on her arm again. "Trust me. I know what I'm doing. You've got what it takes! I'll work closely with you, and believe me; I won't let you fall on your face. You'll be great!"

With that, he left a twenty-dollar tip and ushered her outside to his shiny cherry red Lamborghini. He gave another twenty to the young man he had solicited to keep watch, and fifteen minutes later, they arrived at a quiet tree-lined lane where expansive estates were hidden behind large fences and gated drives.

"We're going to Gisele and Martin Nethers' home. They are V³ oversight board members," Ethan explained as he drove. "Her grandfather was a prominent American industrialist and he is from British aristocracy. They both come from old money and are well known and highly respected globally. They wield enormous power." He touched her hand. "You're lucky. They're important people to know and they've taken an interest in you."

Megyn sat back and wondered, once again, if she belonged here. She'd been around money and power all her life and wasn't impressed by most of the people she knew who had it. She watched the trees and fences pass by and hoped the evening would go by quickly.

They were greeted at the gate by the security guard and directed to proceed to the front door where Ethan relinquished his keys to the valet. Another young man escorted them to the solarium at the back of the property. Ethan pointed out Gisele, who was engaged in conversation with three Callers who Megyn recognized from the previous two season's shows.

She was surprised at how natural and easy going Gisele looked. She wore comfortably fitted Armani blue jeans, with a white T-shirt and navy blue blazer. Her shoulder length hair was dark brown and she had penny loafers on her feet. She looked classy and casual.

Ethan announced their arrival and made introductions.

Gisele gave Megyn a friendly squeeze. "Welcome. We're so pleased you could join us. I feel like we're family already. What would you like to drink?"

Megyn hadn't attended a cocktail party since she lived at home, and the same dread she felt then eased its way back into her mind. She reminded herself that this event was different. Her mother wouldn't be here to become drunk by the end of the evening and her father wasn't going to show her off as his best invention yet. "I'll have a sparkling water. Thanks."

She observed Gisele engage each guest with interest and acceptance. She watched her listen and offer friendly advice without judgment. Gisele called them all her family and seemed to mean it.

"Now that everyone is here," Gisele said. "Let's take our seats around the lovely table the staff have prepared for us."

Megyn and Ethan sat on either side of Gisele. To the left of Megyn was Paul, one of the former Callers. He looked shorter than she remembered from watching him on TV.

The center of the round bronze terrace table held a large dessert sampler with enough sweets to serve three times the number of people in attendance. The platter rotated on an ornate lazy Susan that facilitated uninterrupted service while the conversation moved forward.

"You'll love your year with the V^3," Paul said, leaning close to Megyn's ear. "I was nervous at first, but the ACN staff does most of the work. You just show up and be yourself."

"I remember you," she said. "Didn't you work on environmental issues?"

He examined the selection of desserts. "They like to position you in an area of personal interest. Mine is definitely mother earth and going green. The best part of this experience is the opportunities that open up for you after the show. I'm now working full time with Gisele and Martin on global projects. You'll soon learn more about their efforts and I know they'll invite you to join us as well."

He took a bite of a small custard filled cream puff with chocolate topping. "This is excellent. You should try one." He finished the pastry and sat back. "How about you? Where will you be focused?"

"We don't have our assignments yet. I'm pretty open, as long as I can make a difference. To me, that's what this is all about; joining together to serve our planet, and our fellow human beings."

"You're also going to love Gisele. She's like a mother to us," Paul said. "She seems to know which Callers need family and steps in to fill the needs. You can tell her anything, and she's always available when you need her. She helped me out with money, and she ran interference when we confronted a large corporation who wasn't cooperating with our environmental requirements."

A tall gray-haired man entered and greeted the guests. Gisele stood, her arms outstretched. "Megyn, I'd like you to meet my husband Martin."

"Welcome," he said, his British accent pronounced. "I've heard quite a bit about you . . . all good, of course. I know you'll be brilliant."

Megyn turned red. She didn't like the attention and wondered who he had talked with.

The conversation changed to stories of seasons gone by, and advice and ideas for upcoming service opportunities. The evening ended with Ethan delivering her back to her shared quarters.

"You were a big hit," he said kissing her cheek. "See you tomorrow."

She floated back to her room and thought about her day. She had driven five and a half hours to attend the welcome briefing, walked around the campus, got a tour of her living quarters, met for coffee, obtained a new family, and was kissed by Ethan. She was exhausted, and invigorated.

It was midnight, but she knew sleep would elude her. She wondered how she could ever live up to Ethan and the Nethers' expectations of her.

CHAPTER SIX

The gray dawn sky could barely be seen behind the heavy red and gold drapes that covered the large rectangular window of her bedroom. The clock read 6:57 a.m., but Megyn knew she wouldn't be able to go back to sleep. The Callers were scheduled to meet Ethan in the gymnasium in two hours. Hopefully, she would get answers on what to expect over the next year. The only thing she knew so far was that Ethan would guide them through today's activities.

She was eager to get to know the Callers since she'd been unable to join them the night before, and decided to venture into the kitchen to hang out. She made a pot of coffee and while it brewed looked around. Through a set of French doors on the far side of the room, a patio faced the golf course. It had an extra long pergola, large potted plants, barbecue, pizza ovens, bar, refrigerator, fans, and plush sitting and dining areas.

The LA morning sun was warm as she stood in the opening and looked out. The sound of the last bit of water cycling through the brewer brought her back inside where she assembled a tray of dishes, cream, and sugar. A quick note on the blackboard invited the others to join her for coffee on the patio. She had just settled in when someone walked out the door.

A tall, sturdy young woman rounded the sofa, groaned, and soundly dropped into a chair. "I'm Annette."

Megyn lifted the coffee pot and grabbed a cup. "I'm Megyn. Coffee?"

Annette yawned and nodded.

Megyn remembered her from the day before. "You're up early. I guess you're still on Atlanta time?"

Annette fidgeted, "I'm nervous about the day ahead of us. I wish I knew more of what we'll be doing. I don't like being kept in the dark."

"I don't know either, but I'm excited to find out." Megyn said. "Have you met the other Callers yet? I got tied up last night and was sorry to miss the introductions."

Annette wrinkled her brow. "I met them. They're okay."

"Yo, Meg and Ann. Can I join ya'll?"

Megyn thought about Vince's promotional package. He was athletic, over six feet tall, with beautiful bronze colored skin, dark eyes, curly lashes, and a shaved head. He came across as the friendliest of the Callers, but she wasn't sure about him. Something seemed a little off.

She greeted him and motioned toward the sofa. "I see you've got your own pink concoction. Want coffee too?"

"I'm not a java man. I like to have a protein drink and bottle of water after I work out. I've already been over to the exercise room. Man, it's the best. It's got everything."

Vince seated himself across from Megyn and sipped his strawberry shake. "Ya'll excited about the show? Trianna and Jason seem like good people. I'm not sure about Ethan and Mary though."

Annette slouched to the side and ignored them.

Megyn smiled. "You speak like a Southerner. I thought you were from Washington State."

"I've only been in Kirkland for about six months. I'm originally from Texas; born and raised." He looked Annette over. "What's with you?"

"I'm not sure I like it here. I get a bad vibe. I don't trust these people either, especially Ethan and Mary."

"Well, I love it here," said Vince. "I love what we're going to be doing. I mean, helping others. How about you, Meg?"

"I'm a little scared, overwhelmed, and excited at the same time. I keep pinching myself to see if this is real. I like everyone I've met so far, even Ethan and Mary."

Vince sipped his drink. "There's something about those two that doesn't seem right. Ethan comes across as packaged. He doesn't seem real. And, Mary doesn't say much. I feel like she's observing us."

"They give me the creeps," said Annette who abruptly stood and walked back into the house. Megyn and Vince watched in silence as she slid her large frame through the door.

"What's with that chick?" Vince said. "She was like that last night too."

"I don't know. Maybe she's nervous. I know I am. People handle stress in different ways."

Vince stretched his long limbs and slowly exhaled. "About your dad? He help you get this gig?"

Megyn stiffened. "No, he didn't. I haven't talked to him in over three years. Apparently, someone on his staff heard me when I called into the radio station."

Bret walked out with Carla. "Look who I found sitting alone in the kitchen."

Carla motioned for a cup. "I need my space in the morning, time to wake up slowly."

Bret served Carla and helped himself. "Are we ready for the big 'working session' today? Anybody got an idea what we'll be doing?"

Megyn shook her head along with the others.

Carla examined Megyn. "We missed you last night. Where were you?"

She didn't want to invite questions from her new roommates regarding her time with Ethan. "I had a long day yesterday and went for a walk after the meeting. I needed to unwind and relax a bit. It's hard to be cooped up in a car for six hours and then sit in a meeting all afternoon."

Carla tilted her head. "It would've been nice to have us all here the first night, but I'm sure we'll have plenty of time to get to know each other over the next year. Seven people living and working together twenty-four/seven should prove to be very interesting."

Everyone laughed nervously.

Bret got up and headed for the door. "How about we gather in the front room in an hour and walk together to the gym for our first adventure with ACN? I'll write a note on the blackboard to let the others know."

~

Ethan and Mary sat in the control room and watched and listened to the Callers from wireless cameras and microphones hidden in the patio area. "So far so good," Ethan said. "Megyn and Bret are already the obvious leaders. We called that one right. And, as long as we manage them, we'll also be able to control the others."

Mary looked at Ethan. "You mean you, not we. You know I'm no good with people. Don't forget. I'm the media guru. I'll support you with technology, but managing the people is your problem."

"They'll be easy," Ethan grinned, his white teeth gleaming. "Annette's the only one I'm concerned about. She's opened up more to Megyn than anyone else. I think I'll get Megyn to take her under her wing." He smiled mischievously. "Besides, I think Megyn likes me. She'll be happy to help out."

Mary's expression turned stern. "There's more to that girl than you think. She hasn't talked to her parents in ages. That takes a lot of guts with a father like hers. She should not be underestimated. She could be real trouble for us down the road."

Ethan continued to grin.

Mary glared at him. "I'm just saying. Don't get cocky. We still have a long way to go."

CHAPTER SEVEN

M egyn, and the six other Callers, entered the gymnasium, and in unison stopped and stared. Around the room were, what looked like, seven stores. Each had a banner with the Caller's name. Camera and lighting crews stood off to one side waiting to document each individual's every move.

Ethan greeted them. "First you'll get made up and outfitted. Each Caller will have a unique look. We want to be trendsetters and provide attire our fellow Vanguarders will want to buy from our V^3 store. The shop with your name on it has clothes specifically chosen for you by your personal stylist. He, or she, will help you mix and match for the latest trends. Hair, makeup, and nails people are also in your booth. Have fun. See you back here at 1:30 for lunch and work."

Megyn spent the next few hours with her stylist. A camera followed her as she received a fresh new look; and was given an extensive wardrobe, complete with jackets, shoes, purses, jewelry, sweaters, pajamas, bathrobe, and slippers. The new attire was to be delivered to her apartment and put away, and she was asked to either store, or get rid of, the clothes she had brought with her. Only the outfits furnished by ACN could be worn over the next year.

A set of high-end suitcases was also furnished. They were filled with every kind of marketing give-away imaginable, golf shirts, mugs, silicone wristbands, T-shirts, billed caps, pens, sweaters, jackets, sweatshirts, and many other items. All had the V^3 logo. She was told these promotional items would be worn, or used, by the Callers and the stylists would let them know what to wear when.

At 1:30 sharp Megyn headed outside to the two limousines lined up and ready to transport them to lunch and the new V³ studio. She felt self-conscious and over done. She never wore much makeup, and the new clothes showed off more of her curves than she was used to. Ethan whistled as she approached, and Bret, who was standing next to him, nervously glanced at the ground. Megyn turned red and looked back in hopes a new arrival would distract their attention.

She was in luck. Annette had just come through the doors. Her long, straight, dark brown hair had been trimmed and styled with fresh auburn highlights that glistened in the sun light. Her large frame was outfitted to show off her waistline and long legs. She was dramatically changed. She even walked with more confidence.

The cameras continued to roll as one at a time the remaining Callers rejoined the group. Those already assembled commented on the newcomers' updated looks and marveled over each transformation. The young women giggled and laughed while the guys complained about the amount of time they were going to need for the upkeep of their new hairstyles.

Ethan invited Megyn and Bret to join him in the first limo and ushered the others to the second. Megyn seated herself in the luxurious back cushions while Ethan followed and smoothly positioned himself to allow his elbow to touch hers. He then guided Bret to the space in front of them.

Megyn tried not to read too much into the fact that Ethan had asked her to ride with him, until he'd obviously arranged things to make sure he sat next to her. She wondered if she'd been wrong. Was he attracted to her after all? She found if she positioned herself just right, she could watch him from the side without being obvious.

The limo pulled out onto the street and Ethan honored them with one of his famous smiles. "You two look great!"

Megyn happily blushed and Ethan continued, "In previous conversations, we've talked about your natural leadership abilities and how we would like to tap these characteristics. Today, I had a chance to further observe the other five Callers as they were introduced to a new situation. You probably didn't notice, but none of them moved toward their booths until the two of you took the lead. The calm assurance you both demonstrated, and your willingness to try something new, helped them conquer their fears and uncertainty."

Ethan sat forward. "With my hosting duties, I can't be everywhere and do everything. As I've said before, I need your help. Let me ask you, if you had to choose the two to three people in the group that need the most support, who would you name, and why?"

Bret spoke first. "I'd say Annette is number one. She makes skeptical comments about everything. But that could just be her way of dealing with new situations."

"I agree. I think she's nervous and it comes out negatively sometimes," Megyn said. "Maybe she'll feel more comfortable as things progress. She looked happy after her makeover."

Ethan nodded. "I'd like to enlist you both to go along-side her, answer her questions, and help her feel confident, and to trust what we're doing. Who else should be considered?"

"Carla is another one we should check on," Bret said. "She tends to be quiet and keeps to herself. There's probably nothing wrong, but we should keep an eye on her also."

"It's hard for me to guess what the others might be thinking," Megyn said. "Besides Bret, I've only interacted with Vince, Annette, and Carla, and that was this morning. Vince is excited about everything and, I agree, Carla seems a little distant. Then there's Bret; I have my doubts about him," she teased.

Bret laughed. "I talked with Tawny and Sami last night. Tawny regaled us, in her soft spoken way, with stories of her spelunking adventures; and Sami shared her backpacking travels, and life working on a thousand acre ranch."

He glanced at Megyn for agreement. "It's only been a couple of days so we don't have much to go on. I'm sure we'll both make a point to get to know the other Callers better."

The limo slowed and Ethan glanced outside. "Looks like we're here. Enjoy your lunch and I'll see you over at the studio in an hour. Let's check in with each other once in a while. I truly appreciate your willingness to help."

Megyn exited the vehicle smiling. *Working with Ethan is going to be fun.*

CHAPTER EIGHT

Ethan seated the Callers in the front middle section of the new auditorium, grabbed his wireless microphone, and climbed the stairs to the stage. "Welcome to our brand new broadcast studio. In the back, and around the edges, you can see a balcony with ample box seating. You're located in the stadium area on the bottom level. Mary's up in the studio control room behind you, and will direct the vast array of technology available for our use in each show. Her crew and I have put together a sample of our capabilities to help you become familiar with what we'll be doing. So, for the moment, sit back, relax, and enjoy."

Megyn felt like she was on a theme park ride. Loud music pulsated from every direction while a huge screen in the center of the stage, and several, various-shaped, smaller ones on either side, showed clips of happy young people feeding the poor, cleaning homeless shelters, and sharing hugs. Bright multi-colored lighting surrounded the collection of panels and provided an overall international atmosphere. Youthful voices sang a melodic chant that cycled through multiple languages.

It starts with me
I make a choice
I VOLUNTEER
I raise my VOICE

I join with you
We take a stand
Courageous VANGUARD
Throughout the land

I am the VANGUARD
You are the VANGUARD
We are the VANGUARD

We do good deeds
We serve all needs

At the end of the video, as in the one they had seen the day before, each of the seven Callers gave the V^3 hand gesture.

The film faded and a single spotlight focused on Ethan. New music vibrated softly in the background, and Ethan pointed toward the large screen. In an instant the V^3 home page popped up. With another point, he changed the focus to the center video box. It grew larger as he turned to the Callers and welcomed them to the show.

Megyn was intrigued. He was on the stage talking to them, and, he was also in the video box on the V^3 Web site illuminated on the big screen.

"Things have changed from our prior seasons. This is how each episode will work this year," he said. "Everything is interactive. The V^3 homepage will serve as the guide. "When it's time for commercials . . . ," He pressed his controller. "I point to the appropriate sponsors. Their boxes grow bigger and their message becomes the focus. When we talk about ways to improve our environment . . . ," He punched it again. "I point to the resources section. Up pops a page with links to other Web sites, books, articles, and a video library from previous shows. The same holds true for environment, spiritualism, money and giving, technology and communications, and health and wellness."

He continued to move his cursor around the screen. "There's a social networking tab where Vanguarders can interact anytime, day or night, from anywhere in the world. Multiple languages are accommodated. All our profiles can be accessed under the 'About Us' tab along with our mission, goals, and anthem.

"The V^3 store is located under the logo icon to the right. We'll encourage visitors to register and join at no cost, and everyone who signs up will be sent a free silicone wristband with our name on it, and a purple T-shirt with the slogan, We Are the Vanguard."

Megyn felt Annette nudge her elbow and heard her whisper. "Doesn't this seem a little much? Everyone will dress alike, sound alike, and act alike. I remember studying Hitler's rise to power when I was in high school. He used a youth army to help accomplish his goals. I think this is scary."

Megyn shook her head. "You're over reacting. This is brilliant marketing. Especially when the target audience we want to engage is youth. It has everything; a grand purpose, a look, a catchy anthem, prizes, money, and the latest gadgetry in communication technology."

Annette bumped her arm again, but Megyn placed her finger over her lips and turned her attention back to Ethan.

"We also have a section, where videos can be submitted by our Vanguard of Volunteer Voices. There are two reasons to submit film. The first is a post where Vanguarders can share what they're doing. The second is a weekly contest. These entries will be reviewed by our Oversight Board who will pick the best five to showcase each week, and the V³ audience will vote the winners."

Ethan winked and smiled. "We've allowed one week lead time to film the five winning showcases. Don't worry. Our people will walk you through your roles. You may only be asked to say a few things, nothing, or a lot. Since you all represent V³, it is important to have you visually involved in each broadcast." Ethan grinned again. "Depending on your abilities and comfort level, you may even be invited to participate on stage during our live broadcasts."

He paused and looked down at the Callers. "We don't have time to go through the entire Web site right now. It has, however, been placed in our shared drive, and I encourage you to take time to become comfortable with its content. It's important you keep up-to-date. Vanguarders will ask you how things work and you will need to be able to show and tell them. This won't be officially launched until our first show of the new season, a week from now, so you'll have plenty of time to check it out."

Annette looked anxious. "I need to go to the bathroom," she said to Megyn, and bolted up the aisle and out the door to the lobby.

Megyn started to go after her but decided to give her some space. It had been less than an hour since Ethan had asked her and Bret to support Annette, and she was already regretting her commitment. She sighed. *If she doesn't come back soon, I'll have to go check on her.*

Ethan took the headset off and walked down to the area where the Callers were seated. "I know I've given you a lot of information at one time. Do you have questions I can answer?"

Sami spoke first. "I'm not sure I completely understand what we'll be doing."

"I can tell you exactly what you'll be doing this week. Since you are from a farm, we have chosen you for a showcase that involves Vanguarders who invite children who are physically challenged to come out and ride horses. Our staff will orchestrate a conversation between you and our contestants around what they do and why. It will be like two friends talking. You don't have to do much. The ACN people will have a predetermined direction they want you to take and will provide you with detailed talking points. Don't worry; they'll make sure you're comfortable. If you make a mistake, you can start over. They shoot lots of footage and there's plenty of flexibility."

Megyn felt her stomach tighten with anticipation. She admired Ethan's confidence and tried to take comfort in his earlier promise not to let her fail.

She noticed that Ethan was studying the group. She looked at their faces and saw she wasn't the only one who was anxious. "Don't worry," Ethan said. "We'll walk you through your activities."

Megyn was impressed by how Ethan seemed to care about each of them. She felt as if she could trust him. He wouldn't ask her to do anything that would make her uncomfortable. And if he did, he'd be there to walk her through every step.

"Any other questions?" Ethan asked."

No one spoke.

He leaned his hand on the back of one of the chairs. "The five weekly winners will be invited back to the studio for the next broadcast. They'll each be awarded a check for ten thousand dollars to be used toward enhancing their activities. And, similar to previous seasons, Vanguarders from around the world will call in and vote for the top winner who will receive the one hundred thousand dollar grand prize. This year we will emphasize unity, equality, and service."

"Wow," Sami said. "Maybe I should resign as a Caller and enter the weekly contest."

Heads nodded and several "me toos," were voiced.

"Nothing like a little incentive to make the world a better place," Sami added.

"Especially since the money can only be used to further their Vanguard activities," Ethan said. "We truly want to mobilize the youth, and cash prizes will help many of them expand their efforts. We dream of the day when young people throughout the world will raise their hands, make the three V^3 hand gesture, and proclaim, "We are the Vanguard!"

Megyn smiled up at Ethan. She was proud he had chosen her to mentor and hoped he liked her as much as she liked him.

Her cell phone buzzed, alerting her of a new text message.

Was right not to trust. Discovered something BIG. Meet me on patio this evening. Going for a walk. Need time to think. Annette

~

Megyn sighed. *What now? Probably another problem that doesn't really exist.*

CHAPTER NINE

Megyn filled six glasses with ice and set paper plates and utensils around the bar for dinner while Tawny folded napkins and handed them to her.

"I guess Annette's not going to make it back in time to join us," Megyn said.

"Doesn't look that way," Tawny said, locating the Parmesan cheese and red peppers. "This place has everything."

Megyn laughed. "We don't have a cook."

"Pizza's here," Vince yelled from the front door.

Sami entered from the side. "Just in time. I'm starved."

Carla slid into the middle barstool. "Once again, we're together, and one of us is missing."

"In a couple of days, when we return from shooting our showcases," said Bret, "let's plan to share at least one meal together."

Vince mixed himself a protein drink. "I don't know about ya'll, but I thought today was unbelievable. This is big. It seems unreal that we get to lead it. All we did was name a song on the radio."

"After today," Megyn said, "I feel like we really can, and will, change the world." She bit into her pizza, trying not to think about the calories she was consuming. Maybe later she'd go for a power walk to burn them off.

"I started to cry when the new song played," Sami said, pouring a Pepsi over ice. "I can't wait to meet my showcase people. I love horses and am eager to learn about their program. As far as I'm concerned, everything about this experience is perfect. What do you think Bret?"

"I think the doorbell just rang. I'll go check it out."

Megyn heard Bret talking to someone and then Ethan entered the room followed by Bret.

"I'm afraid I have bad news," Ethan said. "I just got off the phone with our producers, Trianna and Jason Newberry. Annette was taken to emergency about an hour ago. Someone found her lying on the sidewalk and called 911. Apparently, she's had an allergic reaction to something. At least, that's what the doctors think right now. I've called her parents and we've chartered a flight and made accommodations for them. Unfortunately, since they're in Atlanta, Georgia, it will be early morning before they can get here."

Megyn leaned on the counter. She remembered Annette's earlier bolt from Ethan's orientation. She should've followed her. Ethan had asked her to look after Annette and already she'd failed him. "I'd like to go see her."

"I assumed you would all like to go and have lined up two vehicles, and drivers, to take you over. They should be here in the next fifteen minutes."

"How's she doing?" Sami said.

"Not good. Her blood pressure and oxygen levels are extremely low and she's lost consciousness. They don't expect her to make it. Did anyone notice if she was sick earlier?"

Megyn moaned. "I did. When she hurried out of the auditorium, she looked pale. It was when you talked about the necessity of our participation on camera. I thought she was probably nervous. And, she was always complaining. I didn't think she was actually sick."

Ethan put his arms around her. "It's not your fault. You didn't know."

Megyn buried her head in his shoulder. "I almost went after her, but decided to give her space instead. Maybe, if I'd gone, I could have saved her."

"Annette's parents didn't even know she had allergies," Ethan said. "They told me she has asthma and I passed on the information to the doctors. They said people with asthma are often susceptible to allergies too. Apparently, this is the first time something like this has happened to her. Unfortunately, she was alone when the attack occurred."

"There's the doorbell again," Vince said. "That's probably your rides. I'll get it."

Carla hesitated. "I think I'll stay here. I don't really know her, and I don't like hospitals."

Vince stopped in the doorway. "I'll pass on the visit too. Medical facilities aren't really my idea of a good time either. And, I agree with Carla. I just met Annette."

Ethan squeezed Megyn's hand. "I'll take you with me in my car."

CHAPTER TEN

Megyn glanced at the Callers who stood around Annette's bed. They looked concerned and somber. Sami crossed herself and Bret offered a quiet prayer. Megyn couldn't stop herself and tears filled her eyes.

This afternoon Annette had looked the picture of health. But, this evening, lying here in intensive care, her lips were blue and her face pale. Her breathing was labored and a tube was taped to her neck. Her updated hairstyle and fresh makeup from earlier in the day now served to enhance the contrast between her newly found life— and impending death.

Megyn watched her sleep and thought about her own guilt. If only she'd followed Annette to the restroom, asked her if she was okay? Why hadn't she been kinder to her? Then Annette's eyes flickered, and opened slightly, as if trying to focus. Together, the Callers let out a soft gasp. Megyn leaned forward and whispered. "Annette, it's me, Megyn. Can you hear me?"

Ethan entered the room and put his arm around Megyn. "How's she doing?"

"I think she's waking up. See?" Megyn pointed.

Annette turned her head, looking from Tawny, to Sami, to Bret, to Megyn, and then stopping her gaze on Ethan's face. A tear slipped down the side of her face. Then her eyes lost their focus and her monitor beeped. Medical personnel flooded into the room and simultaneously ushered them to the waiting area down the hall.

Ethan assured the worried Callers he would hang around the nurses' station and let them know Annette's status as soon as he could obtain news.

~

The waiting room was windowless and dreary. Megyn sat down near the fish tank. Bret took a seat across from her, his face in his hands. The others milled around. Megyn wondered if they blamed her for not following Annette.

Sami stopped her pacing and looked at Bret. "Would you say a prayer for Annette on behalf of all of us?"

Bret took a deep breath and studied her face. Megyn could tell he was weighing his answer carefully. She wondered why. Wouldn't prayer be something he would do naturally? "I'd be happy to if everyone agrees," he said.

They nodded and Bret and Sami bowed their heads and closed their eyes. Tawny and Megyn stood respectfully in the back.

"Dear Lord," Bret began. "We come together as one voice before you knowing you are the great healer. We ask for your restorative touch to Annette's body. The doctors have told us there is no hope, but we know with you, all things are possible. We also acknowledge she is made in your image and you love her beyond our wildest comprehension. We love you, trust you, and place her in your hands. In the name of Jesus Christ, our Savior, Amen."

The Callers took a seat to wait.

Megyn had heard prayers like this when her grandparents were sick in the hospital. Well meaning church people had left their fate in God's hands, and he had let them die.

Tawny was the first to speak. "What a day. I'm emotionally exhausted. Then we're on flights tomorrow to film the winning vignettes for the first show. I feel like we're on a roller coaster. I'm excited one minute and scared and depressed the next."

"I've never known anyone who's died," Sami said. "Especially not someone as young as Annette. I can't believe this."

Megyn stared at the floor, her heart full of anger. *This is wrong. Annette is a young woman. She should have years and years of life ahead of her.* She straightened herself and looked at the others. "This makes me all the more determined to work for the Vanguard. We don't know how long we have." Her gaze hardened. "We need to do all we can while we're able. We need to use this opportunity to its fullest."

Ethan entered the room and rested his hand on Megyn's shoulder. "I couldn't have expressed it better." He bit his lip. "I've just talked with Annette's doctor. They weren't able to save her. She's gone."

No one spoke.

A tear ran down Megyn's face.

Ethan waited a minute and then continued, "I'm sorry, but I won't be able to stay. Trianna asked me to join her and Jason to talk with Annette's parents and offer our help. Bret, if you could make sure everyone gets back to the house?"

"No problem," Bret said.

"Can we stay a few more minutes?" Sami said. "I have a couple of questions for Bret before we go."

No one moved. "It's all right with me," Bret said. "And since no one has headed for the door, I assume it's okay with everyone else too. What's on your mind?"

Sami examined each member of the group and rested her gaze on Bret. "I want to know why we pray for people to be healed and they aren't cured."

"That's a question that's been asked for thousands of years," Bret said. "To me the premise of the question gets to the character of God. Who is he? Why does he allow one person to live and another to die?"

"The question should be, is there a god?" Tawny said. "I'm not sure what I believe. Every spiritual group claims to have a god, and all of them assert theirs is the right one."

"These are some heavy questions. Maybe I can answer both together. Let me tell you how and why I decided to become a follower of Christ. I think it will provide the context for my beliefs.

"I was raised in a home where going to church was part of everything we did. My parents taught Sunday school classes. We attended vacation Bible school, and my sisters and I, went to church camp every year.

"We also were a family who loved the outdoors. We shared ownership of a home at a local lake where my parents fished while my two sisters and I swam and hiked. We enjoyed the trees, the mountains, the water, the wild life, and the sun, moon, and stars.

"One Sunday evening near dusk, I recall waiting for my parents to stop talking so we could go home. I was about nine years old and it was a school night. Alone and bored, I walked down to one of the

Sunday school classrooms. The lights were turned off and a dim glow from a distant street lamp reflected through the windows and partially illuminated the room.

"I sat in one of the little chairs, wrapped my arms around my knees, and rocked back and forth while humming praise songs. I pondered if I really believed all this stuff or if my faith was my parent's and not my own. It didn't take me long to think about our camping trips, about the birds, the fish, the sun and moon; about the ants and spiders and dogs and cats. These things didn't evolve out of nothing, I reasoned. The world is too complex. There had to be a higher being—a Creator.

"This explained God, but what about Jesus? I thought through what I knew about the Bible; what it claimed to be and what it said about Jesus. If there was a God he would have had a plan, and I, and everything around me, would be a part of that plan. It also made sense that he would send his son to redeem what had been lost when Adam and Eve chose to disobey him in the Garden.

"At this point I was satisfied. Creation had taught me who God was and my commitment to him was solidified. Throughout the years God has continued to prove his existence many, many times."

Megyn fidgeted.

Bret crinkled his forehead. "Why I pray gets back to my view of God. I believe he created everything and it all works together. I believe he was, and is, and is to come. He cares more than we can ever know. I believe death is not the end. We are eternal and when we trust in him we live with him forever."

Megyn straightened and rose from her chair. "Your life has been an easy one. The god I know is not the same one you describe. I can't buy any of this." She headed for the door. "I'll wait downstairs."

CHAPTER ELEVEN

Mary leaned back and sipped hot chocolate. Her mind raced with excitement. She was in a private room where numerous monitors provided a window to an unsuspecting world.

This was the place she was most happy. Ethan could deal with the people. She liked the latest media toys and could find, capture, modify, transmit, and/or broadcast almost anything from her personal command center located in the V³ studio.

She glanced at the clock on her monitor. As usual, Ethan was late. She swiveled her chair to the right and leaned forward to better view another monitor labeled Modesto, California. Her people were in place and ready for Megyn's appearance this afternoon.

The door's quick series of security beeps alerted her of Ethan's arrival. "It's done," he said. "I just got off the phone with our gray-haired British friend."

The front monitor caught his eye. "Is this the Modesto Web site you've been telling me about?"

"First I want to hear everything that's gone on since last night."

Ethan placed his hand on the chair next to Mary. "Pretty much as planned. The doctors ruled the death allergy related. I gave our condolences to the parents, and provided them with generous financial assistance. The Callers were shook up but are headed in different directions today for filming. By the time they get back, this will all be a distant memory."

"Did Megyn mention Annette's text message? I erased it within seconds of transmittal, but wasn't sure if I caught it in time."

"She was caught up in thinking she should have noticed Annette's illness. She feels guilty and believes she could have saved her life if she'd taken action when she first noticed a problem."

Ethan took a seat. "As a matter of fact, because of this incident, she's more committed to the Vanguard of Volunteer Voices than ever. Last night at the hospital, she challenged the Callers. She told them that, like Annette, 'We don't know how long we each have.'"

"What a great opportunity to promote urgency to join the V³. I hope you're going to take advantage of this."

"I just came from marketing. We've got a plan to memorialize Annette's life and use her as the 'poster child' for urgency. I'm sure her parents will support us. They were delighted with her involvement and had hoped this would be an opportunity for her to gain confidence. I believe we'll also be able to use them in promotional ads."

Mary shook her head. "I'm glad I'm on your good side. I'd hate to be your enemy."

Her expression turned serious. "You mentioned our British friend, Martin Nethers, contacted you. What did he want?"

"An update, and to re-iterate the seriousness of the situation. He also told me his international colleagues were eager for results and to stay on task, or else."

"What does he mean, 'or else'?"

"I think he means exactly what he said. If we don't want to end up like Annette, we'd better do what we're told."

"Then I guess we need to get to work." She rolled her chair closer. "This is the project I told you about. Once Megyn was identified as our seventh Caller, I knew we could use her to help launch and market our multiple Web sites throughout the world. These new sites will mobilize Vanguarders in each local area in a way that will coordinate with our hub. I chose Modesto as our model since it's just fifteen minutes north of Turlock, where she's from. It's a good-sized city and I have contacts already living in the area. My guy, Simon, and two other local techies have been working with my staff to mobilize the youth in that city, and the greater California Central Valley. I made sure they entered our weekly contest and talked them up with the selection committee."

Mary sat forward and gave Ethan a smug smile. "Of course they were chosen as the grand prize winners. They were made in our image. Our legal team has designed a contract to strengthen the relationship, and it's noted in the fine print that we have unlimited access to their system should specific circumstances come about."

Ethan leaned back and clasped his hands behind his neck. "We should have complete control of the Modesto Web site by when?"

"Since we have a working model and a contract in place, we anticipate the triggers for our involvement should take place within the month."

Mary brought up a map of California. "All high schools, colleges, and universities in the Central Valley are also involved. We anticipate Redding, Sacramento, Fresno, Bakersfield, and Chico will be online soon after Modesto. The template is in place and the momentum is building from previous seasons.

"The California model will be introduced during our premiere show and followed throughout the year. We will offer money, technical support, and promotional items for other cities, and existing groups to participate. We will insist on rallies and membership enrollment, and run contests all season to see which communities can show the most growth for the Vanguard.

"As local Web sites join the network, it will be easy to track and manage many more people and activities. Our staff has been busy, since last season, with the student groups that have been established as the ground troops for use in future days. Our efforts fit nicely with the militia Martin is already growing. I think he, and the others will be quite pleased."

CHAPTER TWELVE

It was 1:00 p.m. when the Gulfstream III landed with a small bump on the tarmac of the Modesto City—County Airport. From her seat Megyn watched as the stairs were lowered and her luggage loaded into a luxury black town car that must have been waiting for her arrival. She was nervous. All she knew about her visit was that she would receive a detailed briefing from a resident ACN staff member, learn about a community Web site created by local Vanguarders, spend the night, and fly back tomorrow.

A chubby young woman with four-inch stiletto heels, bright red lipstick, and soft curly black hair rushed to meet her at the bottom of the stairs. "I'm Stephanie from Associated Cable Network," she huffed. "I'll be your host in Modesto." She handed her a piece of paper. "Here's your updated itinerary." Sweat dripped down her neck. "Sorry about the weather, one hundred and three in the shade . . . and, no breeze at all." She motioned to the waiting vehicle. "I'll go over the details of your visit as we travel to your first appointment. How was your trip?"

"Short."

The girls settled into the back seat of the town car.

"Corporate airplanes sure take the pain out of flying," Stephanie said. "Would you like a cold water?"

Megyn glanced down at the schedule Stephanie had just handed her, then checked the time. "Am I reading this right? Do I have a media interview in fifteen minutes?"

"It's an eight minute radio spot. Since you're a local girl, they'll ask you questions about how you were chosen to participate in the Vanguard of Volunteer Voices, what you've done so far, and what you expect to happen going forward. I set this one up first so you could get used to how things work. It'll be easy. They just want your personal impressions."

Megyn gulped. "I've never done this before. Will you stay with me?"

Stephanie put one hand up and said, "Excuse me," she took a long drink of cold water. She then dabbed the perspiration flowing from her brow. "Sorry. I've been running all day. Yes, I'll be there too. Don't worry. It'll be over before you know it."

She pointed to the next agenda item. "Then we head for the main strip. We'll gather for the rally in an area similar to the one in which movie mogul, George Lucas, modeled his popular coming of age film, *American Graffiti*. Even though the motion picture was filmed someplace else, it depicts his teen years in Modesto through the lives of two early 1960s high school graduates who plan to leave for college the next day. They spend the evening struggling with growing up and going away to school. They cruise a boulevard alongside other teens. They listen to popular tunes, meet for burgers, try to hook up for the evening, and drag race in the end."

"I don't think I've heard of that movie."

"It was before our time, but it fits in great with the theme. It starred Richard Dreyfuss, Ron Howard and Harrison Ford when they were young. An old movie, one of the best films ever made."

She reached into her briefcase and pulled out a folder. "Here are pictures of some of the scenes that have been used in our promotional materials. We're contrasting the old with the new. Back then teens cruised the strip, hung out at the diner, and pulled pranks on local authorities. Today we cruise the Web, hook up in social networking sites, and form alliances based on interests rather than proximity.

"Our message is one of urgency. Things have changed since the sixties. The world is in trouble environmentally, socially, economically, and spiritually. The youth of today have to grow up faster. Our futures are on our shoulders. We have to work together to find the solutions. We have to team up and take action.

"We're expecting several thousand young people at the rally. We've arranged buses and parking, and will distribute free movie posters and V³ T-shirts and caps." She took another sip. "Because of the heat, cold water will be available. Print, broadcast, and Internet media have also been invited.

"Carefully selected scenes from *American Graffiti* will run on big screens on either side of the podium. I'll welcome everyone on behalf of ACN and present you. You'll, in turn, introduce our local Web site facilitator, Simon. Here's his bio for you to read. He'll lead the rally and I'll help you follow along as needed. Afterwards we'll shoot footage to be used in this season's premiere telecast. There will be additional media interviews and one more tomorrow morning. Then you'll fly back to Los Angeles. You'll be home before 1:00 p.m."

Megyn was feeling overwhelmed and her stomach fluttered. She tried to concentrate on the work before her. "Are there themes, or points I should emphasize during my interviews—talking points?"

"Excellent question. I forgot you have a marketing background. You can help us get our numbers up. Persuade people to join V³ and participate in sharing their efforts with others. The ACN corporate staff also suggested we have you encourage them to communicate with you via various technology sources."

Megyn flinched. "I don't have time to take that much work on right now."

"Don't worry. We have people who will help you manage your social network and stay on message."

"I believe in what we're doing. And, as long as I have help from headquarters, I'll do my best to promote whatever you want."

Stephanie scooted forward. "Great. Are you up for interacting with the crowd? I can work that in too."

"Sure. Anything I can do." Megyn swallowed. "I'd like that water now."

CHAPTER THIRTEEN

Megyn was blinded by multiple bright flashes from the cameras of paparazzi who lined the Los Angeles airport's executive lounge. Surprised by the crowd, she froze not knowing what to do or where to go. Her hesitation was enough to give them an opening and they immediately crushed their way forward while simultaneously pelting her ears with rapid fire questions.

"Megyn!"

"Megyn!"

"Megyn, is it true your dad got you your role on the Vanguard of Volunteer Voices?"

"Megyn, how much money did your dad donate to the V³ in order to obtain a place for you on the show?"

"Megyn!"

She knew she needed to make a move. She guarded her eyes with one hand, stuck out her elbow like she'd seen people do on TV, and moved forward. She couldn't see through the commotion, and was now sorry she'd asked the limo driver to wait by the car. She had a headache that grew worse by the minute and wished beyond measure she'd used the lavatory on the plane before they landed.

She was close to panic when a firm hand took hold of her extended elbow, brought it down to her side, and guided her to the right. "The restroom is over here, Miss Buckman," whispered the chauffeur. "I'll remain here and help you to the car when you're ready."

Before he released her arm he said. "You're doing fine. Now, when you come out, smile, wave your hand and say, 'sorry no questions today,' and I'll swiftly move you to the car."

"Thank you," she mouthed and turned.

Once inside she knew she couldn't waste time. She was eager to get home and away from the notoriety of the last two days. She took care of business, washed up, checked herself in the mirror, headed for the door, and braced herself for the next round. As promised the chauffeur appeared by her side. He efficiently moved her through the maze of bodies, cameras, and microphones. With his help, she safely reached the vehicle, where he opened the door, and deposited her inside.

"Thank you," she said. "I don't know what I would've done without you."

The windows were tinted and Megyn's eyes needed a minute to adjust from the camera flashes and bright sunlight to the darkness of the interior.

"Welcome back," she heard a woman's voice say from the seat directly facing hers. "I thought you might need a friend today."

Megyn blinked. "Gisele, . . . Hi."

"Would you like to come over for a quiet afternoon, talk a little, and relax for a couple of hours; just us girls? Then Martin and Ethan will meet us for an early dinner? I promise we'll have a restful time."

"Sounds good, but I'm exhausted and was planning to go home and relax in the spa."

"Why don't you join me in ours? It's quite comfortable and has great views of the Los Angeles cityscape. I've got bathing suits of all sizes and am sure I can help you find one that will fit. Martin and I even have a personal masseuse we use for occasions such as this. She's wonderful. Believe me, she'll have you feeling relaxed in no time."

The last two days had been disastrous and it had been a long time since Megyn had been pampered. "You've talked me into it."

~

The swirling bubbles and rockets of hot water pulsated across Megyn's body. Gisele sat across from her on an underwater ledge, sipping iced tea and gazing at down town Los Angeles in the distance.

"How did you know?" Megyn asked.

Gisele set her glass down. "I saw the interviews on TV and figured you'd need a friend." She shifted to better observe Megyn. "Am I right?"

Megyn had learned from an early age to guard her emotions and her words. She felt safe with Gisele, but surprised herself when she blurted, "What a fool I've been to think I could keep my family background a secret. This show's too well known. It was bound to come out. It's just that I've been away from them for so long . . . when the questions came about my father's involvement, and how I felt about being an heiress . . . and then the implications that he used his influence to get me on as a Caller. People can be so cruel. They don't know the situation, or me."

"I'm truly sorry this happened to you. I'm surprised you weren't briefed by Associated Cable Network staff on what to expect from the media before you left."

Megyn sipped her lemonade. "The first interview was the worst. I was totally blindsided. I didn't expect I'd be the story. I've let the Vanguard down. I'm wondering if I belong here."

"Some advice from someone who's been in the limelight much of my adult life. You'll get national and global questioning along this same line over the next week or two. Then this story will die out. People will move on. The audiences love you. Young people throughout the world already want to be like you. Don't falter on your desire to do good things. Many opportunities are in your future."

Megyn shrugged. "Maybe you're right. But my experience with my parents is that this won't go away. My father loves the limelight and will find a way to keep both of us in it."

Gisele pulled the tip of her towel down and dabbed at her forehead. "Don't underestimate the influence I have. I will protect you. We're family, remember."

"I hope you can."

"Don't give up now, Megyn. You're the whole package, intelligent, beautiful, kind, well-spoken, and dedicated. Believe me. You'll do great things as Caller number seven. The Vanguard of Volunteer Voices needs you."

Megyn wasn't so sure.

CHAPTER FOURTEEN

Megyn descended the Nethers' massive staircase feeling rested and relaxed. She spotted Ethan, glass of white wine in hand, talking earnestly with Martin. Both men turned to greet her. Martin handed her a sparkling water. "I understand you don't drink alcoholic beverages."

Ethan gave her a welcome-home hug and gentle kiss on the forehead. Her cheeks flushed as his lips touched her face. She wondered if he could feel the heat she radiated.

Gisele entered from behind. "That's right. Megyn grew up with alcoholism in her home and promised herself she would never drink." She escorted them to the dinette table where taco salad makings were attractively arranged.

Martin handed the corn tortillas around and asked. "How was your trip?"

Megyn and Gisele exchanged knowing glances.

"We had over twenty thousand in attendance," Megyn said. "It far exceeded expectations."

"I heard," Martin said. "That's the largest crowd we've had in one location. Even our major metros haven't been able to draw that many. You're quickly becoming a super star, Megyn."

"I hope not." She shuddered. "There was a room full of paparazzi when I got back to LA. Not something I want to experience all the time."

Ethan grinned and gently squeezed her arm. "I think it's too late, sweetheart."

The term of endearment caught her by surprise, and Megyn fumbled as she passed the salsa to Gisele and tried to stay focused on the topic. "I noticed a large number of protestors yesterday. They were over to one side and too far away for me to read their signs. I've never noticed them on the news reports. Who are they? And, why would anyone want to protest what we're doing?"

Ethan assembled a monstrous taco. "We've had protestors since the middle of last season. They're right wing Christians who hold on to conspiracy theories. We've met with them and tried to educate them on the facts, but their leaders continue to misrepresent our direction and motives."

Martin interrupted. "We have many spiritual groups involved and plan to have a national day of prayer where all can come together around common beliefs. We've invited them to be part of what we're doing, but so far, they've refused."

"Maybe we should get Bret to help persuade them," Megyn said. "He seems to be a leader among the Christians."

"I thought you were a Christian too," Gisele said.

"I used to be. Now I'm not sure what I believe. There are a lot of things I don't understand about the god Christians follow."

Martin quickly glanced at Gisele, refreshed their drinks, and suggested they adjourn to the terrace.

Gisele took a seat across from Megyn. "Have you had experiences with any other religions?"

"No, just Christianity." Megyn frowned a little. "Oh, yes. I had a brief encounter with a Ouija board."

Gisele, Martin, and Ethan exchanged quick glances.

"Encounter?" Gisele said.

Megyn wondered why she'd mentioned that childhood incident. She'd pushed it to the back of her mind and hadn't thought about it in years. But the Nethers' home was a place where people listened and cared about each other. She nestled back into the large chair and told them about her experience, ending with DS's threats."

Gisele laughed lightly. "Did you say DS?"

"He said it stood for Demon Spirit."

Gisele shifted, leaned toward Megyn in a conspiratorial way. "You may be surprised to hear this. I've talked with DS myself; although I manage to avoid him most of the time."

Megyn sat straighter in her chair.

"I thought my little confession might shock you," Gisele said.

"Well, yes. I didn't expect to hear this from you."

Martin and Ethan sipped their drinks and listened.

Gisele sat back. "Why? There's nothing strange or wrong about talking with angels. Many people do it. I've talked with a number of them. I've even met Jesus."

"*The* Jesus, the one in the Bible?" Megyn gripped her drink, wondering if she had heard right.

"An angel. He's an angel like the others. Some are good and some are bad." Gisele licked her lips, her eyes wide and intense.

Megyn was confused and uneasy with the conversation. "I used to talk to Jesus when I was a child but he never talked back," she said.

"You probably weren't trained to listen," Gisele said. "What a loss you haven't been able to converse with him all these years. I can introduce you to him and others too, if you're interested."

Megyn squirmed. "I'm not sure. My last experience with *angels* wasn't that great."

Gisele got up and took Megyn's hand. "You've had a long day and this is a topic that requires more time than we have now. I can see there's a lot you haven't heard about. Next time you come over, we can talk about this a little more. It's too bad you met DS first. There are many good angels too. Ones that can help you obtain your dreams. Ones that give you wealth and power."

Gisele handed her off to Ethan who nodded agreement and escorted her toward the door.

Megyn didn't care about wealth and power. She'd seen first-hand how destructive these things could be. She wanted to make a difference, to do something important, to live her life with purpose.

CHAPTER FIFTEEN

Coalinga, California

Mildred Fletcher inched herself to the edge of the bed where she flexed her knotted, aching joints and eased her walker into place. "Gladys," she called to her sister in the bed across the room. "Wake up! I've had another visit."

Mildred watched as Gladys yawned, rolled over and looked at the large red numbers of her bedside clock glowing 2:30.

"All right. I'm awake," she said as Mildred stood and stretched.

"Oh, Gladys, it was just like before." Mildred shuffled across the room and stood by her sister's bed, ignoring the pain in her right hip. "A bright light appeared in the center of our room, and a voice flowed from it exuding both power and peace at the same time. It spread over me and through me. I heard and felt the warmth and power of the message. It was as if I was in a giant multi-media room. Then, just as before, the voice declared, 'I will pour water on him who is thirsty, and floods on the dry ground: I will pour My Spirit on your descendents, and my blessing on your offspring.'"

Gladys sat up and put on her glasses. "Oh, Mildred, this is wonderful. We've been praying for so long."

"At the same time the voice spoke I saw faces," Mildred felt her voice growing stronger, "hundreds of faces, all around the room; old and young, and of different races. The faces looked lost and were pleading for help. I would not have been able to bear the agony in their eyes had it not been for the comfort and assurance of the voice and its message. The faces then blurred and faded, and the most beautiful singing I've ever heard surrounded me and filled my being. My spirit was stirred and I joined in the praise. 'Holy, holy, holy is the Lord God Almighty, who was, and is, and is to come.'"

Gladys took her sister's hands. "Praise the Lord, Mildred, our waiting and watching and calling on the Lord to heal our land is growing roots. It's time to wake up as many others as the Lord sees fit. Let's call Pastor Sharpe and tell him about your new visit. A great battle for people's souls is close at hand. We need many more to join with us in prayer.

~

Bret answered his personal cell phone on the second ring.

"Pastor Sharpe here. Thought I'd check in and find out about your first day in the field."

"Good timing. I just walked in the door." Bret sat his luggage down and plopped onto the sofa in his little apartment. "They sent me to Vancouver, British Columbia. I was there for a Question and Answer session about the use of the arts to promote community service. This was set up by ACN staff and included approximately fifty young people from around BC. I answered inquiries about the importance of artistic expression to bring balance and direction to a person's life, and since the group was small, I created an environment for everyone to share. The majority of the time was fun and productive. But, there were a couple of guys that pressed me about my Christian beliefs."

"How did you answer?"

"I reminded them this was an open forum with many beliefs represented and I would be happy to talk with them individually about my personal faith afterwards. One guy in particular seemed determined to get me to share, but I held firm. It was kind of weird how hard he pushed."

"Sounds like you handled it just right. We want to stay true to the contract you signed going in. Besides, I just got a call from Mildred and she's had another visitation. A spiritual battle like no other is brewing. Don't give Satan a foothold. God will provide the opportunities to share in his time. You're there for a reason. Be strong and courageous. Stand firm. We're mobilizing prayer warriors. May God be with you."

CHAPTER SIXTEEN

The red Lamborghini eased its way into the parking spot next to the one labeled MEGYN BUCKMAN, CALLER SEVEN. She had been quiet on the ride home. So many things had changed in the last few days and she was deep in thought. Ethan's hand moved toward the door and she gently touched his elbow. "I'll go the rest of the way alone. Probably best not to give my roommates something to talk about." She leaned over, kissed him on his cheek and exited the car.

She had enjoyed the company of her new friends, but the discussion about spiritual beings was a surprise. She wondered if her grandparents had been wrong after all. Maybe Jesus *was* just another angel. She wanted time to think and was eager for a quiet evening alone in her small apartment. This was the way she'd lived her entire life and found refuge in small cozy places, and refreshment in her aloneness. Her luggage was already delivered and all she had to do was make it past anyone who might be in the common areas without creating hurt feelings.

The front door was unlocked which allowed her to move quietly through the spacious living room. The kitchen was another problem. Excited voices rang loud with conversation. It was obvious she wouldn't make it to her room without being spotted. Her self-imposed seclusion would have to wait.

"Welcome home, fellow traveler," Sami said as she grabbed a goblet and pointed to the open wine bottles. "Red or white? We're talking about our recent adventures."

"Sparkling water please. I'm exhausted and ready for bed."

She slid into the nearest barstool and looked around. "Is everyone back?"

"All but Carla," Vince said. "She's always the one griping about missing people. Now she's the absent one."

Megyn raised her glass. "Here's to us!"

"And Carla too," Vince laughed.

Megyn swiveled her chair in his direction. "Where did ACN send you?"

"I was part of a group of about two thousand athletes. It was awesome. There were people who had formed teams and clubs and were brought in from around the world. Over half were participants from prior seasons. We had a facilitator who helped us form working crews and set goals for the future."

"What kind of goals?" Sami said.

Vince leaned back, tilting his chair slightly. "Well, you see, since we're all physically fit." He lifted his shirt and rubbed his six pack abs. "We figure we can do almost anything. There were dozens of ideas ranging from doing chores for old people, to enforcement of the new healthy living guidelines from the Universal Health Organization. In the end we focused on activities that will most impact and benefit the majority of people. Things like the health and wellness issues. We'll follow the Universal Health Organization's guidelines and recommendations, and oblige the masses to participate."

Bret refilled his iced tea. "Tawny, you've been quiet. What've you been up to?"

"I wish I could say I've been involved in a program connected to spelunking the last two days, since that seems to be my claim to fame. Vince has his athletes, Sami, her farm friends, Bret, the artsy crowd, but no, I stayed here in town and met with a delegation of nerds."

The Callers cracked up.

"We met in the same room as our V³ welcome and orientation luncheon."

Vince nearly tipped over. "You mean, T, you didn't even leave the ACN campus?"

62

"I just walked out our front door and over to the conference center. Mary led the forum. It appears they've met a number of times before, and the entire meeting was focused on bringing together the world's youth utilizing advanced technology."

Megyn brightened. "Sounds interesting. I wish I could've done that instead of what I did."

"It was. I met a number of the world's leading brainiacs and hackers, and learned tons. They talk in another language, but I was able to follow along most of the time. And, I met Nathan from Arkansas. He lives on a large farm—"

The Callers let out a collective, "And—?"

Tawny continued. "And, I've introduced him to my new roommate who also grew up on a big farm, and—"

Sami's face transformed into a red glow and she fanned herself in a pretense of cooling down. "It's the wine," she offered defensively.

"Need I say more," Tawny said. "The evidence speaks for itself."

Bret stood. "I guess this is my cue to turn in. We've got our first joint photo shoot tomorrow and it's already late. I'm headed for bed." He stopped at the corridor. "How about we meet in the front room in the morning and go over together." He didn't wait for an answer and headed down the hall.

The remaining Callers set their glasses on the counter and made small talk as they dispersed to their apartments.

"Oh, I almost forgot," Sami said grabbing Megyn's arm. "You received a package this afternoon. I was the only one here, so I signed for it. I placed it behind the large chair in the living room. No one ever goes there."

"Why the secrecy?" Megyn asked.

Sami shrugged. "I don't know. I had a feeling its arrival should be kept quiet. I get these kinds of concerns sometimes and am usually right to pay attention to them."

Megyn headed for the front room. "I'm not expecting anything. I wonder if I should have ACN staff check it out first. In case it's from a crazed fan." She laughed over her shoulder. "Thanks. See you in the morning."

She found the package, just as Sami had described, behind the chair in the living room. She brought it back to her apartment, placed it on the nightstand, changed her clothes, and climbed into bed. Her latest novel sat next to her pillows where she'd left it the night before. She thought it would distract her from her disastrous media interactions in Modesto and picked it up to read. But, instead of finding refuge in the story, she found herself going over the same paragraph several times. She stared into space, thankful no one had mentioned her calamitous interviews. Maybe they hadn't seen or heard them yet. Hopefully Gisele was right; all the questions about her family would soon be a distant memory.

She was deep in self pity when she remembered the package. She reached over and picked it up. The box was small and covered with packing tape, and she couldn't find a way to get inside. She reached into her purse, grabbed her keys, and sliced the edges.

She pulled the lid up and found a cell phone wrapped in Kleenex. The battery had been removed and was encased in tissue and placed next to it. A note was neatly printed on the soft paper. ANNETTE'S PERSONAL PHONE.

Megyn frowned and rotated the device in her hands. She opened the back, inserted the battery, and turned it on. The e-mails, text messages, and pictures stored within the phone were definitely communications between Annette and her family and friends. She examined the wrapping again but there was no return address. She decided to check out Annette's Internet activities. Again, nothing of interest turned up. The last place to look was the video content. There was one file and she clicked on it. Annette popped up holding the phone away from her face and talking into its camera. "Megyn, I think I'm being followed. If you're watching this then something has happened to me. Otherwise I would have retrieved it myself."

Megyn's stomach flipped. She sat forward in her bed and watched Annette continue.

"I left you a text that I'd found something. I've recorded it here. When I left the studio I was headed to the bathroom and ran into an old classmate of mine. We talked and I convinced him to show me the media command center. I thought it would be the place to find evidence that would confirm my suspicions that something was wrong. I was right."

Megyn's full attention was on the tiny screen as Annette swept the video camera around the media room. There were monitors that showed Ethan's live presentation to the Callers in the new studio across the hall. And, there were other monitors. Several were streaming film of the Callers on the patio, in the kitchen, in the front room, in the gymnasium at their makeovers, and live from the studio with Ethan. The audio had been turned down on these screens, but the mere appearance of their privacy being violated sent a chill through Megyn's body. There were also folders that lay on the tables with pictures of each Caller, seven DVDs with each name, and voluminous paperwork attached.

Annette ended. "Be careful what you say and do. I don't know where all the cameras and microphones are, how much they're recording, or why. Talk to Bret. He'll know what to do."

She watched the video several more times and decided to review the text message Annette had previously sent. She grabbed her ACN phone, but the text was no longer in her inbox where she had left it. She frowned at the phone, and a half hour later penned a handwritten note to Bret.

CHAPTER SEVENTEEN

Megyn and the other Callers arrived at their joint V³ promo photo shoot and were greeted by the ACN administrator, Maria who escorted them through a red, windowless warehouse door marked, ENTER. They walked down a short hallway. "We'll start here," Maria said. "Hair, make-up, and wardrobe. Girls in the room on my right. Boys on the left. I'll meet you in the craft services area when you're ready. It's straight ahead. You can't miss it. There's lots to eat."

~

Megyn rejoined Maria, Carla, Tawny, and Vince near the food and beverage table, in her hand was her note to Bret, neatly folded so no one would notice it. She glanced around, didn't see him, and approached Maria who told her Bret had arrived earlier and wandered off to look around.

Megyn, now aware that her every move could be monitored, peeked into the warehouse. Her neck muscles tightened when she saw the massive space. The walls and floor were shamrock green. The ceiling was high and lined with tracks that held props, lighting fixtures, and cameras to be moved around for filming. Several ladders were off to one side. Metal poles and three-legged stands with additional lights and umbrella looking reflectors were mounted and dispersed throughout. Cables were neatly bundled and cameras were arranged around the vast space.

Sami and Bret showed up next, along with a tall wrinkled man with a horned nose and miniscule glasses. She wondered how she was going to find an opportunity to pass the note to Bret.

"Welcome. I'm Ernie Bristol and I'll be directing you," the man said. "We're doing a couple of things today. First, we'll take several group stills. Later on, others will join us and we'll shoot video of the Vanguard of Volunteer Voices anthem. Backgrounds, words, and music will be edited in later. You'll have to trust me and do what I ask, when I ask. Timing will be important. I know none of you are professionals, so I'll run you through it right now and we'll do several takes when the others arrive. It's important to relax and have fun."

He led them in to the warehouse and walked to the middle of the room. "Megyn, you will start. The lead-in music will play and you will enter and stop in the center. The first verse will play in the background. It is sung by a lone young woman.

"It starts with me
I make a choice
I VOLUNTEER
I raise my VOICE

"The words, UNITY, EQUALITY, and SERVICE will overlay the video and fade in and out. As I mentioned, these will be added during the edit.

"Just prior to the second stanza I will cue Megyn to extend her arms and invite the rest of you to join in from both sides. Next, Callers from previous years will enter, and finally, several hundred others.

"I join with you
We take a stand
Courageous VANGUARD
Throughout the land

"Digital renderings will be added during the edit as the shot pulls out to show a globe with millions of young faces singing the final verse.

"I am the VANGUARD
You are the VANGUARD
We are the VANGUARD

"The final scenes include multiple videos of Vanguarders helping and serving others.

"We do good deeds
We serve all needs"

He looked around at the Callers. "You'll have to move in quickly without appearing to be in a hurry. The song will repeat with everyone holding hands and mouthing the words. It doesn't matter if you can sing. The soundtrack will contain the voices. Vignettes of Vanguarders doing good deeds will also scroll during this time. Finally, the camera will return to Megyn, then slowly pull out on the Callers, widen to include the others, and continue on until the globe with millions of Vanguarders is seen from a distance.

"In the beginning, each of your white outfits will show up in the video in different colors. Then as the Vanguard grows larger, the colors begin to meld together into the final color—purple. As you know, that's the Vanguard color and will signify unity, equality, and service. The extra people will join us in about an hour. We need to hurry and get the group shots of this season's Callers done before they get here."

Megyn wondered why she was chosen to start the video. She didn't like the attention and didn't want to cause tension between herself and the other Callers. She squeezed the folded paper deep into the palm of her hand. She watched Bret who seemed comfortable anywhere. He joked with the ACN staff and showed genuine interest in their activities. She didn't understand his ease and confidence in any situation. She tried to look casual as she perused the area for hidden cameras and microphones. She noticed Carla standing to the side and tried to give her a smile. But, the gesture was ignored as Carla scurried off.

A young woman approached, ushered her to the first shoot, and positioned her in the middle of three large yellow square blocks. Bret was placed directly behind her with the others on either side. Megyn reached her hand back and touched Bret's. She pushed the tightly folded paper into his palm and squeezed his fingers tight around the wad. She turned and looked up into his face, her voice purposeful. "I know how you love donuts. You may want to try one from the table *later, when no one will be around* to witness your splurge."

His eyes widened. She could tell he was curious, but thankfully he didn't do anything that would give her away. "Thanks. I'll *check it out later.* When there won't be anyone around."

Megyn's heart beat as if she'd been running a mile. *I hope I'm doing the right thing.*

CHAPTER EIGHTEEN

Megyn walked to the giant bookstore down the street from her living quarters and perused the shelves. She ordered a soy latte and found a table in the corner of the small coffee shop inside, and waited for Bret. He arrived ten minutes later and ordered Chai tea.

Megyn glanced around and leaned close. "Thanks for meeting me like this," she whispered. "You didn't bring your phone, did you?"

He examined the room, leaned close, and matched her tone. "No. Your note said to meet you here and to leave all electronic devices at home. What's up?"

"A package was delivered to me yesterday." She handed it to him. "There was no return address, only what you see."

He looked at the note and then the phone. "Hmm. There must be something interesting on this or we wouldn't be meeting in secret."

Megyn left a tip and picked up both drinks. "Let's walk around a bit. I think this is better viewed in private."

Bret activated the device and followed her out the door. "What am I supposed to look for?"

"Check out the video."

They found a small park a block away. There was a fountain with a cement bench encircling it and Bret sat down.

Megyn paced while he opened the phone, hit the video key and watched.

He viewed it a second time and handed the cell back to Megyn.

She disassembled it, gently wrapped the pieces back in the tissue, and inserted them back into the box. "Let's walk while we talk."

He was quiet for a few minutes. "You've had more time with this than I have. What do you think?"

"I have more questions than answers," she said pocketing the small box. "How many cameras do they have, and where? And, why are they filming us? I don't get it."

Bret scrunched his forehead and sipped his tea. "I wonder who *they* are. Annette says she filmed this at the studio media center. Mary must be involved. I wonder who else. Maybe Ethan?"

Megyn flinched. "I don't think Ethan would have anything to do with this. I was wondering if it could be Trianna and Jason."

"No. They don't seem like the types," he said.

Megyn drew her arms to her sides. She couldn't believe he suspected Ethan, but not the Newberrys.

He stopped and cleared his throat. "Maybe we're getting ahead of ourselves. Let's explore reasons why someone might do this, and then figure out who would be involved."

"I've been thinking about this since I opened the box last night. We're nobodies saying nothing to each other. It's all small talk. Why would anyone care what we have to say? It doesn't make sense."

Bret framed his words carefully. "Have you considered there could be more going on here than meets the eye?"

"I don't understand what you're asking."

Bret took a deep breath. "What do you think about the increased emphasis on unity, equality, and service this season?"

"I think it's brilliant marketing."

"Do you really want to be equal with everyone else? Equal pay, housing, food, medical? Should I take from you and give it to anyone I deem more needy? Anyone I think should have what you have." He stopped walking. In front of them a mother was pushing her child in a swing. "Before you answer, think about the people you know. How many of them would you trust to do the right thing with the money you've worked hard for? If we don't trust the people we already know to make good decisions on our behalf, why would we trust people we don't know? Taking from one person and giving what's been taken to another doesn't make the less fortunate person better off. It just makes everyone the same—at a lower level, not a higher one."

"I don't get your point," Megyn said. "To me, these words express fairness. They convey that no one is more important than anyone else. We are all equal in value. We are unified in our goals. We can do more together than individually. What could be wrong with that?"

Bret softened his voice. "There are people who think these words could be literal. By that I mean, equal means equal. Not equal in value. That unity means sameness, alikeness."

"That's crazy. Why would anyone believe that?"

"What about the video we just shot? Our clothing colors changed as we became unified in the song. At the end, everyone wore purple. Then there are the V³ hats, T-shirts, arm bracelets, and numerous other items. In a way, wearing them makes us all look the same."

Megyn frowned. "I think you're making something out of nothing. Trust me. I know marketing. This campaign is brilliant. What do young people want more than anything else? To be included. To be a part of something. To do something important. What you've described meets these needs. It also helps recruit more Vanguarders. It's marketing." She gave him a smile. "And makes tons of money for the network."

Bret stopped walking. "But, what if there were something more going on? Is it possible someone might want to keep tabs on us to make sure we cooperate with the new direction?"

Megyn turned toward home and steered Bret in the same direction. "I asked you here to help figure this out. Now you're spouting outlandish theories. Let's get back to the privacy issue? We need to find out what's going on. I suggest we ask Ethan what he knows."

"I think that's a bad idea."

Megyn quickened her pace and wondered if sharing the information with Bret had been a good idea after all. "Well, I think we should talk to Ethan," she snapped over her shoulder.

Bret caught up. "Please consider my concerns. I'm not the only one who questions the focus of the Vanguard. There are thousands of people throughout the world."

Megyn stopped. "What are you talking about?"

"All those people who protest at Vanguard events. Why do you think they're there? They're concerned this movement could change into something controlling and coercive."

Megyn raised her voice. "Now I get it. I know who they are and why they're trying to disrupt our good work. They're Christians who think they're the only ones who know anything. They want to exclude groups they don't feel measure up to their standards and bring disunity to the cause. They think they're better than everyone else. Besides, I happen to know that some of the board members have tried to engage the leaders but have had their overtures refused."

"Megyn," Bret said, his voice soothing. "I don't know where you're getting this information, but I ask you to hear me out. There are two sides to every story. You're wrong about Christians, and more importantly, you've misjudged Jesus."

Megyn glared into his eyes. "I've heard enough. Of course you would have this point of view. I'm sorry I included you in this mystery. I'm going to talk with Ethan and he'll give me some straight answers."

Bret tried again. "Please, Megyn. I want the same things you do. I want to know why our privacy is being violated, and by whom. Let's work together on this."

She crossed her arms and stared into the distance while he talked.

"All I ask is that you pay attention to the direction the V^3 is moving and how the messages of unity, equality, and service are being used." He moved closer. "Also, there's been a man following us. I first saw him at the bookstore. He's too obvious. I wonder if he wants us to know he's there?"

Megyn turned to leave. "I know. I've noticed him too."

"Will you do what I've asked? Will you, at least, think about it before you involve Ethan?"

"I don't see any reason to keep this from Ethan. You're wrong about him."

~

Megyn stormed into the shared living quarters, glad it was empty of her fellow Callers. Once in her room she made herself a cup of hot tea, plopped into her comfy chair, and turned on the TV.

Her anger was eased by the thought she would finally get some cherished time alone.

The phone rang.

Ethan's picture showed on her screen and she voice activated the talk capability.

"I was thinking about you and hoped you'd meet me for a quick dinner." He sounded good. "I don't have much time, but decided to take the chance you might be available."

His smooth tones and the thought of talking with someone she trusted drove out her need to be alone. "I'd love to."

CHAPTER NINETEEN

Ethan Strong punched the End button on his phone and positioned himself in front of the expansive mirrored closet doors of his master bedroom suite. He swiveled around to admire every angle of his tall buff frame and grinned. He thought about the evening ahead; her long slender body, her gorgeous eyes, her perfect figure, and her eagerness to do anything he wanted. He knew he would ask her to spend the night and he knew she would agree. Many had come before her and many would come after.

He sighed. That would have to wait. An immediate problem needed to be solved. Mary'd called a few minutes earlier and told him Megyn had somehow obtained evidence of the Caller surveillance. Mary was checking the possible source of the information, but he would have to intervene right away and find out what she knew. Now he was forced to interrupt his evening plans to meet with Megyn and smooth things over.

He adjusted his sweater. Megyn was a beautiful girl, and she was a super rich heiress. He grinned into the mirror. *She definitely has a crush on me.* He repositioned a loose hair. Perhaps he would someday marry her, agree to a generous pre-nup, and later, get a divorce when she discovered his philandering ways. He didn't think she was the type to tolerate his lifestyle, and he definitely wasn't interested in changing it.

~

The dinner booth was private and away from fans and cameras. Megyn greeted him with a soft kiss on his cheek.

"Since I don't have much time, I preordered our dinners," he said. "They should be served any minute." He leaned back and looked her over appreciatively. "How was the photo shoot? I hope they captured your creamy white skin, stunning violet eyes, and silky black hair. Those are my favorite features."

She blushed and took a sip of water in an effort to stay focused. "It was good. Ernie and his staff are fun to work with. I can't wait to see the final products."

He placed his arm around her shoulders and gave her a comforting squeeze. "How are you? Everything all right?"

She marveled at how well he could read her moods. She had wanted to talk to him about Annette's message, but now that they were together she felt hesitant and avoided his question. Maybe she should take more time to think about Bret's arguments. "I'm good. Tell me about you. We always talk about me."

He stretched one arm across the back of the booth. "What do you want to know? My life's an open book to you."

"Of course it is, to me and to millions of other people too. We've all read about you on the Internet and in the tabloids for years."

"Okay. So you think you know everything? How about I tell you the things the media have gotten wrong."

Megyn snuggled in closer. "Oh yeah? Like what?"

"Like, I've never been engaged, even though they have me in love, or almost married, every time I'm seen alone with a female."

He took her hand and gently massaged the tops of her fingers with his thumb. "What else do you want to know?"

She tried to stay focused. "Tell me more . . . your relationships." The lights were dim and soft music played in the background. She barely listened to his explanations as every part of her body was alert to his nearness.

He kissed her ear. "Heard enough?"

"No," she sighed. "I don't think I could ever hear enough."

"Sorry to ruin the moment, but I see our server coming with our food."

They waited while the food was delivered and the water glasses replenished.

Ethan started to take a bite of his salad. "Something else I need to tell you. We've hired a security firm to watch over the Callers. We received a threatening communication last week and are concerned about your safety. You may see them around here and there. Could you let the others know when you get back? We don't want anyone to be alarmed by their presence."

She sat up straight. "I walked down to the local bookstore last night and saw one of them. He watched and followed me the entire time. It was unnerving. I'm glad you told me. I'll let the others know."

Megyn sighed. *The Caesar salad is delicious and Ethan has gone out of his way to see me. He and the ACN staff have even hired a security team to guard our safety. I need to trust him.*

She made her decision. *Bret is wrong about Ethan. He is a good guy.* Her hand moved to her purse. "You asked if everything was all right earlier. There is something I'm concerned about." She pulled out the note and phone and handed them to Ethan." I got this package the night before last. Check out the video."

He watched the tiny screen and immediately began to laugh.

Megyn moved away. "You think this is funny?"

"Yeah. Don't you?"

"Did you happen to notice the privacy violations?"

"What?—Oh, you think someone's been watching you?"

"It sure looks like it to me."

"No, you've got this all wrong." He shifted. "We've always had audio and video equipment throughout our facilities. It's sound and motion sensitive. It was installed for a couple of reasons. Conferences, events, and meetings are held all over the campus. Many of these are recorded digitally—thus the cameras and microphones. Also, security has become an issue in the last few years. Believe me. This technology has helped us identify and convict a couple of law breakers."

"But why didn't anyone tell us this? We're not saying or doing anything we shouldn't, but it would've been nice to have been informed."

"You're right. I thought someone had told you. That's why I was laughing."

"What about the DVDs and file folders with our names on them? How do you explain those?"

"It's no secret we have video footage and still shots of each of you. We have background checks and signed contracts. That's a normal part of business. The Callers granted permission and participated in these activities. You know this."

She felt like a fool.

His face grew more concerned. "I hope you didn't share this with anyone else. I'd hate to think the others have the wrong impressions too."

Megyn didn't want him to think she was any more naïve that he already did. She decided not to tell him about Bret. "I'll let the others know as soon as I get home."

Ethan dropped the phone in his pocket. "I'll have this sent back to Annette's parents. They should have it as part of her belongings."

Megyn felt protective of the phone but couldn't think of a good reason to keep it herself. She didn't say anything.

CHAPTER TWENTY

M egyn heard voices in the distance when she opened the massive front door to her living quarters. She followed the sound and found three of her roommates in the media room with popcorn and a movie. The video was gigantic and the sound vibrated throughout the room. She raised her voice to be heard. "What are you guys watching? I feel like I'm soaring over the mountains along with that plane. I've never seen a picture so clear or sound so good."

Sami twisted in her large chair to see who had entered. "This the first time you've been in here? Where have you been?"

Vince and Carla nodded in agreement.

Megyn didn't want to answer the question. "Are Bret and Tawny here? I have something to tell everyone. It'll only take a minute."

Vince pointed down the hallway. "They're in their rooms. I'll get Bret if you get T." He got up and handed the remote to Carla. "Would you mind pausing this for me? I'd do it but it takes several key strokes to get everything stopped."

Megyn hurried to Tawny's door and invited her to join them. She was in her pajamas but agreed to come.

Bret and Vince followed them back to the others.

They waited for Megyn to speak. She couldn't bring herself to look at Bret. "I just talked with Ethan, and he asked me to pass on some information. ACN has hired a security team to ensure our safety. Apparently, there's been a threat."

"What kind of threat?" Vince said.

"I don't know. I didn't ask." Megyn watched their faces. "All I know is security people have been hired to follow us around. They will stay at a distance, but you may notice them. Don't be alarmed. They've been retained for our protection."

She glanced sideways at Bret but saw no reaction from him.

"The second thing he wanted me to tell you is to be aware there are cameras and microphones throughout the campus, including in our common areas."

All except Bret looked around the room. "You mean, like in here?" Tawny asked. "Why?"

"He said the technology was installed long before we got here. Apparently, the various spaces are used for meetings and conferences. Participants often want a record of the event. We can use this capability too, if we want."

Vince moved around the room looking for possible surveillance equipment hiding spots. "Are they on all the time? Like now?"

"Ethan told me they're motion and sound activated." Megyn felt Bret's eyes watching her every move.

Carla slid her fingers across the top shelf of the entertainment unit. "Who has access to the recordings? How long do they keep them?" She looked at the others. "I don't like this."

Megyn stepped forward. "The media center stores the information. I'm not sure who has access." She extended her hands. "Come on. I think we're worrying about this more than is necessary. Who cares who sees or hears our conversations? We aren't saying anything we wouldn't want others to hear."

Sami wiggled her feet on the chair's foot rest. "You haven't been around much, Megyn or you'd understand why we're concerned. We've talked a lot about the show, what we like and don't like, who we like and don't like." She straightened. "Some of our conversations have been private. We've talked about family problems and relationships. Things we don't want to see broadcast to the world. Why didn't someone tell us this up front?"

"I don't know. I think everyone thought someone else had told us. It was an honest mistake." Megyn shrugged. "We can ask Ethan all these questions next time we see him. All I know is they are planning to keep them going because of the security threat."

"Is that the doorbell?" Tawny said.

Bret headed out of the room. "I'll get it."

The Callers grew quiet while they waited for Bret to return. Vince and Carla examined the tops of furniture and light fixtures. Megyn wondered why Bret wasn't saying anything.

Bret returned with an opened package. "It's a DVD of our V³ anthem and photo shoot, with a note from Ernie thanking us for our good work."

"Let's see it," Vince said reaching for the disc. "Let's continue the privacy conversation another time, and in another place. For right now, grab a seat everyone."

Megyn was rattled. She hadn't expected the Callers to react so harshly. She was sure they would feel differently after they talked with Ethan. *Why would anyone care what we say or do?* She couldn't look any of them in the eyes and was glad the DVD had arrived and changed the subject.

Vince inserted the disc and positioned himself in what he was now calling 'his' chair. He touched the screen of the remote, the lights dimmed, and the music began.

There Megyn stood, clothed in bright blue. The overlaid words UNITY, EQUALITY and SERVICE scrolled across the scene and faded discretely in and out as she stretched her arms to welcome the others, red, yellow, and green. More people and colors joined them and then the colors slowly melded into purple.

The video was familiar until it reached the end. The singers' voices were removed and only the orchestra, playing the melody, remained. Ethan's deep baritone continued the narrative. "Hi, I'm Ethan Strong, host of the Vanguard of Volunteer Voices—the television show. To date, over one hundred million young people from countries around the world have joined us to make the world a better place. This year we are stepping up our efforts. In the past we have encouraged individuals and small groups to share their good works and compete for prizes. This season we'll bring your ideas and activities to a whole new level. Join us on October third for two hours as we kick off our new season by sharing our vision for unity, equality, and service. Let's join together and come prepared, lift our voices, and take a stand."

Megyn's heart leaped with excitement as the promo ended. She couldn't wait to do more for the V³. She sensed Bret's presence to her left. She thought about their earlier conversation. *Why did Christians have to be so negative?*

~

81

Bret wrote a note on the blackboard in the kitchen telling everyone to meet at 9:00 the next morning for a walk to breakfast, and no electronics.

He then walked out the front door and headed back to the fountain area where he had argued with Megyn earlier. He pulled out his personal phone, dialed Pastor Sharpe, and filled him in on the day's events. They prayed together for over two hours.

CHAPTER TWENTY-ONE

Eleven faces popped up, one at a time, on to the large flat panel. Each participant had joined the meeting from a different location. Gisele and Martin Nethers welcomed the Council members from the comfort of their in-home media command center and confirmed the agenda.

"Everything is moving along on schedule," said Gisele. "We've finally reached the point where our corps of young people has fully infiltrated the foundation of the Vanguard of Volunteer Voices. It's been two long years but well worth the slow pace we'd agreed to from the beginning. No one has any idea what our true goals are. By the time they figure them out, it will be too late to undo our efforts."

An old man sat in the shadows of one video box. His unkempt hair prickled out in a variety of directions and his large ears sagged with the weight of age. He spoke in a slow cadence, enunciating every word as he turned the statement into a question. "I understand you've had a couple of problems?"

"We all know about the unfortunate situation with Caller number five," said a young Asian woman with long black hair topped by a bright crimson beret. "That's already been addressed. Due to Ethan's quick action, the 'problem' has been turned to our advantage. As a result of Annette's untimely death, the need for urgency was generated, and the subsequent media spots boosted our membership numbers by seven to ten percent in various major metros the first week they were run."

Gisele cleared her throat. "We only have three hours today, so I'd like us to stick to the agenda items. We need an update on our new global headquarters construction project, and a review of the latest flow charts of our organizational structures and plans, including the financials associated with each. I'll also want status reports on our progress related to the unity, equality, and service initiatives. Specifically, as they relate to the one world religion, the global communication and information technology project, and our environmental efforts."

Jahara, the youngest and newest, member of the Council sat forward. "I've got an update on our business connections." He cleared his throat. "Agreements from our corporate partners are growing exponentially. After months of meetings and private discussions, most are now aware of the advantages of working with us rather than opposing us." He smirked and brushed a speck of dust from his papers. "They've had a chance to witness those who have chosen wrongly: Equipment has failed, employees have filed claims for injuries, products have been recalled, and service has been brought into question."

He leaned back and waved his hand in dismissal. "It hasn't taken long for the others to decide that compliance with our demands is well worth the savings. They've made hiring Vanguarders, giving to our causes, and integrating our major focus areas into their organizational cultures and operations, top priorities. We're supporting them and the companies are flourishing." He rubbed his hands together. "It doesn't hurt that a large portion of their competition is now defeated and immobilized."

The old gentleman leaned into the camera. "I've made considerable progress toward the removal of a significant number of world governments. All the new players are in place, ready to take the lead when the current officials are discredited and begin blaming each other for their own demises. This will escalate the inevitable." He leaned back into his shadowed retreat. "Just let me know within a couple of weeks of your timeframe and I'll make it happen."

Everyone smiled. They knew he could, and would.

CHAPTER TWENTY-TWO

The six Callers were somber when they gathered in the large living room vestibule in preparation for their off-campus surveillance discussion. Their usual laughter and sparring was replaced by the stress of a sleepless night. Megyn watched Sami and Tawny look around the edges of the room. She knew they were searching for cameras and microphones.

She wasn't sure what they were thinking and trailed behind on the short walk to the coffee shop. She was the last to enter the private dining area and take a seat. She watched in silence when the server poured coffee and water, and wrote down their orders.

Bret started the discussion. "Last night Megyn brought news that left us all feeling unsettled." He examined the group. "So, what's everyone thinking today?"

Carla started. "I feel like I've been violated."

The rest of the Callers nodded in agreement.

Megyn scrunched her face. "Why would anyone bother to pay attention to anything we say or do?"

The Callers all spoke at once. Carla was the loudest. "Don't you get it? We can no longer speak freely. We'll always wonder if someone's watching and listening. It's creepy."

"Don't they have to get our permission to do this?" Vince said.

"I was wondering the same thing," Sami said.

"Me too," shrugged Tawny. "We should request they remove the surveillance equipment or move us to another location. I don't think I can live like this another eleven months." She took a sip of water. "I've always wondered if they were watching and listening." Bret perused the group. "Does everyone feel the same way?" All heads nodded agreement.

Megyn sighed. She wanted to believe these things were harmless, believe in Ethan. But she was alone in her thinking. Just yesterday morning she had felt the same way they do now. "I guess I agree too. I trust Ethan and the others, but we really don't know who could be watching at any given time. Carla's right. It's not knowing that's unsettling."

Carla rolled her eyes.

"My dad has expensive equipment and fuel around our farm," Sami said. "He's had them stolen and tampered with throughout the years. Consequently, six months ago he bought a number of security, motion activated, cameras. They're targeted to high risk areas. We should ask ACN to only remove the inside electronics. If our safety is the issue, they can provide for our security from the outside like my dad does."

"What do the rest of you think?" Bret said.

Everyone agreed.

The food arrived and the server left.

"Suppose they won't agree to remove the equipment?" Tawny said.

"That's a hard one," Vince said. "I'd like to say I'd just pack up my stuff and leave, but I don't think I would follow through. I love being a part of the Vanguard of Volunteer Voices. This is such a great opportunity. We've already seen how this movement has helped others. This year looks even better than the last two seasons."

"I'd be disappointed too, but I'm with Vince" Tawny said. "I've given up my job and apartment, spent my ten thousand dollar prize money, and signed a one year contract. I can't walk away from this easily. I'd probably just put up with it."

Bret covered his toast with jam. "Fortunately, we don't have to make that decision today." He took a bite. "Let's assume they will accommodate our wishes."

Vince relaxed back in his chair. "What do ya'll think about the new direction for the V³, unity, equality, and service?"

Megyn leaned forward and waited for a response. She was afraid to be the first one to answer after misjudging the Caller's reactions the night before.

Sami finished chewing her last bite of egg and picked up her coffee. "I'm unclear what the changes will be. I got the impression ACN plans to use us to bring Vanguarders together for common efforts."

Carla heaved a sigh. "The visual was obvious to me. There was one person; then more were added. The separate colors melded together forming unity and equality. It means the Vanguard will leverage individual components into a collective to work in concert on an overall strategic plan for service."

Tawny added more cream to her coffee. "My meeting with the techies included Vanguarders from previous years, and it was obvious a strategy had definitely been formulated prior to my participation. Numerous projects have been coordinated and are now managed from one place."

Megyn thought about her conversation with Bret the day before. She reached for one of the coffee carafes left by the server and watched Bret out of the corner of her eye. "What do you think about this new direction, Vince?" she asked.

"Well, Meg, I like it. We can have far more impact if we work together toward common goals than if we continue in small groups and individual projects. My dream is universal healthcare. I envision a day when everyone will have equal access to good treatment. I believe the young people are the ones to make this happen."

"As far as I'm concerned," Megyn said. "It's about time the youth took a lead. In the past our 'adult' leaders have continually botched every opportunity to create positive, sustainable change in the world. They have gathered for global summits on the economy, the climate, women's issues, weapons of mass destruction, disarmament, energy, security, and many other important concerns."

"And nothing has changed," Sami added. "They ignore the problems that do exist and create ones where there are none. They write thousands of pages of documents that generate new programs and pay off their cronies with our hard-earned cash."

"And spend billions of tax payer dollars in the process," Tawny said.

"Who do you think is leading the V^3?" Bret said.

Vince gave him a confused look. "The youth of course."

Everyone responded in the same way. "The youth. The Vanguard. Us."

Bret signed his name to the tab and stood. "Who specifically is leading the Vanguard? Who made the decision to change the focus this year? Us?" He stopped and waited. "Last year's Callers? ACN staff?"

Megyn got to her feet. "I get where you're going with this. We all know the V³ Oversight Board sets the direction officially. But it's the youth who drive the real change. We're the ones who meet and plan and take action." She stopped to check the other Caller's expressions. "We're the ones who are changing the world!"

"Suppose we had a different direction we wanted to go and refused to do what they asked?" Bret said. "What then?"

Sami stood. "Why would we do that?"

"We wouldn't," Megyn said glaring at Bret. "The Vanguarders are the ones who set the agenda. We're the ones who drive real change."

Bret headed for the door. "Are we? Which of your groups suggested that the V³ focus on unity, equality, and service? Which of you worked on the marketing campaign?" He stopped. "I'm not suggesting there's any wrong doing. I'm just asking all of us to pay close attention to the direction we're taking. Do we want to be equal with everyone else? Should we be?"

He walked out the door.

The others stood and followed him. Megyn brought up the rear. "I don't get him."

No one spoke on the walk home.

~

At two-thirty in the afternoon, the Callers made faces at the walls and waved good-bye around their living quarters before they left for the V³ studio. Ethan had promised Bret the cameras would be removed while they were out of the house and participating in their first show rehearsal.

"Did anyone locate the equipment?" Carla asked.

"Nope," Vince said. "Sami, Tawny, and I searched everywhere. We're thinking fiber optics—tiny little fiber optics."

"How will we know the equipment is gone?" Carla said.

Vince opened the limo door. "I guess we won't ever know for sure, Car."

Carla moaned. "Great. Just great."

CHAPTER TWENTY-THREE

The limo deposited the six Callers in the side alley next to the new studio. Maria was there to greet them and escorted them down a long busy hallway with various open and closed doors on either side. There were storage rooms, some large and some small. One contained electronics, the next held props, and another had costumes, fabric, and sewing machines. Along the way, people with hand held communication devices, outlines, scripts, layout renderings, lighting schematics, and other show-related gear and literature hurried by, each focused on a task at hand. Maria told them they had time to explore the back stage areas for a bit before the initial briefing. She pointed out their dressing rooms: "Megyn and Carla will share this one, Tawny and Sami the room across the hall, and Vince and Bret down here. Bathrooms are this way, and craft services refreshments are straight ahead and to the right."

Megyn glanced at the white, eight and a half by eleven, sheet of paper attached to the wall on the left side of the door. Hers and Carla's names were typed in large block letters. She peeked into the dressing room they would soon share. It was small and new. She could smell the fresh paint and carpeting. There was a mirrored area directly across from the door, and a flat screen TV embedded in the wall to her right with two lounge chairs positioned in front. A small sink and built-in vanity were in the back corner. Her stomach churned with anticipation and she wished she had been paired with Tawny or Sami. *Carla always seems so negative.*

Maria disappeared around the corner and Megyn could hear her ushering the Callers into a conference room. She caught up just as the door across the hall opened wide and revealed a large media center. It looked exactly like the one in Annette's video. She stopped to get a better view and immediately located the monitors that had previously held the video of the Callers. They were dark now. She rubbed her arms and dismissed her doubts. *The tapings are routine, like Ethan said.*

"Over here," said Maria touching her elbow and directing her into a spacious conference room.

Trianna and Jason Newberry sat at the far end of the table and were deep in a discussion with the show's band leader, Peter Shore. Trianna glanced up and motioned to the newcomers. "We need a couple more minutes. While you're waiting, grab one of the folders in the stack by the door, find a seat, browse the contents."

Megyn took a binder and sat down.

"Nervous?" Carla asked as she deposited herself in the next chair over.

"Yeah," Megyn took a deep breath. "I haven't been until now. I'm scared to death."

"Me too. I keep thinking about the millions of people who watch this world-wide. I think I may throw up."

Trianna glanced up. "There's nothing to worry about. We'll take things slow and easy. Everything is already planned. You'll see. Just give us a few more minutes."

Megyn's mouth was dry. She sipped the bottled water that had been placed in front of her and reviewed the documents. The first page contained the day's agenda. A detailed overview of tomorrow's two hour show, along with a step-by-step walk through plan. The next section showed her specific schedule noting parts of the show in which she was to participate, the theme and purpose of each segment, and her detailed talking points. It also described the clothes she would wear, the places she would stand, and various other details. Pages outlining the other participants' roles followed.

Carla leaned closer. "Looks like you and Bret have the big parts tomorrow."

Megyn felt like she would hyperventilate. "I'd hoped to start out slow." She sipped more water. "I'm not comfortable with this much attention."

"You really are a natural in front of the camera, you know. Don't you see it? Everyone else does."

"Nowadays, editors can do a lot to make people look better than they are."

Carla rolled her eyes and scooted away. "Oh please. You're gorgeous, and you know it."

Megyn wasn't sure how to respond. Carla was the beautiful one, not her. She was already on edge and afraid she'd say something wrong. She tried to concentrate on the information in front of her.

Trianna stood and welcomed the group. "We've got a lot to cover, so let's get started. Quickly go around the room and tell us your name and what your role is in the show."

Megyn had been deep into the information she was reading and was surprised to see the number of people who'd joined the group. The chairs were full and several staff were leaning against the walls. All had binders and pencils.

The briefing and walk-through went late into the evening. Not only did the Callers slow things down with questions and concerns, but the new studio itself had problems with the sound and lighting systems. Numerous last minute changes and work-arounds were required to meet the deadlines for the live show the next day. In addition, the new direction of the Vanguard of Volunteer Voices created a different program flow from previous years and ACN staff had to be brought up-to-speed on the changes.

~

Megyn finally dropped into bed in the early hours of the next day. She couldn't fail. She wanted to do something important and this was her shot. She was too restless to sleep and tossed and turned for over an hour. She slipped on her flip flops, grabbed her binder and headed down the hall into the shared kitchen to make tea and walk through her responsibilities in the program.

She paced the kitchen while the water heated and wished one of the other Callers was around to talk with. She had never been so scared in her life. This was the kind of opportunity she'd always wished for, but now she wondered if she could live up to the required responsibilities. The mixed messages from her parents flooded her mind. Her drunken mother telling her she would never amount to anything and her father pushing her to do more.

She shoved these thoughts to the back of her mind, settled into one of the bar stools, and read through her binder of materials. She made notes of the talking point answers she would give to the questions Ethan would ask. "Yes, Annette was a wonderful roommate," she would tell the cameras and studio audience during the segment honoring Annette's brief participation and untimely death. The video package documenting Annette's life would then run including an interview with her parents talking about their shared hopes and dreams to make the world a better place. Ethan would emphasize the theme of urgency and, Megyn would continue with her talking points, personalize her support, and reinforce the Vanguard collective commitment.

Her next appearance was with Mary and Simon. Mary would talk about the local area Web site they had launched in concert with the global networking efforts. Simon would tell how the Modesto program was expanding exponentially while video of busy Vanguarders from around the world would flash across the screens behind them.

Megyn was to describe the people she had met and the progress she had witnessed. She took more notes of things she could say to support the pre-established focus of collectively working together. She finished her tea and walked into the dimly lit living room, talking to herself as she shaped and re-shaped the things she would emphasize.

"Hi," came a voice from the corner.

Startled, Megyn tripped and fell into one of the love seats.

Bret hopped up and apologized. "I thought you saw me."

Megyn's hand was on her chest. "Obviously not. What are you doing in here?"

"Praying."

Megyn repositioned herself to face him. "You don't do that in your room?"

"Most of the time. Tonight I'm walking around the house praying for each of us and the messages we'll share later this evening. I heard you in the kitchen, so I just stayed in here to finish up."

Megyn examined her fingernails and fidgeted with her hands. "Okay." *All I need is a conversation about religion right now.* She backed out the way she'd entered, wishing she'd stayed in the kitchen. "I'm going back to my room to try and get some sleep."

She turned and left before Bret could respond.

CHAPTER TWENTY-FOUR

Megyn sat alone in her dressing room. She hadn't seen Carla since they arrived at the studio several hours earlier and could hear Tawny and Sami laughing and talking across the hall. The smell of the five dozen fresh roses sent from her parents overwhelmed her already heightened senses. The flat panel TV showed Bret rehearsing with the V³ band and universal choir assembled to support him in the opening song. "He's got you and me brother, in His hands," he sang out in his deep clear voice. She wondered how he could be so poised and confident. Whenever she allowed herself to think about the various things she was to do, her hands turned clammy and the rhythm of her breathing grew choppy.

She yawned nervously and patted the stage makeup around her lips to make sure it hadn't been disturbed. She stood when Ethan entered the room. He was all smiles as he took her hands in his and pulled her close. "I know you're nervous. Don't try to look at the people, or the cameras. The lights are so bright you won't be able to see them anyway. Look at me. Talk to me. Pretend we're two friends having a chat. No one else is around. You can do that. I know you can. You'll be great."

Carla entered the room with a knowing smile and an exaggerated, "Excuse me."

Ethan backed away. "Just wishing everyone good luck." The TV caught his attention and he watched as Bret began his crescendo through his final verse. "He's got everybody here, in His hands." The choir increased their volume in support and swayed in the background, hands reaching toward the heavens. "I've got to get back out front before he finishes. Good luck girls. Have fun with it."

"Everyone's been wondering," Carla said.

Megyn didn't want to talk about Ethan. "What?"

"You know. You and Ethan. Are you together?"

"We're just friends."

Carla took a seat across from her. "Right." She dismissed Megyn with a wave of her hand. "You know he's got a girl in every port? Sometimes more than one."

Megyn sat down next to her and sighed. "I know. I read the tabloids sometimes. We're friends. Trust me. Nothing has happened. Really!"

"Right."

Bret finished his song and both girls watched as the spotlights blazed down on Ethan.

"He *is* hunky," Carla said.

"I know," Megyn sighed.

Carla poured a glass of cold water. "Maria will be looking for you soon. I just finished my interviews and you're up after Vince."

Megyn tried to breathe normally. She could feel a headache coming on. "How was it?"

Carla shrugged. "They were lined up down the side of the building. I must have talked to at least twenty media people. The interviews were short and ACN staff kept things moving. I was expecting the worst, but it wasn't that bad. They know I'm not a professional and I think they went easy on me because of that."

"I hope I get the same treatment," Megyn gulped. She turned to the TV and pretended to watch Ethan while she mentally practiced the responses Gisele had helped her create regarding her parents involvement in V^3.

~

The evening flew by as Megyn was directed from one scene to another. When she wasn't on camera, she received direction for her next spot. The lights were bright, the music loud and the audience enthusiastic. Busy workers and equipment moved all around her, each with a specific purpose. Her makeup and hair were continually touched up and her wardrobe changed. So much was happening so fast, one minute she felt like she did a great job, and the next wished for a 'do over'.

Two hours later the finale came and the Callers assembled for the Vanguard of Volunteer Voices anthem. Megyn's emotions soared with those in the live audience. The room was electric. The song ended but the crowd continued singing. They raised their hands to make the V³ sign. After the audience finished the song, the Callers hugged and congratulated each other on the way back to their dressing rooms.

Megyn was exhausted to her core, thirsty, and hungry.

Standing in the doorway was the last person in the world she expected to see. "Mom?" The good feelings Megyn had felt just moments before drained out of her. "What are you doing here?"

Mrs. Buckman fidgeted with the designer purse in her hands.

Megyn watched and waited, her feelings a jumble of hope and years of experienced caution. Her mother looked better than she'd ever seen her. She had put on a few pounds and looked healthier. Her dark hair was casual, yet stylish. Things had changed. She was different.

Her mother smiled tentatively. "You did a wonderful job tonight."

Megyn shrugged. She didn't know what to think. She didn't know this woman. "Thanks."

Mrs. Buckman focused on her feet. "I was wondering if we could talk?"

"Right now?"

"We can go someplace private. I won't take much of your time? I've booked a suite down the street."

Megyn wanted to tell her no. She wanted to be left alone. She was happy with her new life. "All right, but I've got to get back and join the others in the next hour."

Mrs. Buckman relaxed. "I promise."

Megyn had heard her mother's promises before and knew better than to trust her words. She retrieved her purse. "Just let me tell someone I'm leaving."

~

The suite was beautiful. Food and drink sat skillfully displayed to one side. Megyn was famished and helped herself to fresh water, fruits, cheeses, crackers, and garnishes.

Her mother brushed an imaginary speck from her sleeve. "Thanks for coming."

Megyn took a seat at the large mahogany table and nibbled her food.

Mrs. Buckman looked resolute. "I want to ask for your forgiveness."

Megyn was silent.

"I know I've failed you as a mother. I'm an alcoholic and I've never been there for you."

Megyn couldn't breathe. She had heard these words many times before.

"When you left home, your father and I were devastated. He handled his hurt, like he always does—working harder. I hit bottom. I checked myself into a rehabilitation program and I've been sober for three years now."

Megyn took a sip of water. There were too many years of broken promises, missed dance recitals, forgotten birthdays, and violated trust. She couldn't respond. She didn't want to be vulnerable again.

"I don't expect you to jump into my arms and forgive me. I know there's too much history. My counselor said we should take it slow. She suggested we start from scratch and get to know each other. Three years have gone by and we've both changed." She sat down across from Megyn and looked into her eyes. "I was hoping we could have lunch together. No pressure. Just talk and get to know each other." She got up and paced. "You don't have to decide today. I know I've surprised you. All I ask is that you consider my proposal. I would like to be your friend, and I would like your forgiveness."

Megyn heard her mother's voice crack and saw the tears in her eyes. She got up and gave her a tentative hug. She felt trapped and didn't know what to say. "Let's plan one lunch and we'll go from there."

Mrs. Buckman heaved a sigh. "That would be great." She blew her nose.

"I don't have my schedule with me," Megyn said. "How about I call you when I get home? I've really got to go and meet up with my roommates."

She walked down the hallway not sure she would follow through.

CHAPTER TWENTY-FIVE

Megyn was eager to celebrate with her fellow callers. She had her mother's driver drop her off at her temporary home and hurried through the front door. She followed the laughter to the patio and greeted everyone with a big smile. Sami pointed to the food and beverages set out by caterers hired by the ACN staff. "Get something to eat and have a seat."

"You haven't missed much," Carla said. "It took forever to get out of the studio. We just got here ourselves."

"Tell your mom and dad thanks for the flowers," Tawny said. "We loved them."

"Us too," Vince said.

Megyn didn't know they'd sent flowers to everyone and didn't want to talk about her parents. She grabbed a couple of things to munch on and turned to the others. "Wasn't it wonderful?"

"It was great, ya'll," Vince said. "I was really nervous at first, but then before I knew it, the whole thing was over. I can't believe how drained I feel. But in a good way. I recorded it and thought we could watch it together once everyone got here."

"I think we missed a lot of the show, with all the wardrobe changes and prep for our next spots," Carla said. "I'm eager to see how it went."

Bret stood. "I know we're still excited right now, but it's just a matter of time before we crash and burn. We better get started." He moved toward the French doors.

Vince jumped up and leaped in front of him. "Don't any of ya'll even think about sitting in *my* chair."

"That goes for mine too," each Caller chimed in one after another.

Megyn followed the others into the media room. She didn't have *a chair* and realized Carla was right in her earlier criticism. She hadn't been around much. She wished she'd had more time with her roommates. It seemed she'd let everyone else be in charge of her life and had missed the chance to get to know the people she lived with better.

Vince dimmed the lights and started the show. The music played and young people throughout the world flashed across the giant screen. Large rallies, forums and individuals laughing, sharing, and serving, moved in out of view in time with the melody. Megyn was deeply moved and glanced around the room. Everyone looked excited.

The stage lights changed and Bret rose from a mist. The universal choir surrounded him and a giant globe of the earth hovered in the middle. Bret and the others looked as if they were in outer space gazing down on the blue and green orb. They appeared to be floating around it, inviting the universe to join them in celebration. "He's got the whole world in his hands," they sang. The sight gave Megyn the chills. "Wow."

"Unbelievable," Carla said. "I wonder how they did that."

Ethan entered next and welcomed the cheering crowd. He told the global audience the Vanguard of Volunteer Voices had more than doubled in the last year and the official registration was now well over two hundred million. He encouraged them to continue to invite their friends to join. He then pointed to the Web site illuminated on the huge screen behind him and walked them through a few key areas of interest.

The promo video of the Callers was up next. The six of them paraded to center stage to be introduced at its completion. The audience roared with appreciation as each name was shouted and the Caller presented. "We look pretty darn good," Vince said.

The Callers exited the stage and Megyn was alone with Ethan. He did a brief introduction and they stepped to the shadows as a video documented her trip to Modesto, California. Simon, the local contact, along with the Vanguard tech leader, Mary, joined them in the dark. The presentation ended, the lights came up, and Mary told about the opportunity to bring people together both locally and internationally. She provided a sophisticated video of how the interactions would work, and showed models of other regions that had already joined the movement.

Simon followed with a visual example of how Vanguarders, with similar interests, had contacted each other on line, formed groups to pursue activities, and taken action. He pointed to Central Valley newspapers that have celebrated Vanguarders' accomplishments of cleaning up Highway 99, one of California's main thoroughfares, trimming trees and shrubs for the elderly, and painting a storage facility for the local food bank. He held up a plaque the council of neighboring mayors had awarded them. Megyn used the Web site to show the V^3 resources available to establish similar local connections. She emphasized this new Web site as a means to promote unity, equality, and service.

Bret was up next with Ethan. His segment was formatted similar to Megyn's, with a video of his trip to Vancouver, British Columbia. It showed the forum he conducted and ended with samples of art created by the various participants. Ethan asked Bret a few questions about his song writing and told the audience that using the arts to communicate a unified message was a key goal this season.

The show continued in the same manner interspersed with performances by hot new stars, dance routines, and state-of-the-art technology and communications techniques. Sami's vignette was presented in 3D, without the need for glasses. Ethan questioned her about the importance of universal health care for the physically challenged, and they talked about the latest in environmentally focused animal husbandry.

Vince was preceded by a choreographed troop of gold metal winning Olympic athletes who performed numerous physical feats with agility, precision, and strength; and he left the audience with examples of ways to live well from the Universal Health Organization. Tawny and Nathan demonstrated prototypes of new communications technologies. Vanguarders in the audience oohed and aahed at what seemed like a magic show.

In the final segment, Carla appeared with Ethan, along with religious leaders from various locations throughout the globe. A rabbi, monk, cardinal, imam, spiritualist, and an atheist smiled out at the audience through individual boxes on the big screen. They talked of unconditional love and forgiveness and emphasized unity, equality, and service through universal connectedness.

The show ended with the V^3 anthem. The Callers remained still in the dimly lighted media room, speechless with emotion. For the first time in Megyn's life, she felt like she was doing something important. She was independent and had a purpose.

CHAPTER TWENTY-SIX

The house buzzed with activity. New assignments had been handed out earlier in the week and the Callers were to be dispatched around the world. Megyn was scheduled for Singapore. She'd visited this small island country, located on the tip of the Malay Peninsula, many times and loved the historic, plantation style, Raffles Hotel where her father held extravagant corporate events thanking his global partners each year.

Attending these conferences had been some of the happiest times of her life. When she and her father were together in this plush setting, he seemed more relaxed. He included her in his activities and didn't pressure her to act in a certain way.

She sat in the kitchen, sipped coffee, and greeted her roommates who hurried in and out grabbing bagels, coffee and juice in between packing and getting dressed. After last night's celebration with her roommates, she finally felt like part of the group and wished she could spend more time with them. She glanced down at the note left on her pillow the night before. It was signed by Gisele and said that a car would pick her up at noon and take her to one of the Nethers' three private jets. She would meet up with several Callers from previous seasons. They would travel together and stay in the Nethers' high rise condominium in Singapore. This would be her home base while she worked with local Vanguarders throughout the region. She would stay a couple of weeks and participate in the next show via the local Singapore ACN studio.

She massaged her temples. She was tired and, as Bret had warned, her emotions had come crashing down from the high of the previous day. Everything seemed overwhelming and she hoped she would be able to relax and sleep on the long flight. The familiar feeling of having her life once again controlled by someone else weighed heavy. And, she dreaded calling her mom to let her know their lunch would be delayed.

Carla popped in for toast and orange juice. "Shouldn't you be getting ready?"

"I'm not leaving for a while and thought I'd hang around out here to say good-bye. I just found out I'm going to be gone for two weeks and am kind of bummed about it."

"What about next week's show?"

"Apparently, they plan to patch me in through a satellite feed."

Carla filled her glass. "If I didn't know better, I'd think you were trying to avoid us."

Megyn wasn't sure if she was kidding. "I can assure you, I wish I wasn't going for so long. I feel like I've missed a lot with our group and want to make up for lost time. Yesterday was a lot of fun."

Carla buttered her toast and started back to her room with it. "I'm running late. See you in a couple."

Bret entered the kitchen, sat his suitcase by the door, and covered a huge yawn with his hand. "Sorry. Carla just told me about your schedule. Two weeks is a long time." He took the pen and paper on the counter, scribbled on it and handed it to Megyn. "If you need anything while you're gone, here's my personal contact information."

Megyn wrinkled her forehead. "Thanks, but I don't see any reason why I would need this."

He poured a cup of coffee. "Probably not, but just in case."

She folded the paper and squeezed it in her hand. "Where are you off to?"

"Tennessee. We're launching a song writing contest. I'm to join ACN staff and attorneys and meet with several of the big music label executives to design a project that will be introduced during next week's show." He took a seat across from her. She could feel his eyes studying her, which made her uncomfortable. He looked thoughtful and concerned. "How're you doing?" he asked. "Everything Okay? I saw your mom waiting in the hallway last night."

Megyn hesitated. Her emotions were all over the place, and she wasn't sure how to get them focused. She wondered how much to share and decided to just go with the facts. "My mom's an alcoholic. She told me she went to rehab and has been sober since I left home three years ago. She asked for my forgiveness."

"What did you tell her?"

She gazed into her coffee mug. "Nothing. I couldn't tell her I forgive her. I grew up with her problem. She would drink, say and do things she felt bad about, ask me for forgiveness, things would get better for a short time, she would drink again, and the cycle repeated itself. I lived with this roller coaster existence for eighteen years of my life. I don't trust her broken promises. I've forgiven her so many times; I don't have any forgiveness left."

She could tell he was thinking about what she'd just said. "Yet, you don't seem satisfied with the way things went," he said.

"I would like to forgive her, but I don't know how. I don't know if I have it in me to try again, and I feel guilty for not wanting to try."

The doorbell rang and Bret put one finger up in a gesture for her to wait a moment and headed for the front door. "Hold that thought. I'll be right back."

Carla and Tawny appeared in the kitchen looking anxiously in the direction of the living room.

Bret re-entered. "Three for the airport. He needs to leave immediately. Apparently, he has someone else to pick up on the way."

The two girls headed to their rooms to retrieve their luggage and Bret turned to Megyn. "I have to go. Can I call you to finish this discussion?"

Megyn felt like the moment had passed and was embarrassed. "That's okay. We don't know our exact schedules, and there's a substantial time difference from Singapore to Tennessee. We'll talk another time."

Bret picked up his bag. "You have my personal numbers. Please contact me if you change your mind. I'll be praying."

The front door closed and Megyn was now the only one home. Vince and Sami had left earlier and she had two hours until her ride was due. She was finally alone, and to her surprise, she was lonely.

CHAPTER TWENTY-SEVEN

The condominium covered the entire floor beneath the penthouse and to Megyn's delight had, expansive views of Singapore, Malaysia, and Indonesia. The three Callers Megyn had met at the Nethers' not long ago, and she, explored the space together and staked out rooms as they went. Megyn was the only female and the guys offered her first pick. She chose a suite that included a spa where she could relax and observe the sea faring traffic in the Strait of Singapore with Indonesia in the distant background. Their luggage was delivered, and they were told someone would unpack for them, and to hurry up to the penthouse for cocktails and hors d'oeuvres with Gisele and Martin. Megyn loved the diversity of food this area of the world offered and her stomach growled with anticipation.

The top three floors were owned by the Nethers and were connected by a private elevator. The Callers took the short ride up and were greeted by Martin when the doors opened. "Gisele's running a little behind. She'll join us in a few minutes." He pointed to the bar and appetizers. "Help yourselves. Dinner's in half an hour. I'll go check on her progress."

Megyn sipped her tea and observed the Singapore cityscape. It reminded her of the time she'd spent with Gisele in the spa with downtown Los Angeles in the background. It was such a relaxing time. Gisele had been there when she needed a friend. Megyn didn't know why but she was uncomfortable. Gisele and Martin seemed sincere and genuine, but she didn't really know them. She had grown up around powerful people with money and had learned to mistrust their words until they were matched with their deeds. She felt guilty for her doubts. She told herself she was just tired from the busy week and would be fine once she rested up.

Paul took the seat next to her. "Remember me, from the Nethers' dinner party your first night in town?"

Megyn laughed. "I know this week has been a long one, but not so long that I've forgotten who you are." She watched the sun set across the harbor. "This is an amazing place. I used to come here with my father every year on his business trips. How about you? Been here before?"

"This must be one of the Nethers' favorite places. They visit here a lot. Fortunately, us previous Callers get to tag along too, but we usually stay on the floor below us. I think we're getting the royal treatment since you're along this time."

Megyn blushed.

Paul continued. "Mark and Josh were invited the first season. I was added last year, and now you. In fact we're around so much these days, everyone refers to us as 'the boys.'"

Mark and Josh joined them with plates loaded with food and a pitcher of fresh iced water. "It's important to stay hydrated when you've been on long flights," Josh said, refilling her glass.

"You're going to love the council's plan for us," Mark said. "We've been working on making it operational all summer and are eager to share the details with you and the international team they've put together. Yesterday, the world was introduced to the priorities of unity, equality, and service. This is the group that will work within the Vanguard to drive this agenda."

Megyn remembered Bret's question. "Aren't the Vanguard members coming up with the ideas?" she asked.

Paul sat forward. "Who would that be? The Callers are the closest thing to leadership there is. They change every year and most of them are not true leaders. They're chosen through random phone calls."

Mark cut him off. "This movement is revolutionary. Imagine the youth of the world, unified and equal, serving others for a better world. It's mind boggling!"

"This season we'll finally be there," Josh said.

Gisele entered the room and greeted each of her guests with a warm hug. She was glowing and elegant in her understated Vera

Wang black dress pants and deep green cotton shirt. "You boys are the best." She smiled at Megyn in appreciation. "Welcome. Welcome, daughter."

Gisele's greeting made Megyn feel warm inside. She wanted this. She wanted a family. She returned Gisele's embrace and blushed with pleasure. Her misgivings from earlier vanished and were replaced by an eagerness to please. She thought of the tension-filled interaction with her mother the night before. That was the old. This is the new. She had finally found the family she'd always wanted.

Martin observed the overflowing plates the boys had assembled. "I told you," he jeered, "We're going to eat in half an hour."

They smiled and continued to munch.

Gisele took a seat next to Megyn. "Sounds like the boys have been filling you in. What do you think?"

Megyn pushed her plate away. "I'm thrilled to be here and eager to get started."

Martin moved toward the door. "Dinner is ready."

Mark, Josh, and Paul joined him.

Gisele gently placed her arm inside Megyn's and escorted her to the huge dining room. She patted her hand and squeezed her close. "I'm so glad you're here. I needed another female to balance out all this testosterone."

The room was long with a shiny teak table that could easily accommodate twenty people. Place settings were at the far end. Martin sat at the head, with Gisele to his right. Megyn was placed on her right. The boys chose chairs on either side of the table.

Gisele lifted her glass of Champagne. "To revolutionary change," she said.

"To revolutionary change," they repeated glasses clanging gently together.

"Unity, equality and service," Martin said.

"Unity, equality and service," the young people repeated.

Dinner was served by slender men in white jackets and black slacks. Megyn didn't pay attention to their comings and goings or the food they placed in front of her. The conversation ignited her zeal to make the world a better place. It was obvious Martin and Gisele were extremely powerful people. Her billionaire father paled in comparison to their connections and influence. She marveled at the ease in which Mark, Paul and Josh participated in the conversation. It was clear they had the Nethers' respect, and she hoped Gisele and Martin would also come to appreciate and trust her counsel.

Tomorrow they would meet with the global team tasked with the roll out of the new V^3 direction: The next two weeks would be spent on updating the target activities, fine tuning the message, and introducing inducements for cooperation. Their time would be facilitated by professionals and include the latest communications electronics for real-time interactions. They would work with the marketing experts, brief media, and engage Vanguarders throughout the world.

Gisele leaned over and whispered. "Don't worry, daughter. I know it seems like a lot at first, but once you get going, you'll be carried along with the others. Everything flows logically and I know you're a logical person. Your marketing background will be a definite plus."

Megyn smiled. "Somehow you always seem to know my thoughts. I was feeling quite overwhelmed and insecure. Thanks."

The evening flew by and Megyn's head was spinning with excitement and new information to think about. She, and the other young people, returned to their living quarters and talked until early morning before finally snatching a few short hours of rest.

CHAPTER TWENTY-EIGHT

Megyn and "the boys" arrived early to the small auditorium. The week's agenda had been electronically sent the evening before. Representatives from throughout the world were in attendance. The majority were young people with a few older activists who'd been invited for their expertise and resources. Allies reconnected and the room buzzed with excitement. Megyn, Paul, Josh, and Mark, took their seats near the front and the meeting began at 9:00 a.m. sharp.

Gisele welcomed the two hundred participants and thanked them for their continued commitment. She talked of the progress they had already made and the exponential growth the Vanguard of Volunteer Voices TV show had allowed them to achieve. The lights dimmed as she delivered her final words, "We are at a critical point in our journey. We'll need to join together to reach our goals. We'll need to work harder than we've ever worked before. We'll sacrifice for the good of the whole. And . . . we'll willingly forfeit our freedoms to give to a cause greater than ourselves. We will unify, equalize, and serve."

Before the final words left Gisele's mouth, the audience was on its feet with cheers and applause. Megyn had never seen Gisele so full of zeal and purpose. The entire experience felt spiritual. The energized participants were now an unstoppable force. She could feel their power and determination.

The room thundered, the lights flashed, money fell from above, and the audience snatched up the bills and coins. A woman took the stage. "This is our new currency," she said. "It will be introduced during next week's telecast and promoted through various media. Anyone who has a TV, computer, or cell phone will get the message. Billboards and print media will also be used.

"Immediately following Tuesday's Vanguard of Volunteer Voices TV show, a nominal amount of these new funds will be distributed to everyone who joins, or has joined, the V³. Opportunities to earn more will be offered through performance of activities that promote unity, equality and service. How dollars are earned will be defined in upcoming communications." The screen flashed examples of currency denominations and publicity samples.

"In the beginning, the money will be exchanged for V³ sponsored items only. Over the next year, the currency program will expand its uses to include tender for education, technology, environmental issues, and our other areas of focus. We will continue to extend our reach until our money becomes the standard of trade for goods and services throughout the world. It will be backed by the Vanguard's sponsors who have now accumulated funds larger than most countries' Gross National Products."

The next hour was spent describing the details of how the roll-out would proceed.

"The reason we can move this quickly," she said, "is because we have formed working teams: teams for health and wellness, technology and communications, environment, spiritualism, and money and giving. These teams are seeded with our people who have been strategically placed to drive our agenda and ensure conformity." She extended her arm in invitation. "If you are participating in one of these groups, please stand so we can thank you for your tireless efforts."

To Megyn's surprise, most of the young people in attendance stood, along with Paul, Mark, and Josh. The remainder of the crowd applauded loudly.

The money woman walked to the center front of the stage. "Throughout the rest of this week you will hear the roll out strategy for each of the teams I just mentioned. The Nethers will complete the week with the overall strategy and implementation timeline." She left the stage to thunderous applause.

The balance of the time progressed in the same way. Spiritualism was the next topic, environmental issues after that, and health and wellness ended the day.

Megyn was overwhelmed. This movement had obviously existed long before the first V³ show aired two years earlier. This was a life work for the Nethers. She wondered who else was involved and why she'd been included at this level. She again thought about Bret's question of who was driving the movement. She liked where things were headed and doubted if the answer really mattered. She was eager to join in no matter who was driving it forward.

She thought of her dad and his huge corporation. He would be surprised to learn that his life was about to change, and that his daughter would be a part of making it happen.

~

The next day Megyn stared at the TV without watching it. Her body eased into the soft cushions of the love seat. Her jet lag had caught up with her and the long first day of meetings had worn her out. She was glad for the time alone and pulled the cozy afghan around her shoulders and sipped her hot Jasmine tea. She wondered what the Callers back home were up to and couldn't wait to share what she was learning with them. She closed her eyes and was awakened by their voices coming out of the TV.

"That was great," Vince said. "I can't wait for my new assignment."

"I've always loved to watch the Vanguard of Volunteer Voices," Carla said. "I wish I'd gotten involved long before now."

"Me too," Megyn said. "I plan to continue long after our time here is done."

"To The Vanguard of Volunteer Voices," Tawny and Sami said together as they lifted their hands showing two fingers forming a V and three fingers signifying "to the third."

Megyn watched the conversation proceed and remembered the encounter. They'd been on the back patio celebrating the completion of the first week's show. Ethan had told them the hidden cameras had been removed the day before. He'd promised their privacy would not be intruded upon again. She had trusted him. She felt sick to her stomach. She thought about the possibility of surveillance in her current situation but dismissed the idea that Gisele would have had anything to do with what happened in Los Angeles. Gisele was her new family. She would never do something like that.

She found the piece of paper on which Bret had written his private contact information, and dialed using her personal cell phone.

"It's Megyn. Do you have a minute?"

"I've got about five. How are you? What's up?"

"Have you seen the latest promotional commercial? It's of all of us on the back patio celebrating the completion of the first show."

The phone was silent.

"Right after the first show?" Bret's voice echoed the unbelief she'd felt when she'd first realized what had happened.

"Yes, it's the part where we all reaffirmed our commitment to V^3 and Tawny and Sami gave the hand sign."

"Have you talked with Ethan or anyone else about this?"

"No, I decided to call you first. I think we should include the others and decide together what to do next."

"I agree. This affects all of us. When are you headed back?"

"Not for another week and a half."

"Hmm. They need to know before that. Maybe we should patch you in via satellite. I'll talk to Vince and see if he knows how to work the video conferencing equipment. I know it's not secure, so maybe we'll try to get help from Nathan, Sami's new techie boyfriend. He can probably come up with a better solution. I assume you're calling from your personal cell. I'll text you with some times once we get things figured out."

"The best time to reach me will be in the middle of the night here. Otherwise, my schedule's controlled by others."

Bret paused. "How're things going? I've been praying for you and your mother and your decision regarding her request for forgiveness."

Megyn was touched by his concern but didn't want to think about it right now, let alone, have a conversation. "Oh. I've hardly thought about that since I left home. This is the first break I've had since I got here. A lot's been happening and I can't wait to share it with you guys."

"Like what?"

Megyn described the day and what she'd learned.

Bret was quiet on the other end of the phone. "I've got to go. Keep me updated on the progress," was all he said.

~

That night Bret called Pastor Sharpe and together they carefully crafted a request calling for worldwide prayer and fasting. They were careful not to compromise Megyn's confidential information.

CHAPTER TWENTY-NINE

Megyn freshened up and headed out the door for dinner with the boys. She'd just completed the final session of the week and was eager to debrief. So much information had been shared, she could barely think anymore. She grabbed the doorknob to exit her room and her foot slipped on a piece of paper near the threshold. It was a note from Gisele and Martin. She had barely interacted with them all week and was delighted to receive an invitation to join them later in the evening to celebrate a successful week and, to make new acquaintances.

She met Paul, Josh, and Mark in the living room. They had also received invitations and told her the new friends she would meet were important.

Paul leaned on her shoulder and peered down into her eyes. "You'll love them. They give this movement its power. We meet with them quite often and each time we're energized and become more fearless for the cause."

"I'm starving. How's the Raffles Hotel sound for good food," Josh said.

"Let's walk," Mark said. "I'm tired of sitting."

Together, they headed for the elevator.

Megyn pushed the button with the star. "I'm nervous. How about a hint as to whom these new acquaintances are?"

"We shouldn't give anything away," Paul said. "All I'm willing to say is, you'll be glad you came."

Josh leaned on her opposite shoulder and talked to the others. "I'll give her a clue. The spirits are what give our movement its power; I know you felt them this week. I could see it in your actions."

Megyn agreed the week's meetings had been like no others she'd ever attended. There was something intangible. It was like an electric current had pulsated throughout the entire auditorium. She hadn't considered a spiritual presence was at work.

~

Gisele escorted Megyn to a room in the shape of a small rotunda. It was round and spacious with shiny bamboo floors and five columns evenly distributed around the outside. The area was lit with hundreds of three-inch round, crème colored candles. On the floor, directly beneath the center of the dome, was a beautiful wood inlay. It was a six feet in diameter circle with a five pointed star in the middle. The form of a man stretched to each point.

Gisele put her arm around Megyn's waist. "Ever seen one of these before?"

Megyn shook her head.

"It's a pentagram." She ushered Megyn to the edge of the circle. "The point, where the man's head is located, represents the spirit. The points with his outstretched hands represent air and water and the points where his feet are extended symbolize earth and fire. The entire picture is of man's relationship with the Creator and his creation. We use it when we communicate with the spirit world."

Gisele released her. "You don't have to participate this first time. Just listen and watch. I'll explain things and answer questions later."

Doors opened from the five directions of the symbol and leaders from the prior week's meetings, joined their small group. Soft music filtered in through hidden speakers as the doors glided shut. Everyone began to chant. Megyn remembered the Ouija board experience and her body trembled.

She felt a cold wind brush past her cheek. The room glowed with the soft light of movement. She took a deep breath and rotated her shoulders. She could hear the beating of her heart in her ears. She closed her eyes hoping to gain control. The memories of Demon Spirit's threats to Sarah crashed through the barrier she'd erected in her mind. *The things that happened to Sarah and her family weren't coincidences. They were done to them. Demon Spirit was responsible.* The room grew colder and her body shook uncontrollably. Her head began to spin and she did the only thing she could think to do, she prayed. *Help. Help me, God. Please, help me.*

A warm arm surrounded her. It led her out the door and to a sofa. Her eyes remained closed as she sank into the cushions. A hot cup of tea was forced into her hands. "Drink this," said Paul. "I'll check back on you later."

She nodded her head.

~

Early the next morning, a woman followed Megyn from the condo and observed from a distance. She recognized her as one of the security detail assigned to protect her and continued to walk. She reached the end of a dock and scanned the night sky. She was confused and embarrassed and not sure what had happened. She looked at her cell and walked back down the pathway. It was two in the morning, but she wasn't sleepy. Today would be her first free day since she'd joined the V³ almost four weeks earlier. She took a deep breath and exhaled. She wondered if Gisele was mad, or worse, disappointed in her.

~

The large digital numbers on her alarm clock read three-thirty when Megyn arrived back in her room. Her bed was turned down and a note was placed on her pillow.

> *Don't worry my daughter. It's my fault. I should have prepared you ahead of time. It's been such a busy week, I didn't think. Let's talk later, when you've had some rest and feel better. Your reaction is not uncommon for the first time.*
> *Love, Gisele*

Megyn sat on the side of her bed and stared out the window. Five minutes later she crawled under a blanket and slept.

CHAPTER THIRTY

The day was overcast and hot. Megyn found a shady spot near a fountain and activated her personal phone. She spoke the number Bret sent and waited. Vince's deep Southern drawl oozed through her cell's speaker, and his glistening white smile gleamed through the six inch screen.

"Hey, Meg. We're just waiting for Car. How's Singapore?"

"Hot, very hot, and muggy. How're things in California?"

"Interesting, very interesting."

Megyn could see Carla approach Vince.

He turned to greet her. "It's about time. We haven't seen much of you lately. You'll have to fill us in on what you've been up to when we get home."

Carla motioned him to keep quiet, and Megyn heard him whisper a response but couldn't understand what he said.

Vince panned the group with his miniature camera. "Say hi to Meg, ya'll."

"Hi," they waved.

Megyn gulped. Loneliness swept over her. She was surprised how much she missed their camaraderie. Things seemed more normal when they were around.

The picture stopped on Bret. "I've told everyone about your call, and Sami talked to Nathan. He did some research for us. He found the promo you mentioned and sent it to our personal cells.

We've all had a chance to watch it. According to him, it was exclusively broadcast outside the United States."

Carla poked her face in front of Bret. "Everyone's ticked off. We've been violated once again."

"We've talked about this ever since Bret told us about the commercial," Sami said directing Vince's hand in her direction. "We should've made it clear the audio and video equipment on the patio would be removed along with the ones inside."

"Even so, they had no right to do this without our permission," Carla said.

"Actually, we're not sure that's true," Vince said. "We signed contracts that allow them to use us for promotional materials." He cleared his throat. "We think they may actually be within the law."

Megyn sighed. "So there's nothing we can do?"

"Until someone tells us differently, we're assuming there are bugs everywhere," said Bret. "Nathan told us technology is so far advanced today that we could be recorded from almost anywhere. Removing devices isn't necessarily going to solve this."

"Bottom line," Vince said. "We think we're stuck. Our conversations change when we're on campus. We're by the waterfall at the park now in hopes it will make recording more difficult."

"This won't help," Sami said. "Nathan told me the waterfall trick only works in movies. Today's technology can filter out background noises."

Megyn could see their surprised looks. "I can talk to Ethan again?" she offered.

No one replied. She knew they didn't trust Ethan anymore, and wondered if she did either.

Bret broke the silence. "I've filled them in on the things you told me about the conference. Anything else to share?"

Megyn explained about the new Vanguard money and how it would be integrated into all aspects of buying and selling over the next year. She told them about the young people planted in the teams and how the strategic direction of the Vanguard of Volunteer Voices had been in the planning for many years.

"Who's behind this?" Sami said.

Megyn took a deep breath. "It's obvious the Nethers are involved. They're part of a global council, but I don't know who else is also on it yet."

"The other day you mentioned that one of the teams is focused on spiritualism," Bret said. "What are they doing?"

"All the teams work the same way. In the beginning they do things that will be accepted and welcomed by everyone. They describe the process as painting a portrait. First you create a frame, or profile, of the person. Lines are sketched but not clearly defined. A silhouette can be seen but lacks the detail needed for identification. You then begin to add more lines, color, and texture. It soon becomes impossible to tell where one color ends and the next one begins. The form gradually takes shape and the image becomes recognizable. This last part is equated to the full integration of a new initiative into cultures and societies."

The faces in the small screen looked at Megyn with foreheads crinkled and mouths open.

Megyn sighed. "Initially, the new target activity is described in harmless, vague terms. It sounds good and is universally accepted. Gradually more pieces are included and people welcome these as well. The process of gradually adding new programs and activities continues unwatched and generally accepted until eventually the new target areas have morphed into programs that are clearly defined and recognizable for what they really are; programs that would never have been expected, or accepted, if they'd been proposed up front."

"How does this tie in with spiritualism?" Vince said.

Megyn thought a moment. "The spiritual team leader emphasizes that all religions should be respected and allowed to practice as they please. Most people agree with this. The statement seems harmless on the face of it. He then proceeds slowly, over time, to the concept of a single god that everyone calls by a different name. This would be more controversial if he hadn't progressed to this new reality over a period of months. This is referred to as nudging people forward. You get them to accept one reality at a time until you finally reach a new norm. The next step moves everyone to the same god, with the same name, and so on."

Tawny's voice cracked. "Are all the activities going to be rolled out the same way?"

"That's the plan so far. But now that I think about it, the expectation of compliance in the current activities has definitely increased. They talked about the programs in a way that left no room for input. The practices were treated as givens. In the next six months oversight teams will be established. They will include pretrained youth leaders who will establish standards and rules for behavior, and most probably, consequences for noncompliance."

"What does that mean?" Bret said.

"It means the youth of the world are being led in a predetermined direction. It will take a while for people to figure it out. Once they do, they will either like it, or not. When I was in the meeting I was caught up in the enthusiasm. Everyone was excited and cheering. Now that I'm away and have had time to think, I can see a few potential problems." Megyn waited. "What do you guys think?"

"What you're telling us seems a little overwhelming," Tawny said. "I like to pick and choose how, and when, I will help others. When the show first started, we celebrated the things people were doing on their own."

Carla interrupted. "Now it feels like someone else is deciding what we will do and who we will do it for."

Megyn hesitated. "I may be wrong in my interpretations. I don't want to get you guys worried unnecessarily."

"Since Bret told us about your call, we've been talking about it," Tawny said. "What you don't know is that we've all experienced some version of what you just told us. The direction of the teams in which each of us participated was definitely influenced by just a few people. We all feel like props for an agenda that is already established and working."

"I kind of agree," Megyn said. "But I'm not convinced there's anything sinister about it. I'm confident the motives come from caring and kindness."

There was a long silence. She wished she could help them understand Gisele the way she knew her.

Bret stepped forward. "We're scheduled to run through Tuesday's program two days from now. We should learn more then."

"It seems like we get the most information about what's going on from watching the show after we've taped it," Megyn said. "That's when we see the new things Ethan's introduced while we were off stage."

"When're you coming home?" Sami said.

Megyn shrugged. "I don't know for sure." She hoped it would be soon. She felt like she was losing her new friends.

CHAPTER THIRTY-ONE

Gisele greeted Megyn for dinner with a hug. "It's just us girls tonight. The boys went out with Martin."

Megyn fidgeted. "I'm sorry for my poor behavior last night. I don't know what happened. I've never done that before."

Gisele handed her a glass of sparkling water. "Some people are sensitive to the spirits and react in dramatic ways. I think you're one of them. That's a good sign. It means you'll be more successful interacting with them than most people are."

Megyn's heart raced. She clenched her hands and tried to control her breathing. She searched for the right words. "I appreciate your support . . . you can't imagine how much . . . but I don't think I can try this again."

Gisele leaned forward. "I agree. It was way too much to begin with."

Megyn cleared her throat. "I don't think you understand. I can't do this. I can't communicate with spirits. I'm terrified. I'll have another panic attack."

Gisele touched Megyn's knee. Her voice was soft and full of concern. "I can't imagine where all this emotion is coming from."

Megyn stared out the window and controlled each word. "My last experience with the spirit world resulted in devastation. One of my best childhood friend's family was destroyed. Her brother blew his brains out in her bedroom. Her sister was raped and had a baby at age thirteen. Her father died of an unknown illness, and her mother developed dementia." Megyn's voice shook as she softly mouthed the last words. "Demon Spirit told her he would destroy her family when she told him she didn't want to talk to him anymore, and he did."

Gisele stroked her arm. "I know there are evil spirits, and DS certainly is one of them, but I can assure you the ones we're involved with are kind and helpful. None of us have ever had a bad experience. Only good."

Megyn stiffened. She wanted to please Gisele, but she just couldn't do it again. *How can I make her understand?*

Gisele stood and poured herself another drink. "Let's change the subject for now. I can see this is upsetting to you. Have you heard from Ethan?"

"We exchange video messages every couple of days. Between the meetings and the time difference, it seems the best way to keep in touch."

"Ethan is a good guy, but . . . I'm sure you know he has a reputation as a playboy."

"He seldom crosses my mind when I'm away from him. But he's really hard to resist when he's smiling his famous smile and holding my hand."

"He breaks a lot of hearts, but, I think you two may actually have something together."

Megyn was surprised to hear this from Gisele. Did she think he was a good catch?

Gisele took a seat near the bar. "How's your mother? Have you heard from her again?"

"Not since the night before I left. She told me she has been sober for the last three years, and asked for my forgiveness."

"What did you tell her?"

"I grew up with a lot of angry words spoken, followed by the promise of sobriety, and later, the request for forgiveness. I don't know if I have any left. I told her I would meet her for lunch, and we'd take it one day at a time. I've been here since then and the longer we're apart, the easier it is to do nothing." She looked at Gisele.

"You're right to take it slow." Gisele soothed. "I'm here for you. You can always count on me."

"I know, and I'm grateful. I'm not sure what I'd do without your friendship."

A server placed an appetizer on the coffee table.

Gisele filled a small plate and handed it to her. "Have you talked with the other Callers? How are they doing?"

Megyn hesitated. She wondered if Gisele knew about the private calls. "I've talked with them a couple of times. They're experiencing some of the same things about the movement as I am."

"Oh? Such as?"

"The scope of the movement. The amount of time and effort that has already gone into it."

Gisele brightened. "It's wonderful, isn't it? Martin and I have been working on this for many years and are pleased to finally see progress." A warm smile crossed her face. "And I'm glad you're here to share it with us. You're like a daughter to me."

Megyn smiled back. She'd witnessed Gisele's warmth and enthusiasm to help others all week. She pushed her earlier feelings of unease to the back of her mind and reassured herself that there were no doubts about Gisele's character and motives. "I'm glad to be a part of this and especially the time I've spent with you."

A tall slender man appeared in the doorway. "Dinner is ready, Madame," he said, and motioned them toward the patio that held a small round table and sweeping views of the Singapore cityscape.

Gisele breathed deeply and considered the scene before them. "This is my favorite place on earth. I love the view from this terrace, and I love Singapore."

Megyn stood beside her. "This certainly is a wonderful place."

Gisele turned to Megyn.

"I want to discuss your future," she said.

Megyn met her eyes and waited.

"I've never been able to bear children and have always wanted a daughter. When I saw your bio and your introductory video I knew I'd found one. You're beautiful, smart, and capable. You come from a wealthy background and aren't impressed by money. You think independently and handle yourself just as I would. I see so much of myself in you when I was younger."

Megyn blushed with pleasure.

"I've been looking for someone to pass along my money and legacy to for several years now, and I believe that someone is you." Gisele grasped Megyn's hands in earnest and a tear rolled down her cheek. "I'd be so honored if you'd join me in my efforts to transform the world for the betterment of mankind. You have what it takes to be successful and I believe you have the same zealousness and tenacity I do. We can be such a great team. What do you think?"

Megyn couldn't breathe. This was everything she'd ever wanted; acceptance, family, significance. But she was afraid. She'd gotten her hopes up so many times before. She was afraid to let her guard down again. She couldn't respond.

Gisele didn't wait for an answer. "I can tell by the look on your face, I've surprised you."

Megyn dismissed the comment with a wave of her hand.

"I don't expect a commitment right now," Gisele said. "Let's take it one day at a time."

"I'm already working closely with you," Megyn said. "What would change?"

Gisele smiled. "I would like to bring you into our inner circle and train you to take over large portions of the movement."

Megyn's stomach lurched. "I've never seen myself as a leader and don't have that kind of experience. Nor do I have the slightest idea what needs to be done next, or how to go about getting it done."

"Don't worry. I'll ease you in." Gisele gazed at the horizon. "I'm thinking you'd stay in your role as a Caller for the show's current season, but we'd also work together at the same time."

"It definitely sounds exciting. But I have to tell you, the whole thing scares me to death."

"Trust me. You'll have every resource you could possibly need, and I'll introduce you to all the right people."

CHAPTER THIRTY-TWO

That night Megyn tried to lie still and breathe evenly. She'd seen a demonstration on how to overcome insomnia on TV recently but none of the techniques she'd attempted were working.

The details of Gisele's offer raced through her mind. They had talked about her future all through dinner and into the evening. Gisele's enthusiasm had been contagious. Megyn had been excited and energized. But now that she was alone in her dark bedroom, she felt inadequate and overwhelmed.

She thought about the things she'd learned. She'd fly back to Los Angeles tomorrow morning. It was a week earlier than originally planned but Gisele wanted her back for the live show. Wardrobe fittings, photo shoots, rehearsals, media interviews, and filming of the next two weeks' programs would fill her time. Then, she'd meet the International Council of Leaders, who was different from the show's Oversight board. They would be introduced at the new world headquarters building site, located just outside Vancouver, British Columbia, and together they would receive updates on multiple avenues of progress in the V^3 movement.

Her mind switched to her mother. She'd promised she'd meet for lunch and try to build a relationship one day at a time. She dreaded the phone call and the emotional toll this process would take. *Our relationship is what it is. It isn't going to change no matter how much we talk and cry. She can never be the mother I've wanted and needed . . . a mother like Gisele who I can talk to and who understands me.*

Then there were her fellow Callers. What would they say when she told them about her new opportunity? How could she make them understand the things being planned were good things? How could she persuade them to join in?

Her thoughts skipped to Ethan. He had barely crossed her mind since she'd been in Singapore. The relationship now seemed frivolous and indulgent in the scope of the opportunities that had been placed before her. The Vanguard of Volunteer Voices movement was currently her primary focus, and somehow he didn't seem to fit in. She considered Paul, Josh, and Mark. They had a common focus with her, but there was no emotional connection. When she was with them, she felt somewhat uneasy. Their zealousness for the cause seemed almost ruthless at times. She wanted someone who wanted the same things in life she did, someone who wouldn't run over others to achieve their goals. She wanted a soul mate to share all this with.

~

The kitchen chalk board had WELCOME HOME scribbled in bold letters that filled the entire surface. She smiled and dropped into the nearest bar stool while her luggage was delivered to her room. The granite countertop was cool and welcome compared to the heat she left behind in Singapore. She rested her head in her outstretched arms and listened. The house was quiet.

"Hey there," a deep voice said from the doorway.

Megyn jumped and toppled the stool. "You scared me."

"Sorry. I thought you heard me come in," Bret said. "Let me help you with that."

Megyn got out of his way so he could set the chair upright. "That's the second time you've snuck up behind me."

"I can assure you I wasn't sneaking. I thought I heard the front door and I knew I was the only one in the house, and, well, maybe I was sneaking. It crossed my mind that someone might have broken in, so I was quietly checking."

Megyn laughed and placed a tea pot on the stove. She located two mugs and offered him a selection of flavors.

Bret joined her by the stove. "Tawny and Sami decided to be domestic and made Morning Glory muffins earlier. They're really good."

"I like mine heated with butter. I'll warm yours too if you'd like."

He nodded. "How was your trip?"

She stared at the microwave. "Exciting. I tossed and turned all night just thinking about everything. Fortunately, I was able to sleep most of the flight home and feel quite energized at the moment."

"Anything new?"

Megyn explained Gisele's proposal. Her voice was animated and enthusiastic.

Bret listened and nodded. "Wow. That's unbelievable. I can see you're delighted."

She leaned back. "Yep. Things just keep getting better and better. I thought being on this show was the ultimate opportunity. But Gisele's offer to mentor me gives me a chance to make a difference on a scale much larger than I could have ever imagined. And without my father's intervention."

"Speaking of family. Have you had a chance to talk with your mother?

Megyn looked down at her hands. "Not yet. I'll call her later this evening."

Bret handed her a cup of freshly brewed tea. "A lot is happening in your life. Do you mind if I pray for God's protection?"

Megyn fidgeted. "Uh. I'm sort of an agnostic. I'm not sure it will do any good." She paused. The tension between them had finally subsided, and she didn't want to start it up again. "But if it makes you feel better, I guess so."

Bret's voice was soft and full of care. "It will definitely make me feel better." He moved to the stool next to hers. "Is it all right if I place my hand on your shoulder?"

Megyn examined the surfaces of the room where cameras might be hiding. "Uh. I guess so, . . . Okay."

They bowed their heads and Bret's hand gently touched her shoulder. She stiffened at the thought of another spiritual encounter and her breath caught in her chest. *Suppose Jesus was just another angel and not who he claimed to be—God?*

"Father God. I know you have a plan for Megyn and have placed her in this situation for a reason." Bret's tone was purposeful and authoritative. "Open her heart to hear your voice and follow your path."

Bret's touch felt reassuring. Megyn's body began to relax and her breathing calmed. Warmth spread throughout every part of her being.

"Protect her from the evil one by covering her with your unconditional love." Bret lifted his free hand towards the heavens. "You are the one true God. You were here from the beginning. You are here now. And you will be here forever. Holy. Holy, Holy are you. None can stand against you."

Bret slowly withdrew his hand but Megyn didn't move. The room was silent. Her eyes were moist with tears and she didn't understand why.

CHAPTER THIRTY-THREE

The hotel's atrium café was bright with the noon day sun. Servers scurried from table to table, arms weighed down with plates full of freshly made lunches, and ice filled goblets of water. Megyn spotted her mother in a far corner booth.

Customers subtly poked their companions when she entered.

"Hi Megyn."

"Love you."

"Keep up the good work," they said when she passed by.

Several pulled out their cell phones to get a quick picture.

She greeted her new fans with a modest smile and casual wave, hoping no one would try to stop her to talk.

"Great show last night," Mrs. Buckman said when Megyn was seated.

"Being a part of this movement is the best thing I've ever done. The shows leave me exhausted, but in a good way."

"You're such a natural. Your dad and I always knew you were special." She chuckled. "And you obviously have a bigger fan base than he does."

Megyn didn't know what to say. Her mother's light heartedness was a new behavior. "I guess you could compare our efforts and impact if you want to. We're both working to make the world a better place. At least that's what he'd claim he's doing."

Her mother let the dig go. Her eyes were full of love. "Tell me about yourself. I feel like I've missed so much. Do you have a beau? I'd think a pretty girl like you would have hundreds of suitors."

Megyn placed her napkin in her lap. "No one special. While I was at University I was too busy for a social life. Now that I'm with the show, the word 'busy' has taken on a whole new meaning. The V3 manages to dominate my time. I've never been happier though."

"I thought I saw a clip on TV that you were seen with the host of the show, Ethan Strong?"

"We went out a few times, but mostly on business. We kept in contact for a while when I was gone, but things have kind of died down since I've been back." Megyn sipped her water.

"That's too bad."

"Not really. I know he's one of the most eligible bachelors in the world, but he's not for me." Megyn straightened her tableware. "How about you? What are you up to these days?"

Mrs. Buckman beamed. "Your dad and I started a foundation two years ago. We have raised millions of dollars and contribute to the funding of numerous causes. I'm the President and I've got a board of international business people who work with me. We've done marvelous work and have great results."

Megyn sat forward. "Really?"

Her mother moved closer. "Yes. I understand when you say the V3 is the best thing you've ever done. That's how I feel about the Foundation."

"I'm speechless."

Mrs. Buckman clasped her hands. "I almost forgot the most important thing, we pray daily for the people, and the organizations, we're funding."

"I assume you're a Christian, like grandma and grandpa were?"

"When my life fell apart and I was going through withdrawals, I clung to God to get me through. I don't know what I would've done without his presence."

The server delivered their salads.

Megyn sat back and watched her mother. "I'm agnostic."

"I'm not surprised. Your dad and I pray for you every night."

"Dad's a Christian too?"

"He saw the difference in me and started to go to a few church services with me. One day he decided to give Christ a chance. The

Foundation Board is made up of Christians too and we approach all activities from a Christian point of view."

Megyn nibbled at her salad.

She could see her mother search her face and make a decision. "Your dad wants a relationship with you too."

Megyn sat back. "Let's just take this one step at a time." She fiddled with her napkin. "You and I are talking and I'd like to leave it at that for now."

"Are you saying you'll consider meeting with him sometime in the future?"

"I'm saying; let's leave it at that for now."

Mrs. Buckman focused on her salad. Megyn knew she wouldn't ask again.

For the first time in a long time, Megyn wondered if it was possible she could have a relationship with her mother. "I would like to know more about your foundation, though."

Her mother smiled. "I'd love for you to come to one of our Board meetings and see what we're doing and meet our members. The next one is tomorrow, but you probably can't make it with such short notice."

"As a matter of fact, I have tomorrow off. I'd like to come. I really would."

~

Megyn walked in her front door and checked her PDA to see who was calling.

"Gisele, I didn't expect to hear from you so soon."

"I wanted to congratulate you on yesterday's show. You were great."

"Thanks. I haven't had a chance to watch it back yet. It's hard to get any perspective when I'm busy trying to remember my talking points and preparing for upcoming segments. The other Callers and I plan to view our recorded copy tonight and celebrate with a home cooked meal by Tawny and Sami. It was so late when we got home last night, we just crashed."

"You must have slept well. You sound pretty energetic today."

Megyn was still thinking about her luncheon. "You won't believe what I just found out. I just met with my mom. I've never seen her like this before. My entire life with her was filled with gloom and doom. She was always drunk and miserable. Today she was fresh and inspiring."

"That's nice, Megyn."

"She's started a Foundation and is helping people throughout the world. It sounds really great."

"I thought you were concerned about the ups and downs of the relationship? I'd caution you to take things slow. I'd hate to see you hurt again."

"I will. I can't get over how different she was, though."

"Just be careful."

Megyn didn't need reminding.

CHAPTER THIRTY-FOUR

Megyn waited in the kitchen for Sami and Tawny to finish making dinner. She yawned, stretched her arms and legs in both directions and almost slipped out of the kitchen barstool. "So you guys met Chef Pierre from the *Cook's Cook* show and he's taken you under his wing?"

Tawny flashed her new Cook's Cook apron with the culinary hat and Cheshire cat smile logo imprinted in blaze orange on a backdrop of royal blue. "Yep. One of our V³ promotional gigs was to be guests on his show. He's quite flirty and one thing led to another. Before we knew what happened, he had us over for dinner and was sharing his secret recipes."

Megyn covered a big yawn with her hand. "Well, I'm tired of eating out all the time. I'm ready for a home cooked meal.

Sami modeled her matching apron. "It's not only home cooked, it's down home. We're having fried chicken, mashed potatoes and gravy, green beans, salad, and biscuits."

"Everything's made from scratch," Tawny said. "We've been cooking all afternoon."

"Mm." Vince said. "I could smell that home cooking all the way down the hall." He pulled out a chair. "Are we ready to eat?"

"Head on out to the patio," Tawny said. "We'll bring the food right behind you."

Vince put his arm around Megyn's shoulders and guided her outside. "Are you as tired as I am Meg?"

"Yep. What have you been up to?"

"You know," Vince said, "the usual: photo shoots, rehearsals, interviews, wardrobe fittings." He paused. "One thing that is new is the promo I did on that show the ladies watch. It was a lot of fun. I was surrounded by beautiful women who convinced me to take off my shirt so they could check out my abs."

Megyn elbowed his ribs forcing his arm to drop from around her shoulders and laughed. "You're crazy, Vince."

The screen door opened with Bret, Sami, and Tawny carrying hot dishes of wonderful smelling food.

"Where's Car," Vince asked.

Bret turned around. "She was right behind us."

"I'm here." Carla looked around. "We're all here."

Tawny pulled out her PDA and took a picture. "I want a copy of my first Chef Michael dinner."

Sami examined the small screen. "Let's switch places and I'll take one of you. We can send each other copies."

Megyn couldn't stop smiling. "I'm so happy to be back with you guys. I fit in better here than anywhere else."

Carla grimaced. "You don't like all the special treatment you're getting?"

"Yes and no. It's fun to be in the center of the movement, and I love working with Gisele and her team. But it's overwhelming too." Megyn poured gravy over her potatoes. "You forget that I've grown up around money and privilege. They have their advantages, but there's nothing like being with a group of rookies that are experiencing the same fears, excitement, and joys I am."

"I know what you mean," Tawny said. "I feel that way when I go spelunking with a small group. We plan together, and work together and rely on each other to get through our underground adventures."

Bret took the pitcher and began filling glasses with fresh ice water. "I can relate. I'm in a management position where I have a staff and people I'm responsible for. Here I'm part of a group. We're all sharing the same new experiences together."

Vince took his cold water and drank the entire glass in one long gulp. "What? What are you guys looking at?" He rubbed his temples and laughed. "I think I got a brain freeze from the ice."

"Well, what's everyone been up to?" Bret said. He looked at Megyn. "What promo did they schedule you for?"

"You won't believe this, but I'm to learn a ballroom dance. They've assigned me a pro to teach me a waltz. I've got four days to learn, and be ready to perform the dance on their elimination show." "Isn't that program targeted at older people? Sami said. "I watch it," Vince said. "They've always got several top notch sports figures. It's fun to see them out of their element. You also get a better sense of their personalities." Tawny poked him in his six pack abs. "You're an old softy, Vince. Or, is it the fancy ballroom outfits the girls wear that attracts your attention?" He smiled and refilled his glass. "What promo are you doing, Bret?" Carla asked. "The Universal Choir and I are one of the performances on the singing competition elimination show. We're redoing "He's Got the Whole World in His Hands" exactly like we performed it on the premiere. How about you?" Carla looked puzzled. "I'm to be a guest on a show where someone in need is given a brand new makeover to their house. I've never seen it before." The other women jumped in. "I have. It makes me cry," they said in unison. Everyone laughed. Megyn was happy to be back and glad no one was mad at her.

~

The V³ show playback was over and Vince returned the lights to normal. "Once again we've outdone ourselves. We were great!" Bret rubbed his stomach. "Dinner was great too! Thanks, girls." "How about that seven layer carrot cake?" Megyn said. "It was divine. Thanks." Tawny and Sami bowed to their compliments, interlocked their arms and skipped down the hall. "You guys can do the clean up." The remaining Callers looked at each other with startled expressions. "I'll take care of the dishes," Bret said. Megyn headed toward the kitchen. "I'll help." Bret followed her. "There's not much left to do since everyone picked up after themselves and the girls put the leftovers away."

"So we should be out of here in no time," Megyn said. She picked up a plate and rinsed it off. "I had lunch with my mom today," she said to Bret when they were alone.

"How did it go? I've been praying for you."

Megyn ignored his prayer comment. "The lunch was much different than I expected." She picked up another dish and ran it under the hot water. "She and my dad have formed a foundation. They've become Christians and started a Christian foundation. Apparently they've raised millions of dollars and are helping people throughout the world."

Bret smiled. "That's wonderful."

"My mom was like a totally new person. I don't know what to make of it. I'm afraid to relax in the relationship and trust her again." Megyn handed him a cup. "But I have to say that this was the first time I've felt respect for her. I felt like we were two friends talking about the things that are most important to us. We have a lot in common."

Bret rearranged the dishes to make more space. "That's a good thing? Right?"

"I guess so. I'm just being cautious. I don't want to get hurt again."

"I'll keep praying."

Megyn took the kitchen cloth and wiped down the counters. "She invited me to their board meeting tomorrow afternoon. I'll get to hear more about it."

"Do you think I could go with you? I'd like to find out what they're doing too. I often get questions about good places to donate money. Maybe I can help spread the word about their charities."

"I'm sure she'd love to meet you. I'll let her know you're coming."

~

Ethan leaned over the side of the bed and retrieved his PDA from the pocket of his jeans. Only minutes before he'd tossed them aside in his hurry to bed his latest conquest who had surprised him with a middle of the night visit. This was the third time in a row the phone had gone off and he decided he better find out who was trying so hard to reach him. He looked at the screen, let out an expletive, and rushed down the hallway. "Gisele. What's up?"

"What are you doing?"

"Uh. I'm spending time with a friend."

"Listen very carefully. I told you last week that if you value your career, you need to stop seeing Carla. Now send her home and get back with Megyn. I need you to keep her on board with our agenda. You've now complicated the situation, and I'm too far away to get it back on track."

He visually searched the room for fiber optic cameras. *Damn.* "I thought you had that under control."

"Your job is to follow instructions, not second guess my orders. Once I get her back to Singapore, I'll keep her here for a while. She's got too many negative influences over there. She's your assignment. Now stick with her."

The communication device went blank.

Ethan slumped into the bedroom and sat on the side of the bed. He stroked Carla's dark hair and kissed her neck. "I'm going to have to break things off for a while. I'm back on assignment." He shrugged his shoulders and forced a nonchalant smile. "It's only for a short time. Believe me. I don't like this any better than you do."

Carla frowned, gave him a long hard kiss, got dressed, and left without a word.

He stared out the window for a few minutes, and then called his administrative assistant. "Order two dozen roses to be sent to Megyn Buckman first thing this morning. Attach a note from me, telling her I've missed her and will stop by later in the day."

CHAPTER THIRTY-FIVE

The town car stopped at the concrete steps in front of the Buckman Medical Instruments headquarters building. Megyn exited the vehicle and looked up at the centerpiece of her father's massive corporate campus of offices and labs interspersed among rolling hills and trickling brooks. The surface of the thirty story building was covered with windows tinted in a light cobalt blue that reflected the environment. "This is it. My father, the greedy corporate CEO, built all of this."

Bret squinted in the bright sunshine. "What makes you say that?"

"He's just like the others. All he cares about is money and power."

"I met him when he was introduced at the V³ kick off meeting and have seen him interviewed on TV a couple of times since then. He seems likable to me."

Megyn stared at the enormous tower. "I hate this place. I shouldn't have volunteered to come today."

"Tell you what: I'll be praying the whole time. And, if you say: let's go, we go. Okay?"

Megyn took a deep breath and headed for the front entry.

Mrs. Buckman spotted the two of them entering through the tall solar powered lobby doors and her face broke into a wide smile. She greeted her daughter and extended her hand to Bret. "It's a pleasure to meet you. I'm so glad you came along."

He returned the gesture. "Mrs. Buckman."

"Please call me Liz."

She escorted them past the receptionist desk and the main elevators and used her pass card to gain access through a nondescript door. They followed a short carpeted hallway lined with bright pictures of the local landscape. An elegant wood paneled elevator was at the end, and an attendant stood to one side with a key inserted to keep the transport in place.

The ride to the top was fast and short, and the doors separated to reveal a granite floor that gleamed from the morning light reflecting through an expanse of windows. A woman sitting behind a mahogany desk greeted them as they passed by. Mrs. Buckman introduced her as a co-worker and assistant, and led them to a room labeled Executive Conference Room.

Eight or nine people were already gathered and met Mrs. Buckman with warm embraces. Megyn didn't recognize any of them.

Megyn and Bret tried to step aside, but a heavy-set Asian woman grabbed her and enveloped her in a giant bear hug. "This must be your daughter, Megyn? She looks just like her beautiful mom. And those amazing violet eyes, like Mr. B's."

Megyn blushed.

Mrs. Buckman put her arm around the woman. "Sharon Wilson is the President of an organization that provides food and medicine to children and families throughout the world. She became very wealthy during the dot com era and has given away everything she had to fund her dreams for a better world." She pointed to the black man next to her. "This is Charles Reilly. He's an engineer from South Africa and has worked to provide fresh water to villages throughout the continent. Next to him is Rashid Dalton, who is from India and has taken on an American surname. He's our skills, education, and training guru. You'll hear more about what he does later."

She glanced at the clock on the wall. "We need to stay on schedule. Feel free to grab some food and beverages from the back of the room, and I'll introduce the others once we get started."

~

Megyn watched her mother take a seat in front and ask everyone to hold hands and bow their heads for prayer. Bret's touch was warm and his presence aroused her senses. She was caught off guard and forced herself to listen to what was going on around her.

Board members praised God for numerous successes in their efforts. They thanked him for the resources he supplied that enabled them to serve others, for the people who now had food and skills to make a better life for themselves and their communities, and for the growing number of foundation members who supported their efforts through prayer, funding, and service.

She heard Bret whisper gentle support and affirmation of their words. Her neck and shoulder muscles began to relax. She felt safe in his presence and was glad he was with her.

The prayers shifted to requests. Sharon asked for God's wisdom and his heart for others. A man from Mongolia asked for God's healing, both of body and of soul, for those they served. A woman from Brazil asked for God's guidance in setting priorities during today's meeting. Others added to the list, and her mother closed with the final request that God's will be done above all else. Everyone said together, "Amen and Glory Hallelujah."

Bret squeezed her hand as an agreement to the prayer and released her.

Once again Megyn's eyes were moist with emotion. She dabbed them with her fist and hoped no one noticed. *What's the matter with me? Why am I crying, and what's with the warm feelings for Bret? He's not my type.*

Her mother introduced the board to Bret and Megyn and provided a framework for their discussion. "We believe the best way to help people is three pronged. First, we meet their immediate needs. This usually consists of fresh water, food, shelter, clothing, and medical care. Second, we provide them with the skills, knowledge, and education to become self sufficient. Some become carpenters, others plumbers, teachers, and farmers. We also teach them about money, bartering, and business. In several instances we've trained them in technology and transportation systems. And third, we build relationships. We teach them about the importance of God and family. And we provide opportunities and associations they would never be able to obtain on their own. All of us have traveled throughout the world giving our time, as well as foundation funds. It's important that we be a part of, and stay connected to, the efforts we support."

Bret raised his hand. "Can I ask questions?"

The faces around the room smiled and nodded encouragement.

"Of course," Mrs. Buckman said. "That's one of the primary reasons you and Megyn were invited."

"As you know, we're part of the Vanguard of Volunteer Voices, which could be viewed as competition. How does what we're doing help, or hinder, your efforts?

Megyn sat forward and observed the board's members' reactions.

Charles was the first to speak. "Thus far, we've not crossed paths in our efforts. This is something we've discussed though, and we definitely realize the possibility of conflicts."

Megyn's shoulders tensed. "What do you mean? Aren't we both working to make the world a better place?"

"Of course," Rashid said. "I'd say the primary difference between us, although there are several, is our commitment to God. We believe he is our creator and we cannot become whole without a relationship with him. Food, water, shelter, jobs: those are all necessary for survival of the body. We're also concerned about the soul. Only God can touch our souls."

Megyn frowned. "So you're saying you would only help people if they become Christians and believe the same way you do?"

"Of course not," Sharon said. "God is Love. That's his primary attribute. He loves us so much he gave us his only son who died upon a cross as a sacrifice on our behalf. He loves us even if we don't love him back." She sat forward. "We're made in his image and we strive to love others in the same way he loves us. A big part of that includes meeting people's physical needs. It also means our sacrifice of time, effort, and money. "

Megyn didn't respond and the room grew quiet. They were saying all the right things, but her experience with Christians had been different. She didn't want to get in an argument.

Charles sighed. "I know some people describe us as bigots and racists. We reject these labels. Just look around this room. We are all colors and nationalities. We serve people of all races. It matters nothing to us what they look like outwardly. We are all made by God in his image. Are we to refuse or deny his creation? No. We are to love it, and to cherish each person as he does. We know we are not perfect on our own, but through him we are made perfect."

Megyn was barely listening. She was thinking of the Christians she'd known over the years. She hadn't seen much love for others coming from a number of them. She remembered a childhood friend of her father's borrowing money and not paying him back. The man's business grew and he still didn't return the money. She was young when this happened, but she could still see her father's disappointed face when this Christian kept the cash citing her dad's wealth. Her father had shook his head and said, "It's not about the money. It's about the promise. It's about your word." The man shrugged and walked away. Her father later told her he had planned not to accept the money when the man offered. The man missed out on the gift her father had intended to give him, and her father lost his friend.

Her grandparents and a few others had been the exceptions. They'd been loving and kind and accepting. They paid their debts and their word was their bond. Their home had been a sanctuary. She missed them terribly.

~

Afterwards Megyn stood to the side as Bret gave Mrs. Buckman a warm hug. "Thanks so much. I thoroughly enjoyed the day. You've got one of the best foundations I've ever seen. I have some connections who would most definitely be interested in helping out with money and talent. I'd also like to put our youth and college-age pastors in touch with you to explore ways those groups can volunteer during holidays and summers."

She hugged him back. "I'd love that. We have plenty of needs, and plenty of work to meet those needs."

Megyn thought about giving her mother a hug, but shook her hand instead. "I enjoyed the day too. I'm glad I came."

Her mother smiled. "Maybe once you've finished with the Vanguard of Volunteer Voices you'd like to continue your outreach, working with us. I know you were never interested in the corporation, but the Foundation is the kind of thing you've always liked. You don't have to give me an answer right now. Just think about it. It could be wonderful working together."

~

Upon leaving, Mrs. Buckman had a plain cardboard box placed in the back seat of the town car with an order they weren't to open it until they arrived back at their living quarters. The package took up one of the seats and forced Megyn and Bret to scrunch up in the remaining space.

Megyn didn't like her new feelings for him; they were unexpected and unwanted. She didn't have time to get involved with someone who didn't want the same things she did. Besides, she'd seen him interact with numerous people, and he treated them all the same. She sighed, *including me*. She wondered if he had a girlfriend and what she was like.

CHAPTER THIRTY-SIX

Megyn attempted to pick the box up on her own, but it was so heavy they decided to carry it into the house together. They lifted the container from the car and told the driver he could leave since they had the situation under control.

Bret took the lead and tried to hold on with one hand and dig his key from his hip pocket. "Of all the times for someone to lock the front door," he said.

Megyn grimaced. "I've got a good grip on my side. Shift the weight to me."

"Okay, but I'm not sure you'll be able to handle it."

She groaned. "Trust me. I've got it. Just hurry up."

Bret tilted the box in her direction and the contents shifted. Her fingers slipped and the container began to tip. They panicked, over corrected, and were barely able to keep it from falling. Megyn's nerves had already been stretched to the limit. Her muscles were giving way and she started to giggle. He joined her in her laughter and they got so tickled they almost dropped the carton again. Tears were running down their faces when he finally got the key into the lock and the door opened.

"Let's just drop it in the chair," Megyn said, laughing so hard she snorted.

Uncontrolled laughter began again. "Did you just snort?

Megyn fell on to the couch and put her hand over her mouth. "I think I did. I've never done that before."

They both wiped their eyes.

She examined the box. "You've got your key out. See if you can rip the tape and open it."

"Uh. Um," a voice said from the kitchen doorway.

Megyn jumped up. "Ethan! Hi."

"I sent you flowers and a note. Obviously you were out and didn't receive them."

Megyn dabbed at her face. "We were at a meeting with my mother. She sent this home with us, and we've been struggling to get it in the door."

As Bret fought with the tape, Ethan gave her a long embrace. He stepped back, placed his hands on her shoulders, and studied her face. "Leave that with Bret and come with me into the kitchen so we can talk."

She didn't want to miss out on the surprise contained in the box, but Ethan was clearly uptight. She looked down at Bret. He had just broken the last piece of tape.

"It's okay. I'll catch up with you later," he said.

She allowed Ethan to usher her into the kitchen. "I didn't expect to see you."

He tried to pull her close and she resisted. "I've missed you."

She laughed. "That's hard to believe. I've hardly heard from you in the last couple of weeks."

He feigned a hurt expression and stroked her arm. "It's been really busy lately."

She ignored his attentions and walked to the refrigerator and got a bottled water. "Don't get me wrong. I'm not upset about it. I was under the impression both of our feelings had cooled down."

He took a chair and munched on cashews that left in a dish on the counter. "Can we at least be friends? How about dinner? I'd like to catch up."

She smiled. "I'd like that."

Bret entered, dragging the open box. "You'll never believe what she sent."

Megyn looked inside. There were six scrapbooked photo albums. A note was attached.

Megyn,
Thought you and your friends might enjoy these. I tried
to personalize them in a way each Caller would approve. I've

included a few sayings and Bible verses that your dad and I've chosen. Every book also uses a color palette unique to the individual. We've committed to pray for the person when we notice the color as we're going throughout our days. Hopefully, this won't offend anyone.

Love, Mom

Bret spread his book across the counter. "I can't believe she got all my baby and childhood pictures. I haven't seen these in years. My mom will love this."

Megyn emptied the box and flipped through the pages. "I've been telling everyone how resourceful my family is. If they want to do something, they figure out a way to get it done. I'll bet when you call your mom, she'll tell you she also received a book, as well as, additional copies for grandparents, or anyone else. Your mother was probably in on this. She had to have supplied the pictures in the first place."

"I love that they're praying for us," Bret said. "I like your family."

Megyn examined her own book and turned to Bret. "Would you mind checking to see if the others are here?"

Ethan removed himself from his chair, watched Bret exit the kitchen. He kissed Megyn's forehead. "I'll meet you at the restaurant for dinner in about two hours."

~

Ethan called Gisele and was glad to get her voicemail. He knew she wouldn't be happy with his update. "Megyn and Bret attended the Foundation board meeting Mrs. Buckman held yesterday. She's developing warm feelings for her mother, even though she claims she isn't. Apparently Mrs. Buckman invited Megyn to join her in working with the Foundation, but Megyn hasn't given her an answer. She's still leaning toward working with you. I encouraged her to go with you and emphasized the depth and breadth of your activities over the limited capabilities of the Foundation, and I criticized the one religion approach her mother is taking. I also reinforced that she be cautious regarding her mother's rehabilitation.

"Another two things you will be interested to hear." He cleared his throat. "She only wants her and me to be friends. If you ask me; I think she has a crush on Bret. She blushes and giggles whenever he's around. And, this is the most disturbing, she said she was thinking a lot about her Christian roots because of the effect Christianity has had on her mother. I asked how she felt about the power of the spirits and she turned pale. I don't know how you're going to get her past her history with DS."

~

It was barely morning when Megyn awoke. She had a long day ahead with another photo shoot, commercial spot, and series of radio and TV interviews. She thought about her life and wondered how it had suddenly gotten so complicated. She didn't want to choose between working with her mom or joining Gisele. She had enjoyed her time with her mother's Foundation and respected their accomplishments. On the other hand, Gisele's efforts were coordinated globally and much more comprehensive. They accepted all religions and focused on unity, equality, and service. *I can make a much broader difference working with the V³ and championing their goals, but, I don't want to hurt my mother when our relationship is already so fragile.*

Then there's Bret. I, no doubt, have feelings for him. When Carla joined us to look at the scrapbooks, I was jealous of his attentions toward her. The same thing happened with Tawny and Sami. I don't know how to control these new feelings and wish I didn't have them in the first place. He is a good guy who is nice to everyone. He's not interested in me. He's not my type, and I'm not his.

And what's with all the interest Ethan's giving me? He's got girls falling all over him. Why is he sticking around with me? It doesn't make sense.

She reached for her PDA to recheck her schedule. There was a message from Gisele. "Good morning." She smiled. "I've decided to fly in for the next show, and of course, see you. There are a number of new services to be introduced and I know you'll be as excited as Martin and I are to be a part of bringing them forward. We'll be returning to Singapore the day after the show and plan to bring you back with us. I know it's a week earlier than I originally told you, but there's a lot to do, and I want you to be front and center, and by my side, as we go to the next level."

The decision had been made for her, but Megyn was conflicted. She reassured herself that working with Gisele was the better opportunity.

CHAPTER THIRTY-SEVEN

Megyn picked up her binder and took a seat alongside her fellow Callers. The ACN staff had already received the updates for the next show and appeared to have a mixture of reactions to the content.

Trianna tried to call the room to order, but several staff weren't cooperating. She held up her hand as if to stave off their irritated comments. "I know. I know. I've already heard from many of you." She set her binder down and braced herself. "These changes come from people much more powerful than me." The group erupted again and Jason stepped to her side.

Trianna continued. "I've talked with several of them, and there's no changing their minds." She raised her chin and straightened her posture. "This is the way we will proceed. If you don't want to be a part of the show, I need to know today. I'm sorry."

The room was silent. Megyn wondered what was going on that people would be willing to quit over.

"Now let's get to work."

Megyn followed along as Trianna walked everyone through the program. She scanned the pages and examined her talking points. She was surprised to see how much her role had grown. They had her working alongside Ethan in almost every segment. She made notes on her parts and tried to figure out the concerns of the staff.

~

The Callers were reviewing the menu when Megyn arrived at the Japanese restaurant's back room. She plopped down next to Sami and perused the food choices. "I want something light, maybe a Sushi appetizer."

Vince stretched and yawned. "I don't usually eat at midnight. I wish they had a protein drink."

Carla groaned. "Me either. This was one long day." She looked at the others. "I can't believe the staff's reaction to the show's content."

Megyn sat forward. "I know. I don't get it either."

"I heard a couple of people talking and asked them," Tawny shrugged. "They said they weren't happy with the way things are going."

Megyn took a sip of her water. "That was pretty obvious."

Tawny held up three fingers. "Their concerns are with three parts of the program." She pushed down two of them. "First, they don't like the solicitation to the Vanguarders for ways to persuade others to the cause. They think the language being used is borderline coercive." She raised another finger. "Second, they are concerned the future has already been determined, and the actions themselves are nothing but 'smoke and mirrors,' intended to make the Vanguarders think they are the ones driving things forward." She added one more digit. "And third, they are concerned about the growing number of youth who oppose the V^3. They think we should consider their concerns."

Megyn looked indignant. "What are they talking about?"

"Don't you watch the news?" Tawny said.

"I've been busy. I can't believe you guys have had much time to watch TV either." Megyn looked at Bret. "Is this about the Christians who are protesting? What am I missing?"

Sami spoke first. "A growing number of people say they want to continue being 'self determined,' as opposed to part of a collective, all doing and saying the same things."

"That sounds a lot like 'selfish' to me," Megyn said. "We can accomplish so much more if we all work together for the common good. Individuals alone can't do nearly as much as unified groups can."

Bret sat forward and spoke softly. "Who decides what's best for everyone? A group of three? Ten? Five hundred? How can they possibly determine what's right for everyone. Wouldn't you agree there are a lot of conflicting needs in this world?"

Megyn started to object, but he put his hand up. "Not everyone wants to be a part of the V^3. How will they be able to live their lives within this new structure? Suppose people don't cooperate? Does the collective silence them, force them to participate, or punish them in some way if they don't?" He sighed. "These are real concerns people have."

Megyn's zeal didn't let go. "I don't understand why people won't decide for the greater good. Many can be helped that wouldn't otherwise benefit if we'd just let go of our own wants and desires. Like I said, their position seems selfish to me."

"I don't understand why you don't want to let people live their lives the way they see fit," Sami groaned. "Why do you want to control them? Do you think you're the only ones who know what's best? Who made you, or these small groups of deciders, God?"

Megyn stiffened.

Vince extended his arms to embrace the group and laughed nervously. "Now ya'll. Can't we just all get along?" He looked at Bret. "Get us all back on track, leader."

Bret crinkled his forehead.

Vince grinned. "You may not be the formal leader, but it's obvious we all look to you for confirmation and direction. It's time for you to get us back on track."

"We don't have much time right now," Bret said. "But I'll just say that I believe the battle between the sides is spiritual."

Megyn glared. "I don't think about this in a spiritual way, and I'm sure most people don't either."

"I agree," Bret said. "My point is I think the root of the argument is spiritual. How people see the world. Some adhere to the idea that there's a Creator who designed and made everything. They believe each of us is formed in his image and everyone has a unique and different purpose. They push hard to live in a way they feel their creator would have them live. And as everyone lives within God's will, it all fits together and functions best.

"Others' beliefs rest in mankind. They create their own standards and foundations from which people should live. One puts their trust in God, the Creator, and the other looks to man. That's all I'm saying."

Megyn played with her water glass. "But—"

"The response Sami just gave is typical for V³ opponents." Bret said. "They often ask, 'Who made you God?' That's why I think this is spiritual."

Bret stood. "Of course, there are many variables within the framework I've just described, and we could talk about this topic for hours. But that's the simple version of what I think is going on."

He sipped his water, placed a tip on the table, and sighed. "We've got to get to bed. We've a big day tomorrow, and we aren't going to resolve this tonight. We can talk more another time if you want."

Megyn started to stand up, but Sami held her arm. "I'm sorry I jumped on you like that. I was out of line."

Megyn shrugged. "I was coming on too strong too."

Vince pulled them out of their seats and opened his arms wide. "Group hug, ya'll."

"The show must go on," Carla said. "Tomorrow will be exciting, if nothing else."

Everyone stood together and hugged. Megyn didn't like Bret's explanations. *Why did he always make things so complicated?*

~

The sky was overcast, and the air humid. The house was quiet and Megyn had a couple of hours to kill before making her final preparations for the evening's live show. She cuddled up in her overstuffed chair to watch the news. Her heart flipped when they showed the large group of protestors that were already gathered outside the studio.

Many had spent the night in the park near the production location. In spite of looking like they'd slept in a sleeping bag, they appeared to be nice young people. Several were drinking coffee, talking, and laughing. The camera zoomed in on a sign that read, EQUAL OPPORTUNITY, NOT EQUALITY. It then pulled out to show a young man tying his shoes. The reporter shoved a microphone in his face. "Why are you here?"

The guy was caught off guard. He stood awkwardly and looked into the camera. "I believe in helping others. I give what little money I have to charities and volunteer my time. What I object to is the path the V³ is taking us. Through their actions my choices for service are being determined by others and taken away from me."

The camera moved back to the reporter. "As you just heard for yourself, these Christians hold selfish beliefs. They believe that only they know how to serve. They refuse to work with others, possibly because of bigotry and racism. These beliefs will take us backwards, not into a better world where all will be treated the same."

Megyn checked the other news channels. The same message was repeated on most. And a few pundits offered opposing viewpoints. She exhaled. *I can't think about this right now.*

She turned the TV off and ran through her talking points one last time. She thought about Bret and wondered if he was praying for them again.

~

The live show was over and Megyn was due to fly out the next morning. She was tired and confused. She took her seat, along with the other Callers, and Vince dimmed the lights of the media room. They sipped cold water, munched on fruits and nuts and watched the video in silence. There she was, alongside Ethan, welcoming Vanguarders throughout the world. She relaxed into the chair and tried to put on her marketing hat. She watched and listened to the messages they were giving. She heard words like persuade, compel, influence, convince, and argue. She saw images that conveyed these messages. She thought about the newscasts she had watched and the concerns of others. She still didn't see anything wrong with what they were doing. *No one is forced to join the Vanguard of Volunteer Voices.*

CHAPTER THIRTY-EIGHT

Megyn waited in the front room for her ride to the airport and thought about Bret. She wondered why she would have such strong feelings for him. They didn't agree on most things and he definitely didn't share the same vision of the world she did. She wanted to transform humankind in one way and he wanted to change them another. *Was one really better than the other?* She pondered the different approaches and examined his previous explanations. The only conclusion she could come up with was the one he had offered. He relied on God and she relied on her own efforts. She rotated her shoulders to relieve her tension, dismissed her conclusion, and pushed the whole thing to the back of her mind.

Carla walked in and stood defiantly in front of her. "I just want you to know. I've been seeing Ethan. When you were away, we started dating."

Megyn's mouth twisted and her eyebrows rose. "You don't have to tell me this. I don't have any claim on him."

"I wanted you to hear it from me. There are pictures of us together, and you'll probably see them in the tabloids, or on line. Some are video—a bit x-rated."

"Believe me. Ethan and I are just friends. I can't believe he hasn't already told you." Megyn examined Carla's face. She looked smitten. "I'll give you the same advice you once gave me. Be careful. He's quite a lady's man."

Carla grinned and plopped into a chair. "I know, but he's so warm and tender. I really do think I'm different. I think he really likes me."

Bret peeked in from the kitchen. He looked at Megyn's luggage. "So you're off again?"

She nodded. "Yep."

"When are you coming back?" His PDA sounded and he looked at the screen. "Excuse me. I have to get this."

"You two would make a good couple," Carla said after he left the room.

Megyn blushed. "Who? Me and Bret? No way. We're miles apart."

Carla got up and headed back to her room. "It's obvious you like him, and I'm pretty sure he likes you too." She disappeared around the corner. "Have a good trip."

Megyn squirmed. *Good thing I'm getting out of here for a while.* She reviewed her two week schedule. It was completely filled. The only time she would be alone was at night in bed. *Perfect. No time to think about Bret.*

~

Megyn watched the busy Singapore port from the penthouse patio while Gisele sipped coffee and read the morning newspaper. "I can see why you and Martin love it here so much. This is so relaxing"

"Hmm."

"I haven't thanked you for giving me this opportunity. I only hope I can live up to your expectations."

Gisele put the paper down. "I have no doubts, daughter. I'm just pleased we've found each other." She nibbled on her scone. "Enjoy the leisure this morning. There'll be no time for rest after today. We've got a lot to do. The opposition is growing, and we need to keep ahead of them if we're going to accomplish our agenda."

Megyn tensed. "I noticed on the schedule, there's another spiritual meeting this afternoon. What does that mean?"

Gisele placed her hand on Megyn's knee. "You know we look to the spirits for guidance and power. This time it'll be an intimate group. We'll sit around a small table and call on Anima, one of the spirits we deal with all the time." She moved her hand to Megyn's arm. "I promise this experience won't be anything like your time with Demon Spirit."

"I'll try my best to be open, but I don't seem to be able to control my emotions when it comes to spiritual matters."

She took Megyn's hand. "We'll hold hands like this, and we'll take things slow. You don't need to say or do anything. I just want you to be there and see and feel how important the spirit guides are to our success." She paused. "We're at a critical juncture in the roll out. We desperately need to draw on their guidance and power. I need you to be strong. This is the most important thing we do to ensure our success." She turned and looked Megyn in the eyes. "I want you there by my side."

Megyn breathed deeply. She would do almost anything for Gisele. "Okay."

~

Megyn held Gisele's hand on her right and the medium's hand on her left. There were six people around the table, Gisele, Martin, the medium, two leaders from the roll out symposium Megyn had attended on her last trip, and Megyn. They all chanted but her. She didn't understand the meaning of their words and focused on keeping her knees from bouncing all over the place.

A cold breeze entered the room and her fingers tightened around her companions'. She squeezed her eyes shut and waited. The chant stopped.

Megyn heard a ragged voice coming out of nowhere. The woman asked, "What do you seek?"

Gisele said breathlessly. "We seek your guidance and your power, Anima. How do we deal with the people who are against us and trying to stop us?"

"The numbers of those who oppose you are growing, but they are weak. They look to themselves for power, not to the spirits."

Gisele leaned forward. "What is your guidance, Anima?"

Megyn shivered; her hands turned clammy, and she willed herself not to bolt from the room.

"Continue to come to me for guidance." The voice turned soft. "You know I care about you."

Martin spoke up. "We think it's time to take action against them."

The voice turned menacing. "Yes, Martin. It's time, but not too fast. We don't want to drive them to prayer. Our spirits are surrounding your teams and clearing the way. Keep your people working with *us*, praying to *us*. *We* will give them the power to build a new world."

"We plan to target their leaders," Martin said.

The voice answered. "Yes. Yes."

Megyn stiffened. *What does he mean? Target who, and do what?*

The room grew quiet and the cold air dissipated.

"Anima? Anima?" Gisele said.

The medium released their hands. "She's gone. You have your answers."

Megyn opened her eyes and noticed Gisele and Martin exchange glances.

"We need to move up the time for our meeting with the Council," Gisele said.

Martin stood. "I'm on it."

Gisele gave Megyn a hug. "See. That wasn't so hard, was it?"

Megyn cringed. "I guess not."

Gisele followed Martin to the door. She turned to Megyn. "Do you mind if we cancel dinner tonight? We've got a lot to do."

"Uh. No, it would be nice to have a few hours on my own to recover from the jet lag."

~

A warm breeze blew through Megyn's hair as she walked the streets. Most of the time she loved being with Gisele, but now she was confused. One minute she felt understood, empowered, and safe with her, and, the next minute, lonely and frightened. She needed someone to talk to. She thought about Bret. He listened and didn't judge. Even when they disagreed, she knew she could rely on him to respect her thoughts and feelings. Her shoulders sagged. *I can't contact him. I'm growing too dependent and don't trust my feelings when I'm around him.*

CHAPTER THIRTY-NINE

Suburban Vancouver, British Columbia

The room was elegant in spite of the fact that it was not yet completed. Studs were draped with red, gold, and black brocade fabric. A large, round ebony table sat in the middle of the floor and servants rushed quietly in and out setting out dishes filled with Indian cuisine along with a variety of beverages. Blueprints lined the only completed wall, and the Council members moved from one design to another, commenting on the most recent changes to the New World Headquarters compound. Megyn joined them and reviewed the artist's renderings of the buildings and the map of the new site she had just toured.

Earlier that day, she'd flown into their private airport, been driven around the area, and surprised to see the number of completed buildings and parking lots filled with vehicles. This little city had eating establishments, shopping centers, gas stations, offices, boutique hotels, schools, fire, police, and medical services. Eight thousand people were already on staff, not counting the construction workers.

Several Council members introduced themselves and welcomed her to the meeting. She pulled out a chair to sit, and Gisele motioned her to her side. "Up here, daughter. Next to me."

Thirteen Council members took seats at the table and another group seated themselves around the edges of the room, their PDAs at the ready. Gisele called the meeting to order. "I want to thank you for allowing the meeting to be held in this location. Even though the headquarters building is not yet completed, Martin and I thought this would be the perfect place for us to gather, to dream, and to address problems." She smiled and extended her arms to embrace their surroundings. "The decorators have done a masterful job making us comfortable.

"We have a lot to cover today, so let's get started." She looked to the caterers. "Please finish service quickly." Then to the media personnel, "Let's have the update and agenda while we eat."

A high-end video projected onto a screen that now covered a large portion of the one wall. The presentation began by bringing everyone up-to-date on the Vanguard of Volunteer Voices movement. It showed highlights of this season's shows, planning teams working together, and key elements of the recent roll-out rally Megyn attended with the boys, when she was in Singapore.

Each segment emphasized the V³ major areas of activity: money and giving, spiritualism, environment, health and wellness, and technology and communications. All were in the context of unity, equality, and service.

Megyn thought about the Council members she just met. There was a broad mixture of cultures and ethnicities present. She felt young since most looked to be in their forties and fifties. She had caught an older man watching her throughout the morning and was unnerved by his unconcealed interest. She gave him a smile at one point, but he didn't respond. Most members seemed nice, but she still felt out of place.

The presentation ended and Gisele brought the focus back to herself. "Before we get into the business portion of the meeting, I would like for us to address the problem of what to do about our opponents."

Martin sat forward. "Gisele asked me to present the facts regarding this uprising. This should help us understand what we're up against and enable us to build strategies to fight back." The screen lit up with video of various protests around the world. "As you know, rallies have formed in many places. The opposition has targeted the areas where we have made the greatest inroads." The screen showed protestors carrying their country's flag and signs opposing V³ efforts.

"The participants are mostly comprised of people ranging in age from thirty-five to eighty, who identify themselves as the Forces for

Freedom, or F³. There are a few from our target audience age group mixed in. Many hold to some type of organized religion. They describe their lives as family and work oriented, giving, and accepting. So far, the media have not given them much coverage, and when they do, they manage to find the best shots to represent our position. Even people who pay close attention to current events and politics don't realize the size of the groups and how much they are growing. We estimate the opposition to be about five million globally. The problem is these numbers are mounting exponentially."

"What do they want?" a woman named Lurleen from Austria asked.

Martin got up and paced the room. "They say they don't want to be sucked into our movement. They say they're afraid they will eventually have no choice but to join in, or be punished in some way."

Jahara looked around at the others. "Haven't we always said people are free to choose if they want to participate, or not?"

Gisele answered, "Yes, but they don't believe us. They think we're nudging them toward a one-world movement where everyone will be forced to take part. They don't have any evidence to go on; just their mistrust of our motives."

The older man, who had been staring at Megyn earlier, shifted in his seat. "We don't need to talk about this. We need to take action. We need to do what has always been done in these situations—discredit their leaders, accuse them of hatred and bigotry, pick out their fringe nuts and make the world believe they're mainstream for the group."

Lurleen joined back in. "Talking points need to be given to the media right away. We make ourselves the victims. Tell the gullible audience we've tried to work with these kooks but they refuse our overtures. Tell them they are violent and dangerous and need to be silenced and controlled—for the safety of the people."

"Harrumph," growled the older man. "Our timelines for rollout must be moved up. We're talking months instead of years now. This may be the only chance we get to make our changes," he said. "We won't get another."

Jahara suggested they identify the leaders and look into their backgrounds. "If we can't find any dirt on them, we'll just make something up using a half truth; anything that will discredit their message. The media are so gullible they will follow right along. They already think these people are nuts. We can help them along with their research by filling in the blanks."

Megyn sat motionless. Her body tried to disappear into the soft cushions of her chair. *These things aren't true. How could Gisele be leading something like this?*

~

The Singaporean night sky was cloudy, the humidity high. Megyn sat on her balcony in the darkness and sipped iced tea. It was early morning and she hadn't slept all night. *What have I done? How will I ever get out of this?*

She thought about the flight back from British Columbia. Gisele and Martin were fired up. They talked excitedly about the future, about the need to move their program forward faster, before the opposition could gain a foothold. They drank champagne and toasted their impending success. They laughed at the stupidity of their adversaries and regaled in the knowledge that their shill organization, the V^3, had allowed them to gain a much greater foothold than anyone could possibly imagine.

They cajoled her to join in and she did her best to accommodate them. She sipped champagne and feigned exhaustion from the overwhelming day. They interpreted her actions as a good sign and continued their revelry.

The memory made Megyn feel weak. She closed her eyes and tried to relax in her chair. *This is big. There is no escape.* A light shone through the balcony windows directly above her. The French doors opened and someone walked out. She cowered in her chair.

"Ethan Strong," Gisele's voice said. "Where are you? I need you to get to Singapore as soon as possible."

There was a pause, as if Gisele were listening to someone on the other end of her conversation.

"I don't want excuses. You can broadcast your part of the show from Singapore. We can make it happen." She walked to the railing. "Actually, that's the perfect solution. I'm concerned that Megyn might be lonely. You two can work together; throw in a bit of your legendary charm."

Another pause.

"You've told me that before. I don't care what she said. Now get down here and romance her again. No woman can resist you."

Megyn heard the familiar sound of a PDA being closed.

Tears ran down her face.

~

Megyn stood under a tree, away from the street lamp, and held the phone close to her ear as if it were a lifeline.

"Hey. Glad you called. How are things going in Singapore? When are you coming home?" Bret said into his Personal Digital Assistant.

Megyn sobbed at the sound of his voice.

"Hello? Megyn, are you all right?"

"Yeah," she managed.

"What's wrong? Where are you?"

Megyn straightened and took a deep breath. "I'm in Singapore, on the street, several blocks from the condo."

Bret waited.

"I've made a terrible mistake." She sobbed. "I can't believe I didn't see it before. They're out to unify the world, and make everyone equal, whether people want to be or not. They will stop at nothing. I committed to work with them, and now I'm trapped here and don't know how to get away. I know too much for them to trust me and just let me go."

"Wow."

Megyn thought he sounded shocked. But he couldn't be. He'd been warning her all along.

"This doesn't really surprise me," he said. "What we need to do now is pray."

Megyn whimpered in his ear. For the first time, that sounded like a good idea to her.

"Lord, you control the universe. You have Megyn in this place for a purpose. We ask that you work it out in your time and in your way. We pray for your protection for her and that your angels surround her and your Holy Spirit bring her comfort. In Jesus name. Amen."

"She's sending Ethan over to be with me. I feel so trapped. We have no feelings for each other and he's seeing Carla. She told me."

"What?"

"Gisele thinks I'm lonely, and I overheard her telling Ethan to get over here and spend time with me. I could tell by her side of the conversation, he didn't want to come. She wants us to work together

159

on the upcoming show. We'll broadcast our part from here. She thinks that will get us back together."

"I know this is a touchy subject," Bret said, "but have you thought about contacting your dad? He's got almost unlimited resources. I can't believe he wouldn't figure out some way to get you out of this."

Megyn sighed. "He's too busy to worry about helping me."

"I don't believe that. And I know you don't either."

"Also, he's like a bull in a china shop. His way of helping is to charge in and knock everything out of his way."

"I'm going to contact him and find out what he knows about the Nethers. He runs in that circle of people, and he's on the Board of Directors for the V^3. I'd be surprised if he doesn't know a few things."

"Okay." She knew Bret was right. Her father was the only one who had the means to help her.

"I'm going to tell him about your predicament too. We need to decide how you two will communicate. You contacted me on your personal phone, and I assume you've still got the security detail following you everywhere?"

"Yes, and yes."

"I think you need to use a new communication device, one they don't know about. Maybe you could pick up one of those phones you pay for ahead of time. You get so many minutes, and when you're done, you just throw it away."

"My schedule is so tight, there's no way I'll be able to get away. Plus, there's always someone around. I'm sure they report back every move I make."

She started to cry again. "They've been watching us all along. I didn't believe it, but they needed to make sure we were going along with the program."

Bret's voice was tender. "Okay. Okay. Let's think."

Megyn sniffed. "Call my dad. I have no other choice. He'll think of something. And Bret, please stick by him and make sure he's careful. I'm afraid."

"I'm going to notify the prayer team too. They've already gone global on the V^3 situation."

Megyn gasped. "You can't. If word of this gets out, I could be in danger." Suddenly the image of Annette lying in her hospital bed flashed into her mind.

"Give me some credit. I'll make sure no names or direct information is shared." He hesitated. "Call me back as soon as you're able. I'll talk to your dad and we'll formulate a plan. I promise. Hang in there."

Megyn's voice sounded small, even to her own ears. "Thanks. Don't tell the others until I'm safely out of here." Her breath caught in her throat. "Annette . . . I wonder if . . . ?"

"Let's not get ahead of ourselves. You're going to be all right."

CHAPTER FORTY

A trim assistant ushered Bret into the plush executive office, served him a cup of coffee, and told him it would only be about five minutes. This was Bret's second trip to see Megyn's father, and he knew Mr. Buckman was as worried as he was. It had been three days since she called and now he couldn't even reach her on her V³ issued PDA.

Mr. Buckman hurried in and shook Bret's hand. "Any word?"

"No sir."

"Then we'll need to take matters into our own hands. I have an idea. But we've got to get word to Megyn in order for my plan to work." He grabbed a bottle of cold water. "When she was a little girl we used to play spies. I don't know if she told you, but Mrs. Buckman was an alcoholic all the years Megyn was growing up?"

Bret nodded.

"Liz's worked through all that and she's back on track now."

"I met her recently. She's quite an impressive woman."

"Yes, she is, isn't she? Anyway, when her mother drank, Megyn would sometimes hide from her." He took a sip. "It used to scare me to death when I'd come home and find her gone. Because of this, she created a secret code for us to communicate with. Only the two of us know about it."

He paused. "I'm thinking I should send her some flowers and a note telling her how much I love her, and ask for her forgiveness. I've wanted to do this anyway, but I've been afraid she might reject me again. I tried to make amends once before but she refused to talk to me." He gulped and looked down at the papers in his hand. "I don't think I could take being rejected a second time."

Bret shuffled his feet and looked out the window.

Mr. Buckman cleared his throat and took his seat behind his expansive executive desk. "No one will suspect anything. Within the note, I will embed the secret code telling her the plan."

"What if she just reads it and misses the hidden message? It would be easy to do considering the emotional circumstances."

"She won't."

"Okay. What's the plan?"

"I'll pick her up in a private jet and whisk her out of there."

"Singapore's small. Won't the Nethers find out you're in town?"

"Trust me. I can be stealth when I need to be."

"Then what? Where will she go?"

"I've got a place for her. No one knows about it, and she can stay there until this whole thing quiets down." He balled his fists. "I hope her disappearance will be a big blow to these people."

Bret stepped closer to Mr. Buckman's executive desk. He leaned his fists on it. "I want to go with you."

"There's nothing you can do and your absence would be noticed." Mr. Buckman stood. "I travel all the time. No one will be suspicious of my whereabouts."

Bret pulled a small note from his blazer pocket. "Would you give this to her from me? I've written down a few verses. I think they will bring her comfort."

Mr. Buckman smiled and studied him. Bret knew he stood before one of the most powerful men in the world. What did he see? Someone he could trust? Someone who cared deeply about his daughter?

"Thanks, Bret. I will pass these along when I see her," Mr. Buckman said. "Please pray for us."

"I've got an international team already on it. They don't have the particulars of the situation, but believe me, we're covered."

Bret turned to go and then paused and looked back. "The show's in two days, you know. She's supposed to broadcast from Singapore with Ethan. Maybe you should wait until after that's over to make your move. That will buy some time before everyone notices she's missing."

"I'll do it. Anything else?"

Bret shrugged. "Did you decide how we are going to explain my visits to your office?"

Mr. Buckman smiled. "I've been telling everyone that you're my new spiritual advisor." He patted Bret on the shoulder. "You're covering our efforts with prayer, and giving me advice, right?"

Bret grinned. "Right."

~

Megyn's days were filled with endorsements, wardrobe fittings, photo shoots, and interviews. Between meals with the Nethers, work, and playing tourist with Ethan, she didn't have a minute to herself. She'd tried to take a walk a couple of evenings ago, but the security detail informed her it wasn't safe to go out.

It was late night when she and Ethan rehearsed their parts and practiced their talking points for the last time before the live performance. Ethan headed for the door, grasped the doorknob, and turned to face her. "Everything all right? You seem different this week." He put up his hand to stop her from responding. "I don't mean because we're not a couple. You seem quieter, more subdued."

She shook her head. "Fine; everything's fine. I'm just concerned about my new responsibilities. So much has happened in such a short period of time."

He patted her shoulder. "Don't worry. You'll do fine."

~

She slumped into the nearest chair. She hadn't slept well in several nights, and the tension of pretending all the time was wearing on her. *I can't do this much longer. I've got to get out of here.* A tear rolled down her cheek.

She looked for her personal phone but it wasn't in its usual place. Her heart beat faster as she dug through her belongings and checked the rest of her small living space. She grabbed her V^3 communication device and headed for the door. *I've got to try again. Maybe there's another way out of here.* She only had access to one exit from her condo—the elevator, and it was restricted to two places; the Nethers' penthouse and condos, and the lobby. She headed down.

The doors opened to a plush waiting area and reception desk. The security guard sat calmly behind the desk. "Everything all right, Miss Buckman?"

164

"Um, yes." Megyn's heartbeat raced. "It's been a stressful day. I need to go for a walk. I won't be long."

"Can't let you do that, Miss. The Nethers' asked me to keep you safe." He stood up and put his hand on his gun holster and smiled. "You're famous now. There're lots of people out there wanting to make a name for themselves, and you'd be just the ticket to help them do it. It's too dangerous."

Megyn turned back to the elevator. Her shoulders sagged and tears streamed down her face. *I couldn't have used the V^3 phone anyway. Someone might be listening.*

The elevator doors opened on her floor and she shuffled to the kitchen, put a cup of hot water in the microwave, and waited to make her evening tea. She took a seat at the counter and smelled the bouquet of deep red roses that arrived yesterday. They were fresh and flawless. *Even these flowers look happy,* she sighed. *My favorite, much better than last week's assortment of spring varieties.* She touched one of the pedals and noticed a card buried in between the stems. She wiggled it out, made her tea, and moved to her favorite chair in the living area. She pulled the note out and read:

> *Dearest Megyn,*
>
> *I know I was too controlling and headstrong. I apologize from the depths of my soul. Please forgive me. I love you more than you know and am always here for you. Even though we've been apart, I've followed your life and know how successful you've been, and what a wonderful person you've become.*
>
> *Remember the kitten you asked me to rescue when you were little? You'd just put on an animal kingdom play and, after the show attempted to ride away with her in that little red toy car you always used to play with. She ran away and I helped you find her. I feel the same way you did; like my little kitten has run away and I don't know how to get her back. If there's an outside chance we can save this relationship, please don't run anymore. Let me rescue you . . . rescue us. The door is always open to my love.*
>
> *Daddy*

Megyn let out a deep breath and tears flowed once again. She needed him and he was there for her. She studied the note and knew what she had to do.

She slept soundly for the first time since she'd left home.

CHAPTER FORTY-ONE

Megyn stood next to Ethan, ready to welcome Vanguarders throughout the globe. Her mood was upbeat. Before they'd gone on, he'd leaned over and said, "You're acting like your old self again. I like it. Welcome back."

She smiled and told him she looked forward to the evening.

The teleprompter flashed on, and they were ready to roll. The Vanguard of Volunteer Voices anthem played and she looked out on the studio audience assembled at their satellite location. There were at least a thousand diverse young people gathered, and they were chanting along with the music. A chill ran through her body. *If they only knew.*

Megyn opened the program and announced the top vote getters for excellence in encouraging and creating unity, equality, and service in their activities.

Carla and Vince awarded the four second tier winners with ten thousand dollar checks each and the grand prize winner with a check for one hundred thousand, on the main stage in Los Angeles.

The director switched back to Singapore. Ethan set up the first topic; money. Bills and coins fell from the ceilings in both locations.

The cameras moved to Los Angeles where the eager United States audience laughed and crawled around the floor holding up their booty. Megyn shook her head and watched the live feed. It seemed like a long time since she'd participated in the same experience.

Video played in the background that showed the V³ items available for purchase with the new currency. There were the usual T-shirts, hats, and other Vanguard logo products. A number of new things had also been added. One set of items was a small assortment of special PDAs. The audience was told anyone exchanging their cash for the new money would receive one as a free gift. Not only would they have cash to buy V³ products, but they'd also have a new state-of-the-art PDA. "It is a win, win," Ethan shouted over the chaos.

Megyn's heart pounded and her knees began to shake. *Why free PDAs? Surveillance? Tracking?* She shook herself.

The camera directly in front of her lit up and Megyn read the teleprompter. "Look under your seats. Each person attending today's show has a PDA taped to, his or her, chair." Shouts of joy filled the studio.

More crawling around the floor ensued. Ethan handled the rest of the segment while she waited in the wings. When he was finished, the action changed back to Los Angeles for vignettes from the other Callers. She hurried back to her dressing room to watch.

She thought about the millions of viewers and sighed. *Everything's different now. I used to feel the same way they do. I don't like running away, but there's nothing I can do. I'm only one person.* She shuddered. *I'm not sure what they'd do to me if they knew my plans.*

Gisele poked her head in the door, and Megyn's stomach lurched. Did Gisele know what she was planning? "You're doing great, daughter. See you after the show."

Megyn's hands felt clammy.

She watched the monitor as Bret entered the stage and introduced a new singer. The credits showed her to be a nineteen-year-old student from New Mexico. She had long shimmering black hair and huge brown eyes. She was gorgeous. Megyn felt her body heat up with jealousy as she watched Bret hand the young woman a microphone and perform a duet with her. The song was new and spoke of making connections. They smiled at each other and then to the audience. The song ended and the singer gave Bret a kiss on the cheek.

Megyn sighed and wondered if she'd ever see him again.

She watched two more sets and hurried back to the stage to join Ethan in facilitating the last few segments. Her neck tensed as the show seemed to drag to the finale. She had only a small window of time to slip out the back door before she'd be missed. There'd been no time to examine her escape route. She wasn't sure if the security guard would let her pass, or if the car would be easy to spot once she was outside.

All her belongings, except her purse, were left in the condo. The note from her father was ripped up and thrown on the floor in an effort to make people think she was still mad at him, and not look in his direction. Identification documents, credit cards and money were hidden in her clothing. She was ready to flee.

Finally, the show's anthem and closing credits began to roll. Megyn turned to Ethan. "I'm not feeling so good. I've got to go to the bathroom—really bad."

He touched her arm. "No problem. I'll cover for you out here."

"Thanks." She hurried off.

As she walked toward the studio's back door, she heard her heart beating faster in her ears with every step. She passed various staff members and felt like each one was watching her and knew what she was up to. "Good job, Miss Buckman," a gripper said.

"Thanks." She hoped her voice sounded calm.

Her breathing became labored when she reached the door. The security guard stood with his hands clasped in front of him and his feet spread apart. He looked all business.

"I need to go outside."

"I'm sorry, I can't—"

Megyn doubled over, threw her hand over her mouth and hurried past him to the door. "You don't understand. I think I'm going to be sick." She thrust the door open and spotted the little red car and headed for it.

The security guard watched from the top of the stairs and called down to her as she ran. "Anything I can do to help, Miss Buckman?"

She kept running and shook her head. She reached the vehicle and spotted Randall, one of her father's long time employees. He started his engine and leaned over and opened the passenger side door.

She jumped in and heard a voice call her name.

The guard rushed down the stairs holding his walkie-talkie to his ear.

Randall stepped on the gas and exited the alley. When they turned the corner, he handed her a sweatshirt, wig, and ball cap. "Put these on."

She ripped off her shirt and skirt to reveal shorts and a tank top. "I'm way ahead of you, except for the wig. I had no way of getting one of those. I also couldn't manage a change of shoes."

"There are three styles in the back, all in your size. Take your pick."

Two blocks later he pulled into a garage and closed the door. "There's another car around the corner. A pair of sunglasses awaits you there."

She touched his arm. "I really appreciate this, Randall."

"No problem, Miss Buckman. I'd do anything for your dad, and you too. I was there when you were born, you know."

They hopped into a dark blue sedan. "We change cars one more time before we get to the plane. Then we change flights two times before we get to our destination."

"Where's that?"

"I'll let your dad tell you."

Her stomach jumped at the mention of her father. "He's here?"

"Waiting in the plane. He's too recognizable to do this himself. Otherwise he would've picked you up instead of me. I had to fight to get him to stay behind."

Five minutes later they stowed the sedan, transferred to a SUV, and headed for Malaysia.

"I'll handle the border crossing. I've got the correct papers."

Megyn sat back in her seat and relaxed.

"Your dad is waiting at a small airstrip about fifty miles from the border. He's hoping anyone searching for you will explore the more traditional routes of escape first. He's pretty confident no one will look for you here. But, I know he won't be happy until you're in the air and on your way. Thirsty? There's bottled water and snacks in the backpack."

She grabbed the bag from behind her seat and pulled it through the space between them. "My mouth feels like cotton. I was so nervous. It was hard to stay focused on the show." Her hand searched the bag. There're two bottles in here. Want one?"

"Yes, please."

Megyn gulped her water. "I'd say I was amazed at how quickly you guys pulled this together, but I know what my dad can accomplish when he puts his mind to it." She paused. "I almost didn't see the note, though. It was tucked way inside the stems of the flowers."

"Make sure you tell your dad. He'll be interested to hear that. He placed it on the roses himself. I saw him do it. The note looked obvious to me."

Megyn laid her head on the rest, "Hmm."

~

Gisele stood near the studio's back exit with her hands on her hips. "She got in the car; or someone made her get into the car? Which is it?"

The security guard shuffled his feet. "Well ma'am, she said she was sick and ran out the door and down the stairs. I watched her to make sure she was all right."

"Yes, I know all that. Did she get in the car willingly or not?" Gisele felt her face turning red. "Who hired this dumb, muscle bound idiot?"

He rubbed his fingers over his chin and crinkled his forehead. "I thought she got in willingly, but I could be wrong. I couldn't see everything from up here. He could've had a weapon, or something, I suppose."

"How long ago was this?"

"Uh, it was," he looked at this watch, "maybe ten minutes."

Gisele raised her voice. "Ten minutes?"

"It could have been a little more."

"Was it right after the show, or later?" she huffed.

"Uh, ma'am, I think it was right after the show."

Gisele looked at her PDA. "That was over a half hour ago, YOU IDIOT."

One of the makeup artists handed her a purse. "I think this is Megyn's."

Gisele grabbed the bag out of her hands and took it to the guard's desk. She dumped the contents out and moved them around. "Lipstick, wallet, comb, tissue, pen—the usual. This is curious. I can't imagine she'd leave without her purse."

She stuffed the contents back inside. "Ethan said she went to the bathroom. Check the bathrooms."

The guard took a tentative step forward. "But, I saw her get in a car, a little red car. I don't know the make, but it was red—and small."

"Who's in charge of the local police force? Get that person on the phone for me. And, set up a group to search the building." She hesitated. "You can do that, can't you?"

~

Bret sat on his knees in the middle of his living room and prayed. He'd fasted all day and asked millions of believers throughout the world to do the same. He knew communication with Mr. Buckman, or Megyn would be dangerous, and the only way he would learn anything about the success, or failure, of her extraction would come from news accounts.

CHAPTER FORTY-TWO

Megyn fell into her father's arms and wept. "I'm sorry. I'm *so* sorry."

"Me too, Punkin. Me too," he said. "It was all my fault. I was stubborn and controlling."

He extended his arms, and she gazed into his matching violet eyes. Tears poured down his cheeks and his face glowed with admiration and love.

Megyn blushed.

"I'd like nothing better than to spend the rest of the afternoon catching up, but you're not safe yet," he said squeezing her shoulders. "We've got to get you out of here." He motioned to the plush tan leather chairs. "Let's take our seats."

The engines roared and they buckled up for takeoff. He patted her hand. "Your mom wanted to come, but I wouldn't let her. I was afraid it would be too obvious if we both left town at the same time. Someone might figure out we were behind your disappearance. The less people involved, the less likely we'll be discovered."

Megyn nestled in and sighed.

"Hungry, thirsty? We're well stocked with food and beverages."

Megyn smiled and kissed the back of his hand. "I ate and drank in the car on the way here. Right now I just need rest. This has been a tough few days. I've barely slept all week. I'm exhausted."

He patted her hand. "You're safe now. No one will be able to find you unless you want them to. I promise."

Megyn leaned back in her seat and for the first time in a long time felt safe. Her eyes were heavy. She let the world drift away.

~

Mr. Buckman stroked Megyn's hair away from her face. "Time to wake up sleepy head. We're here."

She stretched her arms and legs, looked at her dad, and moaned. "I knew I was tired, but I can't believe how long I've been out. I guess I've slept my way across the globe. I barely remember changing planes." She yawned. "I suppose the stress and sleepless nights have taken their toll."

He clenched his fists and his cheeks turned pink. "I'm so angry for what they've put you through."

She touched his arm. "Don't be. They didn't even know I was unhappy."

"Only because you were afraid of what they'd do to you if you told them."

"Some of the leaders are definitely in it for the power, but most are true believers, Dad. They think they're doing something good. Gisele even referred to me as her daughter."

Mr. Buckman's cheeks burned brighter red, and he slammed his fist into the back of his seat. "How dare her! And what difference does it make whether they believe in what they're doing or not? The end result is the same. It's still about doing things the way they think they should be done. It's still about power and control."

Megyn took his hand and kissed it again. "It's over now. I'm safe." She grinned. "You've rescued the princess once more."

"How'd you like my note? Brought back a lot of memories, huh?"

"I had a little trouble with your handwriting. I got the *rescue*, *after the show*, *red car*, and *door* parts but somehow missed the *back* and couldn't figure out which door to go to. All your secret squiggles at the ends of the key words matched but that one. You doubled back a bit and I passed it over several times. I finally decided that *back* had to be the missing direction. Nothing else made sense."

He looked concerned. "Sorry. I guess I'm a bit out of practice." He shuddered and whispered to himself. "I could have blown the whole thing because of a squiggle."

"Never mind. I figured it out, and I'm here now, with you." She
squeezed his hand and tears filled her eyes. "My favorite part was
where you told me you loved me."

He squeezed her hand. "I *do* love you, Punkin, very much."

He stood and helped her out of her seat. "Ready to see your
new temporary home?"

~

Megyn held her dad's hand and explored the small living
quarters, offices, and laboratory. "You say you built this to develop a
new medical instrument? Why's it empty?"

"The project leader died unexpectedly and I didn't have anyone
to replace her. She was one of the top medical research scientists in
the world. This was her dream facility. She had it built to her
specifications. This business is extremely competitive and our
development projects are top secret. She lived and worked here, and
we paid the bills. She passed away before we were able to complete
the first prototype. It was a complex project and now there's no one
to take up where she left off." He looked around. "It's yours for as
long as you need it. You can fix it up any way you want. All of her
personal belongings were removed a couple of months ago."

"I can't imagine how, or why, I'd change anything. I only need
the living area, and it's perfect, small and cozy." She leaned against
the back of the soft sofa. "I guess I'll be here for a while. The
Council is extremely powerful. I don't see them giving up their
efforts to find me anytime soon. I'm a threat to everything they've
spent their entire lives working for."

Mr. Buckman walked her to the closet in the bedroom and
pulled out a duffle bag. "All you'll need for a fresh identity is in here;
new name, look, and papers. I'm afraid you'll have to dye your own
hair if you don't want to use the wig. I could bring someone in to do
it, but you never know who to trust. The Nethers' have plenty of
money to bribe people with."

He pulled out items one at a time. "I had green nonprescription
contact lenses ordered through a third party. They'll change your
distinctive eye color. The wig is blonde and longer than your current
cut. You'll be wearing glasses too. All these changes will make you
unidentifiable and match the new persona we've given you. Anytime
you go out, you need to use all these things. I'd also recommend you

wear the form shaping undergarments your mom found. They'll change your curves and add about thirty pounds. Sorry."

She dropped into a chair. "I don't think I'll be going out for a while. There's plenty of food here, books to read, exercise equipment, computer, and television." She looked around. "I don't see a phone."

"There aren't any. We can't risk it. Don't check your e-mail or any other social networking sites either. They'll have people and technology that can track those things. You're now Donna Marie, from Missouri. Your background information is also in the knapsack, including information on your hometown in Missouri. Everything you do needs to fit into that context. You can get on line as Donna Marie and use her e-mail and other accounts. No credit cards. I've supplied plenty of cash for food and supplies. You know how important all this is, but I work in high tech and, I can assure you that you can't underestimate their ability to locate you if you make the slightest move as Megyn Buckman."

She pulled her legs up and wrapped her arms around them.

Mr. Buckman pulled a piece of paper from his back pocket. He spread it on the table, grabbed a pen from the knapsack, and began checking off items he already covered. "They'll be searching high and low. From what you've told me, they didn't even know you were upset about the situation. It'll take them a while to figure out what happened, and then—be prepared. The search will move to a whole new level." He rocked back and forth on his heels. "They don't have to explain your absence publicly for at least a week—when the next show airs."

He paced the small living space. "I'll go about my business as if everything is normal. No one is expecting me to know you're missing."

"Suppose they suppress my disappearance for more than a week?" She looked at him with fear in her eyes. "Who knows what they'll do."

"We'll just take this one day at a time." His eyes sparkled and his lip curled up. "But . . . if it does get out that no one knows where you are, I'll raise holy hell and demand an explanation."

Megyn crinkled her forehead. "If you want to hurry things along, you could have Mom try to contact me on my V^3 PDA, and call ACN when she's unable to get an answer."

"Let me think about that." He stopped and rocked on his heels again. "In the mean time, we can keep in touch through several online sources. In the duffle bag there's a folder with a list of chat rooms, bulletin boards, and online games where we can exchange messages. There're also instructions on how we will use each forum to communicate, including appropriate aliases. I'll check them several times a day and you do the same. Be careful. We can't talk directly."

Megyn took a deep breath, and let it out. "I'll be happy to stay right here for a while. The last week has been tough. There was no one I could trust."

She saw him examining her. "You did right in trusting that young man, Bret."

Megyn blushed and looked down at her feet.

Mr. Buckman stifled a smile. "He's a nice guy. Seems to care a lot about you."

"Does he know where I am?"

"I left him totally in the dark. He's an honest young man, and he's better off not knowing. I don't think he could lie very well if he was questioned. And I'm sure he will be."

Megyn swallowed. "Does he have the communication information?"

"I wanted to keep him out of this," he said. "For both your sakes."

Her shoulders sagged.

He softened his voice. "Hopefully, you won't have to be in hiding too long. I'm sure he'll want to reconnect with you."

Megyn sighed and touched his hand. "I really appreciate everything. I don't know what I would have done without you."

"And your mom too. She worked with me on all of this."

Megyn's eyes moistened. "Tell her thanks too. I love you guys."

He shuffled his feet. "I almost forgot. Bret asked me to give you this list of verses. He thought they might bring you peace and encouragement. I brought along the Bible you used to use when you were a kid, in case you want to look them up."

~

Gisele and Ethan sat on the patio overlooking the warm Singapore morning sky. She picked up the coffee pot and poured herself a refill. "You thought she wasn't acting like herself this past week?"

"Yeah. Like I told you last night, she was quiet and seemed preoccupied. I asked her several times if everything was all right."

"I know we've been over this a number of times, but I'm having a hard time understanding what happened. Did she question anything, or give you a hint there was a problem?"

"She said everything was fine. She said she was tired from all the travel, and the climate, and time changes."

"But she was better last night at the filming?"

"She was like her old self, excited and ready to do her part for the V³."

"None of this makes sense. But, something has to be wrong. She left her communication devices in her apartment, and all her clothes are there."

"She can't use the PDA at the studio. Maybe she left it home on purpose."

"Her stylist told me she's always brought it in the past." Gisele thought a minute. "Martin's heading up a manhunt. We'll find her. The local authorities have already discovered the red car. It was parked in a garage a few blocks from the studio—empty and no prints. They're checking city cameras now. Martin has requested all her phone usage information. We've got hidden communication devices in her quarters. Mary is checking those as well."

Ethan sat back. "I heard there was a note from her dad torn up and thrown on the floor. Maybe that set her off."

Gisele clenched her teeth. "We'll get to the bottom of this. Trust me. We'll find her."

"Is anyone checking on Bret? I think they talk."

"We're investigating his movements for the last week as well. If he even breathes wrong, we'll know it. I've never liked that guy anyway, and I want him out of her life."

"Do you want me to question the Callers and find out what they know?"

"Not yet. Let's wait until all the data comes in. Then we'll have something to go on. We'll be able to match what we know against what they say." She gazed out at the cityscape. "There's always a chance she'll show up with a plausible explanation."

Ethan furrowed his eyebrows.

CHAPTER FORTY-THREE

Megyn's new quarters was larger than any she'd lived in since she'd left home. The pantry and refrigerator were filled with things she'd loved as a child and she smiled at the thoughtfulness of her parents. She was listless and bored and flipped her television controller between the news and the entertainment channel. It had been three days and nothing was said about her disappearance. The only books in the small bookshelves were suspense novels and she'd had more than enough of that to be interested in reading about someone else's problems. She looked through the list of online sites for communicating with her father. Nothing there either. *I wish I knew what was going on.*

~

Gisele sat alone in an austere office. She leaned on her black ebony desk that reflected the gold accent pieces, and deep red area rug. Floor to ceiling windows revealed an extensive view of the New World Headquarters compound. "Yes, Mary. I want to see anything you have," she said into the phone. "I told you to keep me updated. This is your number one priority." She swiveled to look out the window. "No, I'll come down. It's easier if we use your equipment."

She rode the elevator to the media center, tapping her foot and pushing the button to hurry it along. *You just can't find good help anymore.*

She walked through the door and everyone stiffened.

"Over here," Mary motioned. "Would you like to take a seat?"

Gisele didn't answer. She continued to stand and placed her hand on her hip. "I'm waiting."

"Here's what we've got so far. First, Megyn. We've pieced together various shots taken of her in her room. Many of them late at night."

Gisele watched the short clips go by. There were scenes of her crying, staring at the wall, sitting on the balcony wrapped in a blanket staring out into the distance, and more crying.

"That's one set. The next two show her trying to leave the building and being stopped by the security guard in the lobby."

"Yes. I know about these." She waved her hand in dismissal.

"Okay. Next we've got her searching for something. She seems rather distraught."

Gisele tapped her fingers on the back of Mary's chair. "Yes, I know what this is about."

Mary leaned forward. "We decided to go back a few days prior to what you asked for—just in case." She clicked the mouse a couple of times. "It took a lot of work, but here's what we found."

Gisele bent over and observed Megyn leave the building. She walked down the block and was picked up by another camera from a convenience store on the corner. It was late at night and there wasn't much traffic or light. The next scene was taken at the wharf where she stood in the shadow of a tree, talking on her cell. She paced back and forth, wiped her eyes, and made hand gestures with her fists.

Gisele eased her way into a chair and watched Megyn return back to the condo. She looked like she'd been crying. *What's going on here?*

Mary tapped on another box. "We have the video from the studio showing Megyn getting in the red car, but I believe you've already seen it."

Gisele didn't respond.

"We also have a copy of the car entering the area and parking. No license plates and no film of the driver other than the hands which were gloved and blurry." She waited. "There's video of them leaving. Again, nothing useful.

"We checked for cameras around the neighborhood where the red car was left, but there are none for blocks. There's a main thoroughfare in the area. They could have easily been picked up, or had another vehicle ready to go." She sighed. "Bottom line, they could have driven away in anything." She looked at Gisele. "Okay, that's all we have on Megyn."

"Now for the Callers. We did Bret first, like you asked. We checked his whereabouts during the same time frame as Megyn's call. There's a match. He also walked down the street with his personal cell. Here's the video."

Gisele's stomach lurched. *That little ingrate. She's used and betrayed me. I offered her everything.* Her fingernails dug into the palms of her hands. *I'll get even if it's the last thing I do.*

She got up to leave.

"There's more," Mary said.

Gisele dropped back into the chair and watched.

Mary continued. "As you can see; Bret leaving the ACN campus, and later walking into the Buckman Medical Instruments headquarters building. Leaving an hour later and revisiting it a second time a few days later."

Gisele set her jaw and clenched her teeth. *They don't know who they're tangling with.*

She stood and walked to the doorway. "Keep on him. I want to know every move he makes." She paused. "See what you can come up with on Arthur Buckman during that same timeframe."

Mary turned pale. "Arthur Buckman? But he's—"

"I don't care who he is. Track him. Don't forget the other Callers too. I want a set of videos in my office, with a detailed log of everyone's activities by the end of the week. I don't care how many people you have to put on this."

She turned and headed back to the elevator, her cell to her ear. "Ethan. Where are you? Call me."

~

Ethan sat on a barstool in front of the Callers who were assembled in soft cushy sofas and chairs around the living room of the Vanguard quarters. "Megyn's missing."

"What? No way," everyone answered at once.

Ethan watched Bret's response which was stoic, with no facial expression. He looked at the others. "Just after the show a few days ago. We think she may have been kidnapped although there's no ransom note as of yet."

The Callers started talking at once, and he held up his hand to quiet them. "The security guard stationed at the back of the studio said she ran out the door with her hands on her mouth and stomach saying she was sick. He followed her to the top of the stairs and saw her get into a small red car parked down in the back alley. He thinks someone was waiting there to grab her, and that he probably had a gun, or some other weapon, in his hand."

Tawny spoke first. "We all get these strange e-mails and threats, but we've gotten used to them. None of us take them seriously anymore."

Carla met his eyes and smiled demurely. "Have they been able to track down the car's owner?"

Ethan grinned back. "They tried. Believe me, they tried. But all paths led to dead ends."

Vince grimaced. "Wow, man. I can't believe it. What are ya'll going to do now?"

Sami scooted forward in her chair. "What about us? How safe are we?"

"We've already beefed up security," Ethan said. "They're going to keep looking for Megyn and hoping for the best."

The Callers sighed, shook their heads, and looked from one to the other. Obviously they were unnerved by this announcement.

"If any of you have information as to her whereabouts, let me know." He looked at Bret. "You've been quiet. What do you think? Has she mentioned any concerns or fears lately?"

"I don't know what to think." He looked Ethan in the eyes. "You've spent a lot of time with her lately. What do you think?"

Everyone looked at Ethan.

Carla tilted her head. "Did you notice anything, Ethan? Did she act different?"

Ethan straightened his back. "Uh, I didn't pay much attention."

He got up to leave and examined the group. "I don't need to tell you this is still under investigation and needs to be kept quiet among ourselves. The ACN leadership asks that you allow them to make the announcement in their own time and in their own way. Please don't share this with anyone else."

Everyone nodded agreement.

He headed for the door and Carla followed him out. He smiled and waved her off. "I'll call you." He got in his shiny red car, and drove away. *Bret knew something. I could see it in his face.* He pushed a button on his dash and called Gisele.

CHAPTER FORTY-FOUR

B ret turned to the group of deflated Callers. "Anyone for lunch?"
"Let's go," Vince said.

"How about we try a new place," Tawny said. "After hearing that; I'd like to change locations. Don't want to establish patterns."

"Ditto on that," Sami said.

On their way out they grabbed Carla, who was standing in the driveway, and the five of them crammed into one car. They headed across town and found a noisy pizza parlor where they could sit in a side room to ensure privacy. Vince picked out the toppings and ordered the sodas.

"I wasn't scared until now," Carla said. She looked around the table. "We all knew this was a possibility, but no one really believes it could happen to them."

"I hear that," Vince said as he handed out the drinks and passed the utensils and condiments around.

Bret leaned forward. "I've got something to say. This is between us only. It does not leave this group. Do I have your agreement?" He made eye contact with each Caller until he got a nod. "Megyn called me the other night. She had just been to the world headquarters for a group headed up by the Nethers."

"World headquarters for what?" Carla asked.

"There was a council meeting that included prominent business, political, and academic leaders from throughout the globe. Their purpose is to utilize the youth of the world to transform it. They created, and are using, the V^3 movement to accomplish their vision of utopia."

Vince laughed. "What?"

"I'm not kidding. Megyn's already filled us in on the rally rollout she attended that introduced the new money, giving back, spiritualism, environment, technology and communications, and health and welfare programs."

Sami and Tawny nodded their heads slowly.

"At the council meeting, Megyn learned about the path these new activities will take the youth of the world. They plan to have us spy on our families, friends, and neighbors; coerce and pressure them to do the right thing; and check up on them through reading their mail and searching their recycling. We're supposed to turn the rebellious ones over to an oversight committee who will have them rehabilitated. The Council has plans for great new ways to unify, create equality, and serve others, plans that will become mandatory. They'll 'nudge' us forward until we all say and do the same thing, what they tell us to say, and do."

Carla stuck her chin out. "Why didn't you tell us this before?"

Tawny jumped in. "Don't you think this is stuff, we might of, kind of wanted to know about?"

"Megyn and I agreed to tell you when she got back. We were concerned about the security of our communications."

"But she told you?" Sami said.

"She was upset and wanted to talk."

Everyone glared at him.

"There's more. The Council also discussed the growing opposition *problem*."

"Yeah, I've been watching that on TV." Vince took a slice of pizza. "Some of those people look pretty mad. Especially those Forces for Freedom folks;" Vince said with sarcasm. "They even swiped our V^3 moniker. They refer to themselves as the F^3." Vince bit into his slice, chewing hungrily.

Bret chose to ignore Vince. "Apparently the Council has decided to go after the F^3 leaders, discredit them, and label the participants as racists and bigots. They'll make up stuff if they have to. They've also moved up their implementation plans. They're afraid the winds are changing and now plan to do in the next six months to a year what they originally planned to do over two to three years."

"Let's back up a minute," Carla said. "Are you saying these people are after power and money? I don't see it. The people I know aren't like that."

"That's what Megyn said too when she only knew Ethan and the Nethers. When she met the Council, her view of people's motives changed. According to Megyn the tone and attitude of the group was far from helpful and caring. She still thinks some are true believers, but the end result is the same, isn't it?"

"Hmm," Tawny said. "So it sounds like Megyn was upset when she told you all this?"

Bret frowned. "She'd already agreed to have Gisele mentor her to take a much larger role once her one year commitment as a Caller was over."

"So you're saying she felt trapped?" Tawny said.

"I'm not here to speak for Megyn. I'm just passing on the information."

Tawny rolled her eyes. "I'd sure feel trapped if I were in that situation. Megyn was brought into their inner circle and a lot of secret stuff was shared. If she wanted out, would they trust her with the information?"

Bret didn't answer.

Sami sat back. "Sounds to me like she's flown the coop."

Carla's eyes got big. "Maybe her parents sprung her?"

"She hasn't spoken to her dad in over three years," Vince said.

Tawny rolled forward in the chair. "But she reconnected with her mom recently."

Sami gasped. "Maybe they found out she was having second thoughts? And—"

"Oh, please," Vince drawled.

Carla looked at Bret. "You know where she is, don't you?"

"I really don't know where she is. I haven't heard from her in several days."

"Do you think they found out and something happened to her?" Carla asked.

"I don't know." Bret stared out the window. "Anything could have happened. I'm concerned."

Carla looked troubled. "Maybe it's like the security guard thinks. Someone kidnapped her."

Everyone ate in silence.

Tawny slammed her hand on the table. "What about us? If what Bret is telling us is true. I don't think I want to be a part of this anymore."

"Me either," Sami said.

Carla thought of Ethan and her shoulders tensed. "Let's see how the next few shows go and then decide. We can quit at any time, can't we? Maybe it's not as bad as Megyn thinks."

Vince smiled, sat forward, and stretched his arms to envelope the group. "I don't' think we can get out of our contracts so easily. Let's allow this to play out a little while longer."

~

Gisele checked her e-mail and buzzed her assistant. "Have Mary get me anything she's found on all the Callers. I want to know if they've kicked a dog, slapped a baby, or yelled at their parents. I want to know everything. She should already have a lot of data since she and Ethan hired investigators when these people were first presented to us. I want to see something now."

She sat back and gazed at the landscape. "Get my media staff up here this afternoon. We're going to work on a new campaign."

She set her jaw and whispered to herself. "No one is going to stand in the way of my plans."

She said Trianna's name into her PDA. "Megyn Buckman will not be participating in the show this week."

"But—?"

Gisele cut her off. "This is how you will handle it—"

CHAPTER FORTY-FIVE

Megyn curled up on her sofa, holding a cup of hot Jasmine tea to warm her shaking hands. Her shoulders were tight and she rotated them to relieve the tension of waiting. The Vanguard of Volunteer Voices show was to start in two minutes, and so far she'd found nothing, on any of the TV, Internet, or news outlets, about her disappearance.

She listened to the familiar V^3 anthem and watched the studio audience sing with delight and gusto. Ethan welcomed the global audience, announced the prior week's winners, and Carla joined him on stage to introduce the next segment. The commercials rolled by and Megyn's heart raced with anticipation.

Bret entered and the tween girls went wild. He smiled into the camera and Megyn's heart melted. Five artists from around the world entered the stage. Bret prefaced his segment. "In prior weeks, we've introduced performers that sing and dance. This week I'd like to present artists that have been commissioned by the V^3 to produce work that epitomizes what we're all about." He walked to the first person, introduced him, and a vignette of the young man's life and work was shown on the big screen. The remaining videos also emphasized unity, equality, and service. Next, the finished products were unveiled.

Bret left the stage and Megyn felt lonely.

The show continued with Carla and Ethan teaming up for each set up. Carla looked radiant with her big brown eyes and shiny, auburn highlighted, dark brown hair. She smiled into the camera and the studio participants happily applauded.

The final piece was presented with Vince at a remote location. He introduced three extreme sports which were demonstrated before a live audience.

Megyn paced the floor and wondered why no one had addressed her absence. Her name was still in the credits at the beginning of the show. *Do they expect me back?*

Vince finished with two guys dressed up like bats, jumping off a cliff and sailing down through a rugged canyon with a waterfall and a fast moving stream below. He'd emerged in a similar outfit, waved to the camera, leaped into the canyon and joined them in their flight. The words unity and equality faded in and out across the screen.

The show's anthem played in the background and the call-in numbers were repeated.

Megyn sat at her computer. She wondered what the viewers were thinking since the show wasn't saying anything about her absence.

~

The Callers gathered in one car and headed out for their traditional after the show celebration—food and drink.

"Did you guys notice no one mentioned Megyn?" Tawny said.

"I think that's weird," Sami said. "You'd think they'd at least say she's unable to be with us tonight. That wouldn't commit them to a full blown explanation."

Carla fastened her seat belt. "Maybe they're hoping to find her first so they don't have to explain."

"She's got a big fan base," Tawny said. "A lot of people will demand to know where she is. Are they just going to ignore her followers' inquiries like they've ignored her absence?"

Bret straightened the rearview mirror. "Has anyone heard anything new since Ethan talked to us?"

Everyone looked at Carla who squirmed. "Ethan says Gisele is leaving no stone unturned. That's all I can get out of him."

They arrived at a Greek restaurant and Bret parked the car. "We can enter through the side, over here," he pointed. "There's a private room set up for us."

"I miss having the freedom to go out without being recognized," Vince said smiling. "I mean, notoriety is great, ya'll, but freedom is good too."

A table for five was set up with a server standing by.

"Water for all," Bret said. "Lots of water."

"It's funny how we're always so thirsty after the shows," Tawny said. "I think it's from the stress and tension."

The drinks and first course were delivered and the attendant left.

Bret leaned forward. "What did you guys think about the show tonight? Everyone still in for next week?"

Sami spoke first. "I feel like things are getting more heavy handed. It's kind of subtle, but not. Understand what I'm saying?"

"I know exactly," Tawny said. "You see and hear things, but you don't believe it's what you're hearing and seeing." She shuffled in her chair. "I think we human beings have a way of filtering information to fit our world view. If I didn't know what I know about the V³, I probably wouldn't even notice a problem. I'd interpret things the way I want them to be and dismiss the rest."

"Like the equality thing we've talked about before," Sami said. "It never would've crossed my mind that equality meant equal. I heard it as treating people equal, not making everyone equal."

Bret sighed.

Vince jabbed Bret in the ribs. "How about you, man? You still in?"

"I'm praying about it, and I have a number of other people praying too. We're getting into territory that challenges my Christian beliefs, and even though I feel called to be here, I'm asking God to reaffirm." He thought a minute. "Maybe another week of two. I'm not sure."

He smiled and jabbed Vince back. "What are your plans? Go or stay?"

Vince got serious. "I'll go when I know it's time to go." He looked at his fellow Callers. "It's not time yet."

Carla looked down at her partially eaten meal and didn't say anything.

~

Megyn scrolled through the postings on her V³ fan page. Most of the comments were from people who missed her and wanted to see her back on the show. Many said they were going to call the station and complain. Some speculated that she and Ethan broke up, and Carla was the cause. Those strings of dialogue thought she was distraught and couldn't face him. Some trashed Carla and a few defended her. A couple wondered if Megyn was pregnant, and others thought she'd been fired. One person noted that Megyn thought she was too good to be a part of the show anymore.

Megyn groaned. *People believe what they read in the tabloids. They don't know me.*

The chatter went on and on. There were thousands of posts and she quickly grew tired of following the redundant strings of conjecture. She drew her knees to her chest, wrapped her arms around them, and heaved a sigh. *This is going to take a lot longer than I thought.*

A banner moved across the screen and drew her attention back to the computer.

MEGYN BUCKMAN FANS
BE PATIENT
ALL WILL BE EXPLAINED NEXT WEEK

~

Liz Buckman sat quietly reading Megyn's fan page while Mr. Buckman paced the floor. Tears filled her eyes. "Megyn has a lot of people who love and miss her. It's so sad how this whole thing hasn't worked out. She was so hopeful."

"I just hate that she's got to live like a prisoner, while these yahoos try to take over the world." His voice choked. "I'm afraid she won't stay put but will decide to go public and fight them." He rubbed his eyes with his fists. "She's got that fire in her belly that comes from the Buckmans."

"Yes, dear." She knew it well and hoped it would be the thing that would get them all through this.

CHAPTER FORTY-SIX

Bret sat at the kitchen counter sipping coffee. The week had been tension-filled among the Callers. Everyone snapped at the other over the smallest things.

Tawny walked in, poured a cup, and leaned against the stove. "Something's going on," she declared. "I can feel it. It's been almost a week since the last show, and we still don't know anything about Megyn's disappearance, and everyone acts like it never happened."

Bret took a sip. "I know. We've had a lot of free time this week too. No fittings, or photo shoots, or media interviews."

Carla walked in. "Aren't you guys concerned about the possibility of cameras in here?"

They both tilted their heads and shrugged.

Tawny yawned. "Anything new from Ethan about Megyn?"

Carla looked away. "I think he's avoiding me" Her voice dropped. "He's not returning my calls or answering his door. I guess he's done with me." She took a seat. "Hopefully, they'll say something about Megyn during tonight's show."

"I have a bad feeling about this," Bret whispered.

~

Megyn was filled with a week of bottled up tension when she turned the TV on to watch the latest V³ show. The program proceeded with its usual format. She clutched her pillow and tried to relax. Her name was in the credits again, but still no mention of her thus far. *Are they trying to drive me crazy?* She checked her fan page. The activity level was through the roof. Angry Vanguarders from all over the world had been promised an explanation regarding her whereabouts and now they demanded answers.

She plopped onto the sofa, watched, and waited. The Callers seemed a little tense and so did the studio audience. She wondered if it was her projecting her own feelings or if something was wrong with them too.

She sat forward with her elbows on her knees. *Come to think of it, I haven't seen any ads or heard any interviews from the Callers this week. Their roles on the show are greatly diminished too. Something is wrong.*

Her body started to shake. She checked the doors to make sure they were locked and turned off her lights. She snagged a blanket from the other room, draped it around herself and the TV to block the brightness, and sat down in front of it. A half hour later, the show was over, and again, nothing was mentioned.

She turned the TV off, massaged her temples, and tried to think. *If I were Gisele, what would I do?* She groaned, grabbed her duffle bag, filled it with essentials, and headed toward the secret exit in the laboratory. She gasped, took a quick detour to the lab's bathroom, and managed to get the wig on over her hair. Her hands shook so much she couldn't get her green contacts in and gave up. She shoved the glasses over her ears and nose, clutched her bag, and headed out. She didn't know where she was going, but she knew she had to get away.

She rolled the cabinet away and opened the trap door her father had shown her the first day. Then climbed through and pulled the small rope to move the bookshelves back into their original spot. The space was dark. She grabbed the flashlight from its holder and eased her way down the steep stairway. The tunnel was clean and well vented, and she followed the passageway to the garage, located her car, jumped in, and drove away. *I've got to get away from here.*

An hour later she pulled into a small neighborhood and stopped the car. *What am I doing? Dad was thorough. Gisele couldn't possibly know where I am. If she knew, she'd already be here.* She stilled her breathing. *I'm just having a panic attack. I'm running out of fear, not reason.*

She turned the car around and headed back to her hideout. She stopped at a gas station and topped off the gas tank. She parked the car, and headed to bed. Her heart was still pounding and she turned on the lamp and picked up a book. She read the same page over three times and tossed it to the side. *Help me, Lord, Help me.*

Her mind shifted to Bret and the scriptures he'd written down for her. She hadn't even looked at them. She dug into her duffle bag and retrieved her Bible where she'd tucked the note. She tried to steady her breathing and focus on the words written in red.

Peace I leave with you; my peace I give you.
I do not give to you as the world gives.
Do not let your hearts be troubled and do not be afraid. (John 24:7 NIV)

She read the verse over two more times and spoke the words aloud. Her breathing slowed down. She looked up another verse.

So do not fear, for I am with you;
do not be dismayed, for I am your God.
I will strengthen you and help you.
I will uphold you with my righteous right hand. (Isaiah 41:10 NIV)

Her body melted into her pillows. She'd read one more verse, then she'd memorize them.

I will lie down and sleep in peace, for you alone,
O Lord, make me dwell in safety. (Psalms 4:8 NIV)

Megyn lay back and repeated the verses. She fell asleep before she finished saying them the second time through and woke up late the next day.

~

Bret was awakened by pounding on his door. He pulled on his flannel pajama bottoms and stepped into the hallway. "What?"

Tawny was beating on Sami's door. "Get Up! Everyone. Get up!"

He rubbed his eyes. "What's going on?"

"Meet in the entertainment room," she told each of the Callers when they answered her urgent knock.

Within a few short minutes, everyone was settled into *their* chairs. Bret watched as Tawny stepped in front of the group. Her breath was labored and her hands shaking. "Watch this and then let's go for a walk. I don't think anyone will feel like eating when we talk this time."

She took the remote and turned on the news.

Bret's mouth dropped open as he viewed himself in various situations, making carefully edited inflammatory comments against the Vanguard. "That's only part of what I said. They didn't finish the statement."

"Who's doing this? Why? I don't understand," Tawny said. "That's not what Bret said."

Sami was indignant. "They make you look like some kind of kook, zealot, nut case. I don't get it. Why would they do this?"

Tawny shushed them. "Later people. It gets worse. Keep watching."

One-by-one the Callers were shown spouting incendiary comments that were edited and taken out of context. Bret's head was spinning.

Tawny switched channels "This is on every network."

Scarlett Jones, an anchor on a major cable station, smiled into the camera. "We've been talking about this all morning and more information keeps coming in." She glanced at her co-host. "Isn't that right, Rex?"

"Yes, Scarlett. Turns out the Callers are from a movement put together by religious zealots to overthrow the V^3's efforts to make the world a better place. Just one week ago, Megyn Buckman walked out and has basically disappeared. Since then, the V^3 has been investigating her absence, and what a web of deceit and intrigue they have uncovered."

"That's right Rex. Apparently, she discovered they were on to her and went underground with the rest of her revolutionary comrades."

Video of the Callers in different restaurants and waiting rooms streamed as she spoke. "It says here, Rex, that Bret Steward is leading the group. Sounds like he's some kind of charismatic cult guy."

Tawny flipped the control to computer mode.

"Here are our V^3 fan pages," she said. "Our *former* fans are outraged. They want us gone. Some of them want us dead."

Bret cringed as he read the X-rated, hatred-filled comments on his page. He grieved at the fans feelings of betrayal.

Tawny flipped it back to the TV mode and the newsman, Rex, was talking. "This just in Scarlett. I'm being told that millions of V^3

donation dollars are missing, and this group is suspected. The FBI has been called in to investigate. They're expecting warrants to be served this afternoon."

Bret looked around at the four panicked faces.

"Leave everything that belongs to the V³. Grab whatever you want to carry, and let's get out of here. We may not be coming back."

"No electronics," Tawny said as they fled to their rooms. "Be back in fifteen."

Carla stopped. "Where're we going? There's no place to hide."

Tawny put her finger up to her lip. "Shh. Talk in the car."

~

Megyn sat in stunned silence as she flipped from channel to channel with the V³ Callers headlining every news show. She wasn't scared anymore—now she was angry. *You can come after me if you want—but not my friends.*

She moved to her computer and pulled out her list of communication sources. She chose a cooking site bulletin board.

> My friends are at a loss for something unique for a dinner party. Looking for ideas of what they should cook. If they decide on lamb, they'll need to know what to put on the lamb? Please help them. lambchop

She checked her post every fifteen minutes. Not much happening on this bulletin board. No one was answering—at all. It was nearing dusk when she found her reply.

> I've got some ideas on how to rescue your friends' dinner party. Will get back to you. I need just the right recipe. supercook

She took a deep breath, sat back, and did something that felt unnatural, prayed.

~

Bret drove his car into the countryside. Out here there would be no video cameras on every corner, and it would be easy to tell if anyone was following them.

"Thank goodness we had a way to get out of the house before the mob of reporters noticed," Tawny said. "I think we finally lost the last of them when you did that U-turn on the freeway and then two more in the park and convention center."

Sami chuckled. "Thank goodness for the golf course. If we hadn't snuck across to the walkway behind the trees on the other side, they would've caught us for sure."

"This isn't funny." Carla groaned. "What are we doing? We can't run away from the law. All we need to do is explain our sides."

"You don't get it," Tawny squeaked. "These people are powerful. We can't argue our way out of this. They've set us up. We're trapped."

"If that's true," Carla said, "why are we running? They'll just catch us, and things will be worse than they are now."

Vince sat between them in the back seat and touched their arms. "Let's don't argue ya'll. We're not the enemy." He looked at Bret in the rearview mirror. "Maybe we should pull over and talk about what we're going to do."

Bret pointed. "There's a river up ahead. Let's get out, stretch our legs, and talk there."

"Anybody remember to grab some food or water on the way out?" Sami asked. "I'm thirsty."

Bret pulled over and popped the trunk. "There's water in the back. I covered it up before we put our packs in."

Sami walked down to the river bank. "I've found a good spot over here," she called back. "There's a nice breeze too. Would someone please grab me a water?"

Bret took a seat on a rock and breathed in the fresh country air. "This feels wonderful. Perfect place to talk."

Carla sat down next to him and sipped her drink. "Now what?" She looked up at Bret. "Maybe we can hide where Megyn's hiding?"

Everyone's eyes focused on Bret.

"That's a great idea, but I really don't know where she is, or how to contact her?"

"So you're admitting you know she's in hiding?" Tawny said.

"I don't know that either. I hope she is, but I don't know for sure."

Carla picked up a stick and wrote her name in the dirt. "You know more than you're saying, though. I can tell."

Bret frowned. "Anything I know about Megyn isn't going to help us right now."

He turned to the group. "Okay. Let's talk. As I see it, there're two choices. We can hide out and try to clear our names, or we can turn ourselves in and accept the consequences since our side will most probably never be heard."

"I don't want to turn myself in," Sami said. "We don't have a chance if we go back."

"I don't want to either," Bret said. "I'm afraid our fates could be worse than prison."

Carla looked startled. "You think they would try to kill us?"

"I don't know," Bret said. "But we need to consider the possibility. We have to assume the Nethers believe we've been told about their plans. I don't think they'd take a chance that we might ruin their life's work."

Sami grabbed a rock and tried to skip it across the water. "Do you think . . . they . . . poisoned Annette?"

Bret gazed into the distance. "I don't see how we can ignore that as a possibility."

"But where can we go that they won't find us?" Carla said.

"We need to check our resources," Tawny said. "Then we'll know if hiding out is even an option. We left in a hurry I'm not sure we grabbed the things we're going to need. For instance; how much cash do we have? Our credit cards and check books are now unusable."

"We need to know about other survival supplies too. Food, water, medicine—whatever," Sami said. "Between Tawny and I, we have great wilderness skills, but we're still going to need basic supplies."

"What's that?" Vince urgently whispered.

Tawny wrinkled her forehead. "Basic supplies?"

"No, ya'll." He put his finger to his lips. "Shhh. I hear something. Sounds like a big piece of machinery . . . a tractor, maybe?"

Bret stood up and searched the sky. "It sounds like a helicopter to me."

Carla pointed to the top of the trees in the field down the road. "It is, and it looks like it's headed straight for us."

CHAPTER FORTY-SEVEN

The Callers ran in every direction trying to hide.

Bret walked back up the bank and stood next to the car. "I'm afraid they already know we're down here," he yelled to the others.

No one came out.

He watched as the helicopter slowly moved in their direction. He could hear Tawny and Sami whimpering under the bridge, and he took a deep breath.

"I knew we couldn't run from the law," Carla yelled back.

Vince walked up the river bank and joined Bret. "I'm not surprised either." He held his hand over his eyes to block the sun as the giant bird landed. "I just didn't think they'd find us so fast."

A young man jumped out and advanced to the group. "I'm looking for Bret Steward."

Bret stepped forward. "That's me."

"Where are the rest of the Callers? I need all of you to get your things and join me in the chopper."

Bret stood firm. "I don't know who you are. I'd like to see some identification. Why should we go with you?"

"My name's not important. A friend sent me. That's all I can say."

"Where do you want to take us?" Bret began to pray under his breath. *Father, please let me know what to do. We need your help.*

The young man clasped his hands in front and stiffened his legs to the sides. "I can't tell you that. All I'm allowed to say is that a friend sent me."

Tawny and Carla eased their way forward. "What about the car?" Tawny said.

"We'll take care of it," the young man said.

Bret wiped the sweat from his brow. "We need to talk first."

"Hurry," the young man said. "If we don't go in the next few minutes, I'm afraid others will be arriving."

Bret corralled the Callers over to one side. "Well?"

"Let's do it," Tawny said.

Sami nodded. "I'm in. I hadn't realized how much I didn't want to go to jail until I thought I was going just now."

Carla shuffled her feet. "Things can't get any worse than they are now."

Vince hesitated. "I don't know. We're already in a lot of trouble."

Bret patted him on the shoulder. "No one has to go with us. It's your choice. Just decide fast."

Vince stepped back. "Hmm . . . Okay. I'll go."

Bret felt a peace flood over him. They were in complete agreement. *Okay, Lord, I'm trusting you.* He headed for the car. "Grab your stuff everyone."

The young man helped them get themselves and their bags loaded and motioned for the pilot to take off. Once they were on their way, Bret looked down at the river. In the distance, he noticed a town car with tinted windows headed in the direction of his vehicle.

They moved over the country side and watched the landscape change to hills, then larger hills, then desert. It was noisy and impossible to talk. The Callers clutched their bags, made anxious eye contact with each other periodically, and three hours later landed in the middle of the desert.

Once the blades stopped, the young man hopped out and motioned for them to follow. Bret acquiesced first and the others trailed behind. Each one stepped to the ground until they stood shoulder to shoulder observing the barren landscape. There was nothing but rocks, sand, and sparse patches of dry looking plants in every direction. The heat could be seen rising from the ground.

"Where are we?" Bret asked.

"We're waiting for your next ride." The young man looked at his watch. "Which should be here in the next half hour." He looked at the Callers. "I've got cold drinks and food in the cooler if anyone's interested."

Vince stepped forward. "My mouth is dry and I'm starving. Need any help?"

Fresh lunch boxes containing sandwiches, chips, fruit, cookies, and cold drinks were handed to each person. The young man set up folding chairs and two umbrellas. They ate in the shade, and waited.

"I like our mysterious friend already," Sami said. "This is definitely better than what we could have done on our own." She looked at the young man. "You're not going to tell us who it is, are you?"

He smiled and handed her a napkin.

~

Just as promised, thirty minutes later, a small jet landed on a makeshift runway. It rolled to a stop about one hundred feet from where they were sitting. The pilot disembarked, and he and the young man exchanged nods of greeting.

Bret walked over to the plane. "Wow. I didn't realize there was a runway there."

"Very few people know about it," their new host said.

They waved good-bye to the young man and the helicopter pilot, boarded the small craft, and relaxed into soft leather seats.

Sami rubbed the soft leather. "Yep. I like our new friend."

The pilot's voice came over the intercom. "I'm Captain George. Please sit back and relax, we should arrive at our destination in a couple of hours. There's coffee and a restroom in the back."

Vince nudged Bret. "Does it look like we're doubling back?"

Bret leaned over and gazed down at the desert. "I don't know. It all looks the same to me. Anyway, we're committed now. There's no turning back. We may as well just relax and enjoy the ride."

Vince poked him again. "But suppose we're being whisked away by the Nethers' and we're going to disappear, just like Megyn?"

Bret sighed. "I don't think so. I think these are the good guys." He closed his eyes and prayed.

One more plane ride and another hour in a car and they arrived at their destination. The young woman driver parked the SUV and told them to wait while she made sure everything was ready for them.

A couple of minutes later, another young woman came out and escorted them into the facility. She held her finger to her mouth and motioned for them be quiet. They walked through dimly lit rooms that looked like a reference library, kitchen, and laboratory. Curious glances were exchanged along the way. At the end of the large space, she pulled out a key and opened a door.

Carla was the first one through. "This is nice." She touched the back of the sofa. "Our new 'friend' has found us a little apartment."

Tawny and Sami walked in next. "It looks like someone lives here already."

Vince, then Bret entered last.

Bret looked into their host's new green eyes and got a huge smile in return. "Well, well, well," he said.

Megyn pulled off her wig, gave him a big hug, and embraced the others, one at a time.

"Welcome. It's nice to have company. I've been so worried about you guys."

~

Gisele's phone buzzed and she picked it up. "Yes, Mary. What is it?"

"I've got good news. They've stopped moving and the red light just popped on. That's our signal. They're with Megyn."

"Take care of them. Make it look like an accident."

"All of them?"

"Hmm . . . all but Megyn. I want her brought to me."

~

Vince walked around the room. "So this is where you've been hiding, Meg. We've worried about you too."

Bret spotted the TV's remote. "Anyone ready to check the news?"

Megyn furrowed her brow. "You're not going to like it. They've dug up every piece of dirt in our lives, and I suspect much of yours is like mine, made up."

Megyn walked into the kitchenette followed by Tawny and Sami. "I've stocked up on extra groceries if anyone's hungry. I don't have clothes, blankets, or beds for everyone yet but I'm sure we can start picking up things, a little at a time. We don't want to draw attention to ourselves."

Sami sighed. "We're safe, but now what? We can't hide forever."

"Let's just relax and enjoy the evening. We've got all day tomorrow to figure that out," Tawny said. "I'm too exhausted to think. It may be early evening, but we've been on the run since dawn. All I want to do right now is take a shower and kick back for the next few hours."

Bret turned the TV off and he and Vince joined the girls. He rubbed his chin and leaned against the refrigerator. "Does it seem like we got away too easy?"

Five blank faces stared back at him.

Vince looked in the cupboard. "Why do you say that?"

"I've counseled with people who've been arrested, some for serious offenses. The authorities just show up and take you in. Sometimes with force, but most of the time without. Information is not leaked to the press ahead of time. Otherwise people would do just what we did—run."

"What are you saying?" Carla asked.

Bret shook his head. "And, all this 'dirt' on us. Someone spent a lot of time collecting and compiling that. It feels like a campaign to discredit us. The people behind this are ruthless. They'll stop at nothing to take us down."

Megyn spoke in a whisper. "I think they killed Annette because she snooped in places they didn't want her to be."

Vince frowned. "Ah, come on. I don't believe that."

Bret stared into space. "Why did they give us a chance to get away, and not take us in first?" He scratched his stubbled face. "Only one reason. To find Megyn and get us all together." He paced the short length of the kitchen. "That's it." He stopped. "They want us all together." He looked at the startled faces. "We're not safe here."

Megyn touched his arm. "That can't be. I was brought here through several backtracks and decoys. I know you were too. Am I right?"

Everyone nodded.

"Then there's no way anyone could have followed you."

Carla yawned. "I'm tired. Let's relax a bit and talk about this in the morning."

Vince extended his arms to gather them together. "We're making way too much of this. We got away because they needed warrants and police documents to take us in." He shrugged his shoulders. "Someone must have leaked the information before they were ready. That's all."

Bret looked skeptical and headed out the door toward the lab. "I'm going to pray."

Megyn pulled out towels, blankets, and pillows. "The girls can use the bedroom and bath in the apartment and the guys will have to use the facilities in the lab. There're a couple of showers and extra towels out there. We can use them for bedding since I only have a few sheets and blankets."

Vince jumped up. "I'll go get them." He picked up his backpack and headed out the door. "Maybe I'll get a shower while I'm at it."

CHAPTER FORTY-EIGHT

Bret couldn't shake the feeling of foreboding. He breathed a deep sigh and entreated God. "Something's wrong. I feel it. Lord, send your angels to cover this building. Guard us. Protect us. Lead us."

He saw Vince go by, heard the shower come on, and then, Vince talking.

"What?" he whispered to himself. "Who's he talking to."

He got up and slowly opened the door to the men's bathroom. There was a tiled wall to his right that blocked the shower area. He stopped behind it.

"Yes. I sent the GPS signal when we got here, and yes, she's here. You're not listening. Bret is suspicious we got away too easily. I've convinced them to stay through the night, but you've got to get here as soon as possible. I think they may try to leave first thing in the morning. I'll call you if anything changes."

Bret heard Vince whistle a cheery song and get into the shower. He eased his way out the door and rushed back into the apartment.

The girls were in the bedroom and bathroom. He knocked on both. "We've got to get out of here . . . now!"

"What? No," Sami said. "I'm tired.

"Vince turned us in. He's been carrying a GPS device, and I just heard him on the phone with someone. He didn't have a southern accent. He's in the shower now. We don't have much time."

The girls froze.

Bret's pulse was racing and his voice was full of urgency. "Get your stuff."

Megyn grabbed her duffle bag, which she now kept in ready-to-flee condition, and stuffed in her computer. "There's a back way out of here and I've got a car. Follow me," she said between choppy breaths. "Vince hasn't seen it and won't be able to tell anyone what it looks like."

Bret and the girls followed Megyn out the same tunnel she had entered the week before. They climbed into the car.

"There's plenty of gas," Megyn said when they were out of town. "Where do you want to go?"

"Just drive for now," Bret said. "We'll figure out where we're going once we're far away from here."

"My name's Donna Marie."

"Huh?"

"That's my new identify."

Tawny gasped. "Does anyone have money?"

"I've got it covered," Megyn said. "And a contact, if we need help."

Bret frowned. "I think we're all going to need new identities. Including you, Megyn, um Donna. Vince has seen you in the wig and green contact lenses. We can't take any chances."

"I'm having a hard time believing Vince did this to us," Tawny said. "He seemed like such a nice guy, with that southern hospitality."

Sami yawned. "No accent? He must've been a plant all along. I can't believe this is happening. It seems so surreal. Like I'm watching a movie about someone else."

Carla groaned and whispered to herself. "I want my life back."

"How're you feeling, Megyn?" Bret said. "It would be nice if you took the first shift driving since you're probably more rested than the rest of us. I'll take the next one."

Megyn repositioned herself. "I'm good for now."

Bret turned to Sami and Tawny. "Okay, girls, it's time to hear your survival ideas."

"Well," Tawny said. "Spelunkers are more versatile than people think. There are lots of opportunities for underground exploration, and I've done many of them."

Megyn shivered. "Just the thought makes me cringe."

"That's what I mean. You're thinking caves. But caves aren't the only places underground. There're old military sites; bunkers and tunnels used in wars. There're also basements of buildings that are hardly ever visited and can be safe and warm. I've been in sewers, transit and utility tunnels, abandoned buildings, and ghost towns too.

"So what do you suggest?" Bret said.

Tawny shrugged. "There're a number of considerations. Many of these are cold, wet, moldy, full of asbestos, and just plain unsafe, even if you had the right equipment. Some are monitored by security guards, have video cameras, motion detectors, and alarms." She thought a moment. "The other problem is other urban explorers. The sites that aren't tightly monitored are apt to attract a stream of my colleagues."

Bret looked concerned. "We need something clean and dry; a place where we won't attract attention as we come and go. We'll also need to use the computer to check on the latest news . . . and to launch our counter-attack."

"The only places I know of that have electricity are basements of buildings that are currently occupied during the day. The risk we'd be discovered if we were there for more than a couple of nights would be great."

Megyn sighed. "If we can find a place that fits the clean, dry, safe, and undetectable criteria, the rest can be taken care of."

Tawny started to laugh. "I don't even know where we are. What state are we in?"

Megyn smiled. "We're still in California."

"No way," Tawny said.

"The Buckman theory is to hide in plain sight, so that's what I did. Your plane landed in the desert, in a place where you couldn't see the city. You were driven to my little apartment on the edge of the greater Los Angeles suburbs which is why you didn't recognize where you were. Besides, you took the long way to get to me. We wanted to confuse anyone who might try to follow."

Tawny rubbed her hands together. "LA sounds perfect. I have just the place. It's got four primary entrances and exits. There's even one that nobody knows about. It was created since the last blueprints were made. It's an abandoned mine with an old shack that was originally used as an office. The shack is concealed, about a mile from the mine's entrance, in the side of mountain. There was an old man there who told me about the hidden passage. He's the one that made it, and the only one who knows about it."

Megyn shifted in her seat. "Where'd you come across this guy?"

"I went to explore the mine and ran into him. He lived in the shack. He was surprised to see me in the mine since most explorers think it's inhabited by ghosts and don't bother to go there. He said I had a lot of gumption for a girl and invited me to supper."

Bret crinkled his forehead. "Can we trust him?"

"I'm pretty sure he's dead," Tawny frowned. "He said he had prostate cancer and had refused treatment. The doctors told him he only had six months. He said he was going to live with a cousin in Florida when he got so sick he couldn't take care of himself anymore. That was a year ago."

Carla slapped her knee. "Sounds perfect. Anything that's not cold, wet, and moldy sounds good. How soon can we get there?"

"I don't know where we are. Get on 210 and I'll direct you from there."

"Megyn checked her GPS and turned around."

Bret reached for the radio dial. "How about some news? We need to find out the latest."

Arthur Buckman's voice boomed out of the speakers. "This is an outrage. I don't believe any of it. Why would my daughter steal money when she obviously doesn't need it? I'm hiring attorneys to fight these preposterous accusations and my own private detectives to find her." He paused. "I'm going to find out who's behind this and why. And when I do, Katy bar the door."

The commentator picked up. "That was Arthur Buckman, billionaire, CEO of Buckman Medical Instruments, and father of his only child Megyn Buckman, Caller number seven from the hit show Vanguard of Volunteer Voices . . . . Now for breaking news. Vince Jackson, Caller number three, was just found dead in the shower of a recently abandoned laboratory."

Everyone froze.

"Cause of death is unknown. Stay tuned. A press conference by the local authorities is planned to take place in the next hour. Along with this story, a call has gone out to all Vanguarders worldwide. A million dollar reward has been offered to anyone who can provide legitimate information as to the whereabouts of the five remaining Callers. Check the V3 Web site for details on the reward and how to claim it."

Sami began trembling uncontrollably. "I wonder what my parents are thinking. They must be sick with worry. And, Nathan . . . will I ever see him again?"

Tawny's voice cracked and tears rolled down her cheeks. "Who knows what my family is thinking too. We'll be safe at the place I'm taking us." She tried to sound upbeat but her words came out in a gurgle. "And, I'm sure you're going to see Nathan again. I'm the matchmaker and when I hook people up, they stay hooked."

Sami gave her arm a squeeze.

Carla stared out the window. "We're going to die. I just know it."

"My dad won't let anything happen to us," Megyn said. "He'll protect us. I know it."

Bret bowed his head and his mouth moved quietly.

CHAPTER FORTY-NINE

Megyn pulled up next to a small wooden structure and parked the car under two large oak trees. They retrieved their belongings, and Bret covered the vehicle with a green burlap tarp that was folded and stored in an outdoor plastic container on the side of the shack.

Megyn stretched and yawned and followed Tawny up the stairs. "We need to get organized fast. We're running out of daylight."

The front porch was covered and held an old rocker and propane barbeque. The inside of the shack was small, the furniture old, and the ice box empty. It was dusty, but otherwise clean and neat. There was only one twin sized bed, and the John was outside and down a path.

"Ugh," Carla said. "I hate outdoor toilets. Can't we go to a nice hotel somewhere?"

Tawny opened drawers and cabinets. "Looks like he's left a few things behind, a six pack of TP and a variety of canned soups."

Megyn opened a cupboard. "Five cans of baked beans over here." She dug around a little further. "Canned fruit and green beans too."

Bret came in. "There's a well. I sent a bucket down to check on the water and it looks clean, but I have no idea if it's good to drink."

"The old man drank it," Tawny said. "He said it made for excellent lemonade. And, I'll have to admit, the glass he gave me tasted good."

"There're a couple of boxes of instant cereal in the cabinet above the sink," Tawny said.

Carla opened a chest. "Blankets and pillows in here." She picked one up. "Hmm, smells like cedar."

Bret opened a tool box and breathed a sigh of relief. "I've found his lighting supplies; two propane lanterns extra fuel, and a pack of three mantles. Looks like he used candles as well." He grinned at the others and held up a box. "Matches."

Tawny looked around the space. "This is just like I remember it. Thank goodness he was neat and organized." She moved to the back of the room and examined the bare wood wall. "Hmm. I think this is it." She touched a small knot and a click was heard. She pushed one of the boards and a section opened.

Carla grimaced. "It's dark in there. It looks cold too."

"You think?" Tawny snapped. "It's a tunnel. This is our escape route. About fifty yards in, it joins one of the mine tunnels." She bent down and picked up a small metal box and pulled out a ruffled paper. "This is a map of the tunnels. There are at least five ways out. Four are documented in official records. One is not."

Bret lit the two lanterns and placed them in the room. "I think we're safe for the time being. Let's get some rest and figure out what we're going to do in the morning. I'll sleep in the car. You girls can have the house."

Tawny looked at Bret. Did you say there's a bucket in the well?"

Bret took one of the lanterns and a plastic container from the counter and headed for the door. "It's getting dark outside. I'll bring some water in."

Carla moaned. "That old lantern doesn't light up very much, does it?"

Tawny repositioned the remaining lantern in front of the room's only mirror and the area filled with light. She smiled to herself. "That's much better."

~

The next morning, the five Callers sat on the front porch drinking hot water. The birds sang and the morning was already warm. Megyn rubbed her eyes. "We need coffee. That's got to be number one on the list of things we need."

We need a lot of things," Carla muttered. "Like a flushing toilet and a shower." She shooed a bug away with her hand. "How much money do you have anyway, Megyn?"

"Enough for essentials. That's it." She watched the birds fly from one tree to another without a care in the world. "I've been thinking. We can probably stay here a while, but we'll have to obtain a number of supplies. I can contact my source and get them ordered for pick up nearby. We need to make a list."

"We have to create a backup plan too," Tawny said. "In case we're forced to run again."

Sami heaved a sigh. "And some kind of warning system too. I didn't sleep well last night. I was afraid someone would find us again, and I heard every little noise."

"I've already started a list," Megyn said. "In general, we need food, clothing, bedding, towels, wash cloths, additional cookware, dishes and utensils."

Bret rubbed the two day-stubble on his chin. "I made a list too. Camp stove, generator, a couple more laptops, propane, and a few tools to fix things up around here."

Carla hunched over. "I guess we're not going to have a refrigerator?"

"He used an ice box which means you need ice to keep things cold," Bret said. "We can ask our new benefactor to check on a fridge that would work efficiently on a generator and not drain it of too much power. We can't run in and out of town very often or someone will get suspicious."

"Let's don't forget. We're going to need new identities too," Megyn said. "And ways to change what we look like."

Sami sunk her face into her hands. "I don't know if I can do this. Five of us are sharing a one room shack with no electricity, and we're drinking hot water for breakfast. I'm dirty. I don't have clothes to change in to. I miss my parents and boyfriend, and, I don't see how we're ever going to turn this thing around."

Megyn put her arm around Sami's shoulders. "You don't have to worry. We'll figure this out. We've got someone powerful behind us too."

Bret got up. "The sooner we get going, the sooner we'll get out of here." He patted Sami's shoulder. "You'll feel a lot better when you have something to do."

Tawny hugged her. "You need some food and sleep too."

Megyn followed Bret inside and pulled her lap-top out of her duffle. "I have one back up battery and then we're out of power until we get a generator, or more batteries."

"Right now, let's just use the computer for necessities." Bret said. "We can check the news through the car's radio."

She got her folder out and perused the list of communication sources. Bret leaned over her shoulder to read the document along with her. At his touch warmth spread throughout her body. She couldn't believe how much she'd missed him.

He moved closer and stretched his arm over her shoulder and pointed. "How 'bout this survival site? It fits with our current situation."

"Um? . . . Yeah. That looks perfect." She powered up and clicked on the Internet icon but got an error notice message telling her there was a problem. "Great. We're not going to be able to get the satellite connection from out here."

Bret stepped back and massaged his neck. "Maybe not. But, I've heard that sometimes satellite connections can come and go. Let's keep trying every fifteen minutes until after lunch. If we still don't get a connection, we'll make other plans." He closed his eyes, leaned over and placed his hand on the computer. "Lord, I know this is a small problem, but could you help us out here?"

Megyn cracked up. "Do you pray about everything?"

"There's a great need. Humankind is at stake."

She wondered how it was he was always thinking about others. She was worried about herself, and getting out of this alive. She felt embarrassed and ashamed.

~

Fifteen minutes later, Megyn dialed in again. Three more times she tried, and the next one connected. She typed in the survival site's address and scanned through the forum choices. "Here it is; Survival Supplies. My dad and his people are geniuses." She input the list of needed provisions and typed in the code name: maggie.

We're a group of women teachers in their fifties that need advice on what to bring. We'll be staying the summer at my minimalist uncle's place with no electricity, a well, and outdoor toilet. Would consider the purchase of a generator and energy efficient refrigerator. maggie

The response was immediate.

I've done a trip like that myself. There were women along too. Let me dig out my supply list and get back to you. I'll have to hunt around in the attic, but can probably find it by tomorrow afternoon at the latest. frank

Megyn wrote back.

Thanks Frank. We're all novices at this. You're a life saver! maggie

She thought of her childhood. He *was* her life saver. Her shoulders sagged as she turned the computer off and closed the lid.

Bret touched her arm. "Your dad is a special man. He loves you very much."

She placed her head on the lap-top and cried. She wondered if she'd ever see him again. If they'd be able to reclaim the lost years. She wanted to crawl in his arms and let him protect her like he'd done when she was a small child and her mother had been drinking.

~

The five Callers gathered around the car and listened. "The police have now confirmed Caller number three, Vince Jackson, was killed with a blunt object to the head. Sources say he was in the shower and probably didn't see his attacker. The police are seeking the whereabouts of the five remaining Callers and have labeled them as 'people of interest' in this case. They are also suspected of embezzling unspecified millions of dollars from V³ donations. If anyone knows of their whereabouts please go to the V³ Web site for information on how to claim the million dollar reward."

Bret looked into the petrified faces of his friends and turned the radio off. "Supplies will be here tomorrow and our lives will become considerably easier. But right now, we need to get a security system set up around our perimeter and develop a plan to clear our names."

The girls shrugged and nodded their heads in agreement.

"Let's form two teams." Bret said. "Sami, would you like to lead the security team?"

She twisted her mouth.

"Who wants to work on security with Sami?" Bret waited. "Okay, Carla, you're with Sami."

Carla eased her way over to Sami. "I want to work on a project where I know I can actually accomplish something."

Bret ignored her comment and turned to Megyn and Tawny. "You two will work on a plan to clear our names. I'll take care of a few maintenance things around here, and float between the two teams." He clapped his hands and headed toward the house. "Okay? Let's get it done."

CHAPTER FIFTY

Megyn and Tawny sat at the small white-washed kitchen table. "I think the Internet is going to be the only means we have to tell our side of the story without getting caught," Megyn said. "But, I'm not sure how to go about it."

"I don't know either." Tawny poured a glass of water. "Maybe we could use the V^3 site as our primary communication source. It gets more traffic than any other."

Megyn crinkled her forehead. "Do you think they can trace us from there?"

"I don't know." Tawny frowned. "Good hackers can probably find us from anywhere online."

Bret walked in and leaned on the front door jam. "How're things going?"

Megyn sighed and showed him her notes. "We've just started and aren't coming up with much."

"Looks like you're on the right track to me," he said.

"Neither one of us have experience with computer applications outside the usual ones. We don't know what can be tracked or how to keep from being detected." Megyn sighed.

"I know it's risky and we'll have to do a bit of research before we start blogging all over the place. But we don't have a choice," Bret said. "We've got to find a way to get people to hear our side."

Megyn sat back. "Maybe we should first determine what we're going to say, and figure out where to say it later."

Tawny snickered. "How 'bout we write that we're innocent and didn't do any of the things we're accused of?"

Megyn grinned. "Works for me."

Bret suppressed a smile and headed outside. "I know you two will figure it out."

The girls stuck their tongues out at him as he left the room.

Megyn shifted her feet. "Maybe I should make a list of the things I've learned about who's behind the V³, and what their real intentions are."

"And I'll make a list of the things we've experienced on our end," Tawny said. "Like hidden surveillance, our security detail, and various things we've been told during the time we've been with the Vanguard."

Megyn tore off a couple of sheets of paper and handed them to Tawny. "Don't forget about Annette." She dug in her duffle for another pen. "Let's check back in with each other and compare notes in about fifteen minutes."

Tawny started writing. "I'm going to put Vince into the mix too. We can decide how we want to handle their deaths later."

Megyn concentrated on her paper. She listed the names of the people on the Council, described their headquarters compound, and made notes of their plans and strategies. Her mind wandered to the time she'd spent with Gisele and how she'd loved and trusted her. She'd shared her fears and concerns and opened her life completely to Gisele. Now Gisele wanted her dead. She shuddered.

She put down her pen and stared out the front door. "You about ready, Tawny?" Megyn asked.

Tawny nodded.

Megyn leaned back in her chair. "I was cooped up in that apartment for over a week and had plenty of time to think about what I would need to do to clear my name. First of all, I don't think we should preach at the people we're trying to convince, or we'll turn them off. I'm thinking we need to take a two-pronged approach. First, we could pose a series of questions that compel them to examine the situation differently."

She got up and paced the floor. "In reference to the Vanguard of Volunteer Voices movement itself, we could ask questions like: What does unity, service, and equality *really* mean? Everyone equal—equal housing, income, health care, food? Does unity mean we all do the same thing, or else?" She waved her hands around. "And who decides what we're going to do? Think about any meeting or class you've sat through. Think about the people who sat in the room with you. Would you want these people to plan your life? How would another group be any better? Even with the best of intentions, will the teams know what is best for everyone? Suppose the teams aren't the ones driving the agenda? Are more powerful people involved?"

Tawny joined in. "Who stands to gain by the decisions that are made? Do the actions help the people they're intended to help? How? In what ways?" She grinned at Megyn. "Don't tell Bret, but this reminds me of the approach he takes with us. He always challenges us to think on our own."

"It's a good technique," Megyn said. "It makes me think for myself. He's helped me sort through a lot of things in my life, just by asking questions." She put her finger over her mouth. "Don't tell him I said that either."

Tawny giggled and put her finger over her mouth. "Mum's the word."

Megyn looked at her notes. The second prong would be that we submit information on the V³'s *real* leadership as our defense." She picked up her paper. "We investigate the Council members and their connections to each other, as well as, their past activities, and financial dealings. We then educate our audience about these details and pose more questions in reference to their true actions on behalf of the V³. Council members' public interviews and writings will serve as additional evidence for our defense.

"We can also use this information to fight their charges of embezzlement and murder. We will challenge our audience to examine the data, and follow the money and motives of each side before they believe we are guilty."

"I love it," Tawny said. "We'll use their words against them. We won't have to make things up like they do about us."

"I would bet they're not expecting us to fight back either. And they're especially not expecting us to go after them personally." Megyn paused. "They're extremely powerful and arrogant. No one ever goes against them." She looked deep into Tawny's eyes. "We have to fight. We know what the alternative is. It's just a matter of time until they find us."

Bret walked in. "Wow. Things look serious in here." He opened a cabinet door and pulled out a can. "Beans anyone?"

Tawny hopped up. "We've got a great plan. Wait till you see it."
She nudged Megyn's shoulder and winked. "She's brilliant. Thought
of most of it herself."

Megyn felt Bret's gaze on her face and she blushed. Would he
be impressed with what she'd done?

"I can tell there's more going on here than I'll ever know." He
opened a drawer. "Anyone seen a can opener?" He moved the
utensils around, found what he was looking for, and proceeded to
release the beans. "The other team's come up with good ideas too.
Let's have lunch and talk. Hopefully we can get to work on
implementation this afternoon."

Megyn stroked her lap-top. "Most of our work will require
Internet usage, but we can spend the afternoon refining our
strategies, and create a detailed outline of the content while we wait
for new power sources."

She opened the computer. "I'm going to check if 'Frank's'
gotten back to us."She tried to connect but got another error
message. "I hate this. How are we ever going to manage our
communications?"

Carla walked in and plopped down on the side of the bed. "It's
a lot cooler in here than it is outside." Sweat trickled down her face.

Sami came in next, grabbed the pitcher, and poured them each a
glass of fresh water.

"You both look like you need to dump that over your heads,"
Megyn said. "What have you two been up to?"

Carla smiled. "We've been foraging through the shed, knocking
down dead branches and dragging them to create barriers, and
rearranging rocks."

Sami checked out Bret's progress with lunch. "Save those cans,
please. We can use them as part of our alarm system."

~

Gisele slammed her fist on her glossy ebony desk. "I didn't
think it was possible to lose someone with today's technology. Have
you checked the satellite images of the area during the time when
they would've left?"

"We did," Mary said. "But whoever chose that location for a
laboratory in the first place, knew it wouldn't be a place of interest
and no orbiting cameras would be focused in that direction."

Her neck veins shone red. "You can't find out who owns the building either?" She got up. "There must be someone we can bribe, or threaten, to give us the information."

"The entire project was handled by attorneys on behalf of a shell organization that dead ends. It's like it exists, but doesn't. And, the attorneys aren't talking."

Gisele glared at her. "So to recap what you've just told me. We don't know the make of car they're driving or where they went? All we've got are their fingerprints all over the place? I'd bet my fortune Arthur Buckman has something to do with that property." Her voice was peppered with sarcasm. "It would be great to take him down along with his treacherous daughter."

She twisted her earring and leaned close to Mary's face. "You've identified, and are keeping tabs on, their friends, right?"

"We've even got several of their phones tapped and are tracing computer communications."

"How about the Buckmans?"

"He and his wife have been invulnerable. Because of the high stakes business he's in, he's already got the latest technology to keep competitors and enemies blocked."

Gisele slammed her desk again and waved Mary out of the room. "Find them!" she screeched.

~

Megyn clicked on the Internet connection icon; finally it opened. She breathed a sigh of relief and quickly went to the survival supplies forum page and found a response from Frank. He listed most of the items the Callers had hoped for along with a few more. She looked for clues on how they were going to get them. The post ended with the words:

> You can pick these up at your local recreational superstore, but I'd advise having them delivered to your home. Most warehouses that can turn around quickly and usually have next day delivery. We did this for our trip, and our lives were much easier. Some of the retailers even throw in surprise packages for free. frank

Megyn responded:

Thanks, Frank. You can't imagine how grateful we are that you took the time to get this list together. We'll definitely take your advice and have the supplies delivered. Happy trails. Maybe our paths will cross some day and I can thank you in person. maggie

Megyn shrugged her shoulders and looked at the others. "He's having everything delivered tomorrow."

"Did you tell him where we are?" Carla said.

Megyn reached into her pocket and held up her GPS finder. She crinkled her mouth and nose. "Oh, yeah; he's sending a surprise too."

CHAPTER FIFTY-ONE

Megyn and the other Callers sat on make-shift chairs on the side of the shack and watched the main road into the area. The night before, Sami had been designated the only one to greet the delivery person. Megyn had loaned her the blonde wig and the small rectangular glasses that had distinguished her as Donna Marie.

"I wish whoever was coming would hurry up and get here," Carla whined. "I need a bath and fresh clothes." She swatted a fly. "It's hot and I'm sick of cereal and beans."

"How would you like to be the one wearing a wig in this heat?" Sami snapped. "It's only our second day here. At least we have food and water." She wiped her wet forehead. "Things could be a lot worse."

Carla got up and huffed her way to the front door mumbling. "I need to get out of here. I need time to myself."

Sami huffed. "Fine. Go."

Bret stretched and moved his seat back into the shade. "We need to make a brief exploration of the mine a priority today." He looked back at the road. "I really do trust your dad, Megyn, but it still makes me nervous that we're not familiar with the exits out of here."

Tawny wiped her brow and moved her chair next to his. "Even if we get out safely, what then? We only have one means of transportation."

Megyn picked up her note pad. "We're just sitting here getting more and more irritable. Why don't we look at the tunnel map and make a plan while we're waiting?" She swatted a small green grasshopper off her foot. "We can explore the mine's exit points later, when it gets really hot." She shrugged. "I assume it's cool in there."

Tawny hopped up and took off. "I'll get the map."

Sami shushed the others. "I think I hear something."

Megyn grabbed Bret's arm and the two of them ran for the far side of the car and crouched down. Her heart beat loud in her ears as she peaked around the hood. She watched Sami move slowly toward the front of the yard, straighten her glasses, and keep her distance as she waved the box truck under a tree and walked around to the driver's side door.

Sami squinted in the bright sunlight, shaded her eyes, and walked forward to greet the man behind the wheel. He opened the door, and climbed out. Suddenly Sami squealed, threw her arms around the driver and smacked him hard on the lips. He fumbled and gently pushed her back. "Excuse me?" he said.

Sami looked rejected. Her voice sounded weak. "Nathan?"

"Sami?"

She laughed and pulled off the wig and glasses.

They embraced again and Megyn and Bret emerged from behind the car, relieved and surprised by this unexpected turn of events.

Megyn greeted him with a hug, "Come on you two. Let's go into the house and talk."

Bret shook his hand. "Glad to see you, man. We can really use some technical support."

"That's why I'm here." He squeezed Sami's hand. "Well, one of the reasons I'm here. Mostly, I wanted to be with Sami. I figured Mr. B had to be involved in your disappearance in some way and I've been bugging him to let me help ever since the news hit and you guys took off. He finally relented."

Sami wrapped herself around his arm and tears ran down her face. "I'm so glad you're here." She pulled him forward. "Come on in and see our home."

He hugged and kissed her and followed her up the stairs.

Megyn handed him a glass of water. "We've got problems using the satellite connection. We don't know how to use the Internet to communicate our message without being traced, and many other technical issues."

"When Mr. B told me where you were, I checked the area out completely. I've brought gear that will solve the reception problem and technology to keep us from being tracked too."

Carla sat back. "So you believe we're innocent without hearing our side of the story."

"Shut up, Carla," Sami snarled. She stepped in front of Nathan. "We can trust him."

Carla rolled her eyes, folded her arms, and leaned against the wall.

Nathan smiled. "Mr. B told me that since he didn't know me, the only reason he let me in on things was because he had me thoroughly investigated and was comfortable that I was legit."

Carla ignored them. "I say we unload the truck and talk later. I want a bath."

Megyn moved toward the door. "Baths will have to wait a little longer. We need to get our generator and refrigerator set up, and explore our emergency exits."

Carla pouted. "I can't help with the equipment and I don't need to know the way out. I'll just follow one of you." She tilted her chin up and headed for the well. "I'm getting a bath and changing my clothes."

The Callers, minus Carla, unloaded the truck. Bret and Nathan set up the generator, fridge, and computers. Nathan ran cabling up the side of the mountain and positioned receiver dishes, while the girls unwrapped the kitchen supplies, cots, sleeping bags, and linens. Brand new clothes for everyone, including Nathan, were packed in separate suitcases with sticky notes to identify the owner.

While Carla was off washing up with water in a bucket, they discovered that Mr. Buckman had sent them a portable shower setup. They attached the pump to the well and tested it with a water fight. Everyone but Carla ran and laughed and created a muddy mess. They washed off again and dried as they sat on the front steps drinking iced cold sodas and talking about water fights from their childhoods.

~

"I'm stuffed," Megyn said, patting her midriff. "It's only been a day of eating out of cans, but when you're not sure where your next meal will come from, barbeque chicken, corn on the cob, and fresh strawberries seem like a dinner from the best restaurant in the world."

"One of my all time favorite meals," Bret said. "Thank you girls."

"How about a little entertainment?" Nathan turned on the thirty-five inch flat screen.

Megyn scooted closer to the table. "What have you got?"

Nathan gave her a Cheshire cat smile and patted Sami's hand, which was still wrapped around his arm. "I've got a little surprise for you." He touched the screen and a file folder icon popped up. Another tap and images representing sheets of paper dispersed across the screen. "I knew from the beginning there was no way you guys were guilty of what they claimed, so I started investigating on my own. First, I checked on this Council your dad told me about. I probed the members and found lots of interesting and damning information." He brought up copies of contracts, property titles, corporate boards of directors lists, bank statements and IRS paperwork. "This is just the beginning."

Megyn grinned. "Finally proof. Has my dad seen these?"

"He's got copies of everything."

Megyn wondered if this would be enough. She knew how powerful the people were that she'd met that day in Vancouver. Her dad was one person; they were many.

"Well," Nathan said clicking a few keys on his computer. "I also wanted to know what happened to the money they claimed you stole."

Everyone moved closer.

"My research isn't complete yet. But I've got a couple of trails I'm following." He looked around at the group. "I only brought two more lap-tops. No one is to use them unless I'm right here with you. I have them locked out and you will need me to let you in."

Carla harrumphed.

Megyn heaved a big sigh. "I'm so relieved you're here."

Bret looked out at the horizon. "It's going to be dark in a couple of hours. I suggest we spend the rest of the evening exploring our exits. We can start fresh on this tomorrow."

Nathan shut the computers down and cuddled with Sami.

Tawny pulled out the map and laid it on the counter. Everyone gathered around and watched her point out the tunnels and exits.

Bret zeroed in on the intersection between the cabin's hidden tunnel and the main thoroughfares. "We should each have a pack ready in case we have to run." He looked at Nathan.

"I'm already on it. I've got a remote control that I can use to shut down and destroy the hard drives if we have to leave in a hurry." He patted the top of his computer. "I also have a backup server that's location is unknown to all but me and Mr. B."

Tawny picked up the map. "Ready to go?"

"What about get away transportation and a backup place to go?" Megyn said. "Maybe tomorrow, Tawny can take the lead on figuring that out. You've done great with this location."

Nathan got up and nodded to Tawny. "We can check out some places online. I'll help you do the research."

CHAPTER FIFTY-TWO

The tunnel was dark and the temperature cool. The compact space was just large enough for an average sized man to walk through holding his head slightly bent forward. Tawny carried a lantern and led the group. Bret took up the rear with another light. Megyn covered her mouth with her hand, tried not to inhale the dusty air, and touched the side of the dirt enclosed walkway to keep her balance.

She was in the middle of the line without much light and only dense air to breathe. Her pulse raged with unexpected anxiety. A cold wind brushed her cheek sending a chill that spread quickly through her body. Something was there. She wanted to run and break into fresh air and daylight, but she was blocked by five other people. Her hands and face turned clammy. She tried not to faint or vomit. "Go away!" her raspy voice whispered.

Something hissed in her ear. "I'mmm here. You can't get away from meee."

"Go away!" she cried.

"Yooou can't win. I'mmm going to tell them where you are," said the voice.

Megyn stopped and placed her hands over her ears. "Nooo!" she screamed.

Bret jumped forward, knocking Sami and Nathan aside. "You all right?"

Megyn shivered uncontrollably. "Just a bit of claustrophobia, I think." She straightened and tried to rub warmth back into her arms. "I'm all right now." She brushed herself off and looked around. Everyone's faces glimmered with concern in the light of the lanterns.

"You sure," Nathan said. "You look kind of pale."

"I'm fine," she said massaging her forehead. She wanted the attention off of her. "Let's go," she said.

The tunnels were confusing and Tawny checked her map frequently. Megyn felt like she'd been walking for hours when they finally reached the hidden exit. They crawled through a long tight tunnel and found themselves in a ravine on the other side of the hill from their home. A small stream ran down the middle with large boulders on either side. Oak trees lined the sides of the hills.

Megyn breathed in the fresh air. She was still shaking and dreaded the trip back.

"This is great," Nathan said. "Lots of cover and fresh water."

"Let's divide into twos and scout the area a bit," Tawny said. "Look for caves, overhanging rocks, or fallen trees with big trunks sticking out of the ground. We can use those for shelter if we need to. Also look for fire trails that we can follow out of here. Notice if there are fish in the stream, or small animals we can capture for food?" She looked at the horizon. "Don't go too far. It'll be dark soon. Meet back here in half an hour. Bret can lead us back, and we can talk about escape plans and alternative living quarters tomorrow after we've had a good night's sleep and a chance to do some research."

Sami and Nathan took off across the stream and Carla grabbed Tawny and they headed downhill. Megyn fidgeted. "I guess it's you and me," she said to Bret. "Looks like the only place left to go is up the hill."

Bret stepped aside and waved his hand. "You first, ma lady."

Megyn climbed over a fallen tree and stepped between rocks and bushes that looked like poison oak. She spotted a broken branch that she picked up and used for a walking stick. "I love hiking. I always feel like I'm on an adventure." She took a deep breath. "Smell the fresh air? This is what's real. Not the concrete and glass of the city."

Bret picked up a stick for himself and followed along. "This is definitely God's country."

A large boulder overhung the water and Megyn climbed on top. "Let's sit and look at the stream a while. Maybe we'll see fish, or squirrels, or rabbits if we're quiet."

The top of the rock was smaller than she expected and they had to scrunch together to avoid slipping into the water. For a few minutes, neither spoke. Megyn could feel his gentle breathing and her shoulder and neck muscles slowly let go of the tension from her earlier encounter.

Bret played with a couple of small sticks he had picked up. "I hope you don't mind if I ask, but what happened back there."

Megyn tensed. "I felt claustrophobic."

"Is that all?"

"Why do you ask?"

"I felt a presence, something evil." His voice trailed off.

Megyn's breath caught in her throat. "You did? I did too."

He fidgeted some more. "Do you want to tell me about it?"

She heaved a sigh. "I don't like to talk about it."

He waited

She told him about the Ouija board and the disturbing results. She described the two spiritual encounters she'd had with Gisele. She began shaking uncontrollably when she explained what the demon told her in the tunnel.

He put his arm around her shoulders, and sat like that until her body relaxed once again. "What do you think about all this?" he asked.

"I don't want anything to do with it; if that's what you mean."

"I'm talking about spiritual things. Megyn, in general, what do you think?"

"All I know is that I feel afraid when I'm with the Nethers and at peace when I'm with you."

"Have you considered why that is?"

Megyn didn't want to face that question. She didn't want to let God have power over her. She wanted to stay in control. She checked the time, scooted down the side of the rock, and brushed herself off. "Please don't tell anyone what I just told you. I don't want them to think I'm a nut case."

~

Megyn got up at dawn and turned the pump on, took a cool shower and washed her hair. She hummed to herself and dressed in fresh new jeans and a T-shirt. She slipped outside their makeshift rope and tarp changing room, and walked into Bret.

"Oops, sorry." She blushed.

"You seem bright and cheery this morning. How're you doing?"

"Nothing like a shower and clean hair to make a person look at the day with brand new optimism."

He clutched his towel and walked behind the enclosure. "Sami's made coffee, and Tawny has bacon and eggs cooking."

She climbed the short flight of stairs to the porch and found the house teeming with people. Between the computers and screens and meal preparation, there was no room to move. She bundled her dirty clothes, hung her towel over the railing, and sat in the rocking chair on the porch. Sami stepped out and handed her a cup of coffee. "Hmm. Thanks."

She breathed deeply and thought about her situation. Even though her life was already in danger, the idea of exposing such powerful people frightened her to the bone. She had seen firsthand the zealousness with which the Council operated and was confident they would stop at nothing to take them down. Even her father and mother were at risk in this high-stakes power game.

A few minutes later, Bret walked up and leaned against the banister. He sighed. "Well, this is it. Today we jump off the cliff."

She looked up at him. "Just what I was thinking." Her hands shook. "I'm scared. We need to pray."

"After breakfast, when we sit down to work. I don't know if Carla and Tawny will want to join us. They can opt out if they choose," he said. "I've prayed with Sami and Nathan before, so I'm pretty sure they'll be thankful for the opportunity."

"That's fine," Megyn said. "I just know I need it. When you pray, it always calms me down."

"It's not me that helps you relax, you know. It's Christ in me. It's his power. Not mine."

"That's what my grandparents used to say." She took a sip of coffee.

"I've got to get word to our prayer partners to fast for the next few days."

"Fast? As in don't eat?"

"Pretty much. Depending on people's circumstances, fasting can vary. Some give up a meal, sweets, or everything but liquids. People approach it in a variety of ways. Most just don't eat for a meal, a day, or more."

"And this helps them, how?"

"In the Bible, God asks us to fast and pray, and there are many examples of people fasting." He looked out at the landscape. "Even Jesus fasted before he began his ministry. I can't explain it, but along with prayer, it draws us closer to God."

Megyn rocked in her chair. She knew so little about Christianity. She wondered what else Bret did that was weird. Whatever, if it helped protect them from what was coming, she was all for it.

CHAPTER FIFTY-THREE

"**H**ere's what I'm thinking," Nathan said. "We're going to post a series of videos on various Internet sites. The packages should be no longer than five minutes each."

Megyn interrupted. "But—"

Nathan rested his hand on her arm and talked over her. "A five minute vignette is more than most people will listen to online no matter how multi-faceted we make it. Three minutes or under would be even better. It's critical we make our clips short and exciting."

Bret was hanging a burgundy sheet behind the screen for a background that wouldn't give away their whereabouts. "This should be easy for you, Megyn. You're a marketing major."

Megyn stared at her notes. "I hadn't even thought of this in those terms. I've been so focused on getting the information on paper that I've lost the bigger picture perspective." She scooted forward and rubbed her temples. "Let me think a minute. We need an overall message, and each video will include a single point that supports it."

She walked out onto the porch and paced. "I've got it. How about this?" She sat back down and spoke while she typed. "The overall message is that we all want the same thing—to make the world a better place." She concentrated. "What's a good tag line for this?"

Tawny tapped her feet. "How about, 'Our target is the same, but our ammo is different?'"

Bret stopped working. "How about, 'Do to others what you would want them to do to you?' Or a little less biblical sounding approach might be, 'Treat people like you want to be treated.'"

Megyn frowned. "I don't know. Your thinking is sound, but I'm not sure we've found the best phrase yet. It will come to us if we just leave it alone for awhile."

She stared into the monitor. "The first video should visually show where we agree with the V^3—making the world a better place. In this one we'll show people giving to the needy, and working together to accomplish goals. The following videos will include a series of comparisons between the two of us in terms of the process and outcomes.

In their scenarios everyone does the same things. They use the same money. They worship in the exact same way. They treat the environment the same. They eat and drink the same things. They redistribute everyone's resources to those they deem to have more need. They limit speech to what they believe is correct. They punish those that don't follow the rules, that kind of thing."

Nathan massaged Sami's neck muscles. "Our side welcomes different religions, races, and points of views. We don't necessarily agree with everyone, but unless they hurt someone else, they are free to do and think as they please. We encourage people to discover their talents and provide avenues for them to find work and grow as individuals."

Megyn cut him off. "We could go on and on with this, but I'd like us to think about the outcomes of these two approaches. One makes everyone equal, the other wants equal opportunities. I know it's a cliché, but one provides a handout. The other a hand up. One decides on the norms and forces everyone else to follow them. The other encourages diversity and freedom of choice. One leads to bondage and servitude. The other leads to independence and purpose."

Bret finished tying off the last corner of the sheet. "It's like I said before. It's spiritual. We become complete—who God made us to be. We can only do that through freedom. He gave us free will to choose—even if that choice takes us away from him."

"Here's another idea for our tag line," Tawny said. "'Join us and you join yourself.'"

Megyn stretched. "We may be able to do something with that."

Sami twisted her shoulders and stood. "This has been a little heavy. I need a break." She looked around. "Speaking of heavy conversations and breaks, where's Carla?"

Bret walked to the porch and glanced around the yard. "Carla!" He hurried down the stairs and around the side of the house. "Carla? Where are you?"

The others left the house and scanned the area.

"Where can she have gone?" Megyn said.

"Maybe we better search the yard." Tawny said. "When's the last time anyone saw her?"

Sami looked at the shadows of the trees. "Anyone seen her since breakfast? From the looks of the sun, I'd say it's almost lunch time."

Ten minutes later they gathered in the middle of the yard.

"The wig and glasses are gone," Sami said.

Megyn's stomach flipped. "She's walked to town. She keeps saying she wants to get out of here. But I didn't think she'd actually do it."

Bret examined their surroundings. "I think we have to assume we've been compromised, whether she's done it intentionally or not. We need to get everything into the box truck and get out of here."

"I don't have another place for us to go to yet," Tawny said. "We were going to work on that today."

Nathan ran his hands through his dark hair. "There's an old underground military bunker in the desert not more than a forty-five minutes from here. It's been deserted for years. We can hook up our generator and I know I can get a satellite signal from there." He grinned. "I saw it when I first reviewed the area."

"What about hiding the vehicles, potable water, and air circulation?" Tawny said.

"There's a lone metal building that can house the vehicles. I've got supplies that can handle the rest."

Bret headed up the stairs. "Let's get packed up. Fifteen minutes, maximum."

Megyn hesitated. "Suppose she comes back?"

Bret shook his head. "Even if she does, we can't be sure she wasn't compromised. I don't like it either, but we have to leave her behind." He exhaled. "They won't do much to her anyway. It's you and me they really want."

~

Megyn descended three flights of stairs of the old military bunker and entered a large circular open space with five concrete-lined tunnels leading off in different directions. She heard a motor start up and welcomed the fresh air sweeping down from the ceiling vents and across the room. The décor was seventies style, complete with chrome, and orange and green fake leather. She walked around the perimeter and glanced down each tunnel. She found the kitchen stocked with everything needed for cooking meals for large numbers of people, along with canned, bottled, boxed, and bagged food of every kind. There were large barrels of water and jugs of different kinds of juices.

She found several offices, bathrooms with showers, and bunk beds galore. She flipped switches and lights came on, along with various other appliances. She flushed and water ran through the toilets. Showers got hot; toilet paper was plentiful.

She extended her arms and twirled around the big room. "This is wonderful," she said.

"We owe Carla a huge thanks," Sami said.

Nathan hooked up the computer. "Let's not thank her too soon. There may be word of her showing up on one of the Internet sites." He touched the screen several times. "Not yet."

Sami crinkled her forehead. "Maybe nothing happened, and she came back and we were gone."

Megyn walked around the room. "If you were missing for a couple of hours, would you expect that we'd still be there when you came back?" She sighed. "I've been worrying about this since we left. Several things finally dawned on me. None of us would have left without telling the others. And none of us would expect everyone to hang around waiting and wondering."

Sami's eyes moistened. "You're right. It's just hard to believe how people can be so selfish. Didn't she even care about us? Our lives are on the line, or at the very least, our freedom. These are things I'm not ready to part with."

Nathan put his arms around her. "I love you."

She cried into his neck.

Bret, shoulders sagging, stood in the doorway. "Just because there's nothing on the computer about Carla, doesn't mean they aren't looking for us, or already know where we are."

"You're right," Megyn said. "There would be no reason for them to provide us with information about what they know or don't know."

Nathan removed his head from Sami's hair and stepped back. "Let's get to work. The sooner we convince the world we're innocent, the sooner we'll get our lives back."

Bret followed him. "I'm not so sure that's possible. These are people who will never give up."

CHAPTER FIFTY-FOUR

Megyn peeked around the corner and saw Nathan and Bret concentrating on the computer screen in what looked like the control center of the facility. There was a white board that covered one entire wall. "This will be perfect for creating outlines of our key points, and video storyboards," she said to herself.

She noticed two wooden bins full of large rolled up documents sitting in one corner and examined their labels. They were maps of the area, and blueprints of the building and its infrastructure. She unrolled the stack containing facility drawings and found detailed exits, and their locations, in each tunnel. She set them aside and dislodged another set and opened it on the large counter. It held schematics with information on sensors that were located at ten, five, and one mile intervals. She flipped through the pages and found more alarms located closer to the bunker with notes that indicated the buzzer would increase in intensity the closer the intruder would get. She flipped to the final pages and smirked. *Hidden cameras—just like our ACN home. But this time we'll be in control of them.*

Tawny and Sami walked in together, and Megyn handed them a stack of maps and blueprints. "Something to do today."

Tawny examined the drawings and grinned. "We'll be happy to check these out."

Nathan looked up. "Be sure to verify their accuracy and make notes on anything you think we might need to know."

Tawny grabbed Sami by the wrist and pulled her out the door. "See you later," she called from down the hall.

Megyn took a seat next to Nathan and watched him create videos from the storyboard she'd given him. She thought about mankind and how self centered it could be. *There are too many people who think their way is the best way. They disregard others honest thoughts and feelings. They believe they're doing good while undeniably harming others.*

She sighed. *But there are others who genuinely do good things. Like my mother's foundation. They help people help themselves.* She remembered a visual she'd seen on a news commentary show. There were two pictures side by side. One showed people standing in long lines during an economic depression. They were waiting to be fed by the government. Their countenances showed defeat and despair. The other picture showed an automobile manufacturing plant. Partially made cars moved down an assembly line of workers. They looked happy and proud of their accomplishments. The commentator asked the audience, "Which *line* would you rather be in?"

She bolted upright in her seat. "Your Choice."

Nathan swiveled his head. "Huh?"

"I've got it. The tag line." She looked at the guys. "Your Choice." She clapped her hands. "It's *your choice* how to best use your talents to change the world. It's you. Not a team of people who decide for everyone. Look at our government leaders, our corporate leaders, heck, all leaders. Some are good and some are bad. Why would we allow a group of people to dictate what we should say and do? Or when we should say and do it?"

For the rest of the evening, she worked with Nathan to integrate the right words and concepts, and he posted the first three video installments on several social networking sights before they went to bed.

~

It was almost midnight. Megyn hadn't been able to get to sleep and decided to check the responses to their videos. She put on a light green cotton robe she found by the shower area, and shuffled into the office. She pushed the hair out of her eyes and spotted Nathan sitting in front of the monitors intently reading comments. "Anything interesting?"

He jumped and grabbed his chest. "Can you make some noise next time? You about scared me to death."

"Sorry," she whispered. "Do you ever sleep?"

"I only need three to four hours a night which is kind of nice, especially in a situation like this one."

She took a seat next to him and Bret walked in shortly thereafter. "I was awake and heard voices," he said, grabbing a chair.

"What are people saying?"

Nathan scrolled through the comments. "They span the gamut. Some believe everything the V³ has put out about us. They think we're trying to ruin the movement; they hate us. Many comments are angry; some are vulgar.

"Opposing them are mostly people who've been on the other side all along. Many are from the F³ group; remember them? Forces For Freedom? Best I can figure is they've grown in size to at least ten million worldwide. They're supportive and want to hear more from us."

Bret yawned. "We haven't even hit them with the best information yet."

"We took this approach on purpose," Megyn said. "The first three videos were designed to get their attention and build audience. We want the Council to continue feeling that we're scared little children, and they've got the upper hand."

Nathan clicked on one of the F³ home pages.

Megyn leaned closer to the monitor.

"There are a lot of these sites we can look at," Nathan said. "Since the movement is a ground-swell of concerned people from around the world, they are loosely formed around neighborhoods, cities, and states. There's no overall structure, just people who agree coming together to protest."

"Maybe we should help them organize globally," Megyn said.

"Not sure about that. They like their independence," Bret said.

Megyn examined the home page. "Maybe we could create a hub for them to loosely tie together. They could remain independent, yet have more power to influence key areas of agreement as a larger group."

"Not a bad thought," Bret said. "We'll have a better idea of interest once we get a little further along with our own stuff."

Megyn chewed her lower lip.

"What is it?" Bret said. "I can tell something's bothering you."

"I've heard most F³ers are white and Christian?" she said.

"It began that way," Bret said. "But these issues affect everyone, all races and all religions. The current profile of the F³ has expanded dramatically. People from around the world are questioning the coercive methods of the Vanguard."

Megyn thought about how much her thinking had changed. Just a few weeks ago she would have argued with Bret on this point. She sat back and stretched her legs. "I guess I can go back to bed now that I've satisfied my curiosity about reactions to our videos." She yawned. "It's pretty much what I expected, but I'm disappointed anyway."

"I'll keep working on this," Nathan said. "I'll have more pulled together by the time you get up in the morning. Remember, there are many time zones throughout the world. Comments will continue coming in all night and into tomorrow."

Megyn returned to her bunk and closed the door behind her. It was dark and she felt a cold chill. She shivered and noticed her skin dampening with sweat. Her mind became disoriented and she backed against the wall rubbing her arms.

"I'mmm here," the shrill voice mocked. "Yooou can't hide from meee.

"Go away!" she shouted in her mind.

She heard maniacal laughter. "Carlaaa told themmm where you arrrre," the voice taunted. "They'rree commming."

Megyn felt her head spin, fumbled for the door, and collapsed as her hand touched the knob.

~

Megyn rubbed her cheek as she carried a fresh brewed cup of hot coffee into the office and found Nathan asleep on a cot behind the big desk. She tiptoed to the computer and checked the headlines.

> Breaking News: Carla Andrews, Caller number two from this year's Vanguard of Volunteer Voices, was found yesterday just outside the Los Angeles area wearing a long blonde wig and small rectangular glasses. She claimed she was lost and had been traveling for days but could provide no evidence to back up her story. She initially refused to answer questions, but our sources tell us she may have

struck a deal with authorities. A press conference is planned for 8:00 p.m., Eastern time."

Megyn skimmed through three other news sites. All reported the same thing. She sat back and clamped her fingers around the back of her neck with her elbows in the air.

Nathan stirred and turned over.

She keyed in her father's name and got numerous hits ranging from Arthur Buckman, the business tycoon, to Arthur Buckman, the outraged father. She massaged her injured cheek and tears filled her eyes. "I miss you Daddy," she whispered to a picture of them together on her sixteenth birthday. That was the year he'd given her the Silver Mustang. It was the car of her dreams. In it, she could escape her mother's alcoholic episodes. She gently stroked his face.

A news icon on the top right corner began flashing. She touched the screen and gasped. There stood a smiling Carla, arm in arm with Gisele and Ethan. Gisele stepped forward and gazed straight into the camera. Megyn felt Gisele's eyes penetrate deep into her soul and her heart began to race. *She knows where I am. The demons told her.* Fear overwhelmed her, and she pulled her feet and arms into a fetal position. "Help me. Somebody help me," she whimpered.

CHAPTER FIFTY-FIVE

Bret walked in and immediately realized what the problem was. He enveloped Megyn in his arms and led her into a small lounge area down the hall. He rubbed her shoulders until her shaking subsided. He held out a fresh cup of coffee. "Drink this. It'll warm you."

She looked up, dazed, and allowed him to place the warm drink in her hands.

"You had another visit. I can tell."

"It told me Carla turned us in. And then I went into the office and breaking news came on with—"

"I saw them when I came in, Gisele and Ethan with Carla."

"Gisele looked at me. I could swear she could see me. It was creepy and scary. I'm afraid of the night now, of being alone." She started to shake again and her voice dropped. "Gisele prays to them for power, and I believe they give it to her. They'll never leave me alone." She grabbed Bret's hand and pleaded. "Please pray for me."

Bret hung his head. "I'm so mad at myself. We were going to pray back at the shack and got sidetracked trying to get out of there." He squeezed her hand. "I'm so sorry we're just now doing it."

He wrapped his arm around her shoulders. "Dear Lord. We lift up the situation we find ourselves in and ask that you use it to your glory. Let your angels surround us, and the blood of your sacrifice, protect us from those that try to do us harm, either from this world, or another realm."

Megyn's body slowly relaxed and warmth retuned. She snuggled into Bret's embrace and absorbed his words.

"We claim you as Lord of all creation and master of the universe. None can touch us that you do not allow. We rebuke Satan and his minions in the name of Jesus. Amen."

He removed himself from her arms. "Megyn, I need to ask you something. And don't change the subject like you usually do."

Megyn's shoulders tensed.

"What do you believe about God? Do you believe in Jesus as your Savior and Lord?"

"I guess I do. I've been thinking about it a lot lately. I've been fighting him. I haven't wanted to give my life over to him. It's hard for me to trust. I've turned my back on him for so long now; I don't think he'll listen to me anymore."

"That's not true. Of course he listens. He loves you even when you reject him. His love is steadfast and never failing." He scratched the stubble on his cheeks. "You've been thinking about him? What've you been thinking?"

Bret wanted her to look him in the eyes, but instead she was staring at the ground. "I studied John Locke in a philosophy course in college," she said. "His arguments fit my thinking. This is my version of what I remember. I exist and I came into existence somehow. I couldn't have come from nothing, so there had to be something before me. Something that created and organized this complex world I live in. Something greater than myself."

She stopped and looked at Bret. Her vibrant violet eyes and long dark eyelashes melted his heart. He could hear the honesty of a child afraid to trust again, as well as, a young woman ready to put away the past. He wanted to hold her close and comfort her. He wanted her to know the God he knew.

She was still talking. "This fits with some of the things you've said before. I guess those conversations are what've got me thinking."

He could tell she had more to say and nodded encouragement.

"I'm made in his likeness and have his attributes; such as reasoning, love, a sense of right and wrong, truth, and justice," she said. "I appreciate his creation and delight in the colors and design of this world. I know that I'm complete and fulfilled when I function in the way I was designed to function. It's like our founders said in the Declaration of Independence, '"We hold these truths to be self-evident, that all men are created equal, that they are endowed by their Creator with certain unalienable rights, that among these are life, liberty and the pursuit of happiness.' These are part of my core being. I want and need them in order to be complete."

Bret was impressed. "I hadn't thought about that line in a long time. It really fits with our current mission."

Megyn tapped her foot and glanced into his eyes. He blushed and looked away. He knew his feelings for her were growing rapidly. He forced himself to focus on the Lord. That is who she needs. *I need to point her to God, not be her God. My emotions are all jumbled up. I wish I could contact Pastor Sharpe to help me get clarity.*

"That's what I've been thinking about, and yes, I'm officially a believer," she said. "I told Jesus that I accepted him back when I was twelve years old at Christian camp and followed that commitment with baptism. Do I need to do it all again?"

"What do you think? Were those just words and false actions back then?

"I've never really changed my mind. I just got mad at God for a while." She sighed. "I'm embarrassed to admit it, but that's what happened."

He took her hand. "Good. Now, when the evil spirit comes back again, rebuke it to leave you alone in the name of Jesus and by his blood."

She looked startled.

"Here's what I want you to say. I'll write the words down for you later." He paused. "Get behind me Satan. In the name of Jesus Christ, you have no authority here." He thought a moment. "These are similar to the words Jesus used to rebuke Satan's temptations when he fasted and prayed before starting his ministry."

"That will make it go away?"

"You are his, and Satan and his followers have no hold on you. Jesus has given his life for you. You are protected by his sacrifice." He hesitated. "Sometimes Satan's servants are strong. If you have trouble, come get me and we'll pray together. There's a lot at stake in this situation; that's why I've also asked others to fast and pray. Sami and Nathan are believers too. We can always enlist them to help us. Don't be scared."

"But I am."

Bret massaged his neck. "People think God and Satan are equal. They're not. God created Satan, and he can't do anything God doesn't allow him to do. He has powers but nowhere near the mighty power of God." He touched her shoulder. "You have his Holy Spirit living in you. That means God is living in you. He's not some kind of being who sits and watches. He's alive in our lives when we invite him in."

Megyn squeezed his hand. "When I'm with you, I feel strong and confident, but when I'm alone, I become afraid. Especially when it's dark."

Bret wanted to hold her, protect her; but he knew now was not the time. "Did you read the verses I left for you with your father?"

"One night I got spooked and ran from the house. I'd convinced myself that Gisele was coming any minute. I drove for over an hour before reason finally took over. I returned to the laboratory and remembered the verses. I dug the paper, and my Bible, out of my duffle bag. I read them over until I fell asleep."

Bret smiled. "I do the same thing almost every night now, and sometimes during the day too. We've got a lot going on. When I can't sleep I recite verses. When I need direction I check the scriptures. When I need comforting I read the stories of those he has comforted. When I need reassurance, I memorize his promises. Any topic, any need, it's all there. The answers are all there."

Nathan stuck his head in the doorway. "Excuse me. I didn't mean to interrupt."

Megyn grinned. "We're just talking about God."

"That's a good thing to be doing right now. I just posted three more videos, and we've definitely upped the ante."

Megyn and Bret followed Nathan back to the office. They examined the monitors.

Nathan touched the screen. "This just came in. I thought you'd want to see it."

Up popped a video. It showed Gisele in a white knit business suit relaxing in a large gold leather chair in the midst of a paneled library. "I don't want to create more problems than are already out there," she said. "but since the fugitives continue to spread lies and smear good people, I have no other choice but to share this with the public. It breaks my heart to do it, but they have left me no choice. As you can see from the attached video, Bret Steward has been creating doubts about the Vanguard of Volunteer Voices all along."

The scene switched to the Callers sitting in the back room of a restaurant talking about the V³. Bret was questioning the Callers as to who was really leading the Vanguard, and Vince was arguing that it was the youth. The camera moved back to Gisele. "We don't have footage of the entire conversation but—" She extended her hand "—Carla here, tells us that he was persuasive and managed to convince the others that he had better ideas and would be a better leader than the young people of the world."

Megyn pounded her fist into the table. "That's not true!"

Gisele heaved a deep sigh and put her arm around Carla who looked frightened and confused. "As you know, Carla has been with the Callers for the last few days. She's too distraught to talk right now but agreed to stand here as confirmation of what I'm about share."

Gisele smiled and squeezed her closer. "Carla tells us—through tears of grief—that she has been held against her will and forced to live in squalor as the refugees have moved from place to place in an effort to escape capture and prison. She says Bret has mesmerized them all, and Megyn has helped him control their every move. She says he quotes scriptures all the time and claims he is God."

Carla blinked at the camera, placed her hands over her face, and shrank backward.

Gisele held on. "As you can see, she's still afraid of his power to control." She paused for effect. "I just want to let it be known that we will stop at nothing to find the people who have done this to her—" Carla began to sob and Gisele patted her shoulder. "And to the Vanguard of Volunteer Voices."

Bret didn't move. "I have to say, I expected something like this. These people are cold-blooded."

Megyn rose and paced. "That's all you've got to say?" she shrieked. "They say these lies about you and you're not mad?"

He reached and grabbed her arm. "I'm angry all right. But yelling at the computer isn't going to change anything. We need to stay focused and build the graphics we talked about. That's the way we're going to fight back. We'll show the relationships of the Council members and the money. They have their evidence which is comprised of half truths and lies. And we have ours which are undeniable facts."

Megyn wrenched free of his hold and paced some more. "This is hopeless. No matter what we say, they will twist it to mean something else. Based on what I just saw; they probably have video of every conversation we ever had. There's always a way to make our words and actions look like they mean something else."

CHAPTER FIFTY-SIX

Megyn watched Nathan input three condemning videos. The first one identified the Council members and provided their backgrounds. The next showed the new headquarters facilities with graphics of their organizational structure. The third explained the members' relationships based on business dealings, including their individual stakes in the Vanguard and the millions that had flowed into their personal bank accounts from V³ activities. The viewers were encouraged to continue to check in to learn more.

She leaned back and closed her eyes. "I know we need to keep working but I feel like we're beating our heads against a wall. Every time I think we're making headway, they counter with something else. I don't see an end to this." She sighed. "It's like ping-pong. We say something; they respond; they say something; we respond, and so on."

Nathan patted her arm. "I've been working on a little project I was hoping to surprise you with later. Since you're so down, I'll share it now."

Megyn straightened.

Nathan touched the screen several times and a grainy video appeared. It was footage of the roll-out rally Megyn had attended in Singapore.

Her eyes grew big and a grin formed across her face. "Do you have the whole thing? All four days?"

"Yep. I received this a couple of days ago and have been trying to clean and edit it ever since. The person who took it is not a professional and was using a cheap video recorder." He shrugged. "The light and sound aren't too good either."

Megyn kissed his cheek. "How long to get this ready?"

"I think I've got the sound, pixel, and lighting problems just about handled. The copy won't be perfect, but at least a person will be able to watch it without subtitles." He smiled. "I figure we can post a long version along with a couple of shorter editions. Viewers can choose which ones they want to watch."

He punched Megyn's arm. "I'll need you to help me identify the people and provide any other information you think the viewers will need."

Megyn was feeling better. She was ready to quit fighting God and, with his help, take on the real threat to her independence.

~

The five refugees sat around one of the tables eating a dinner consisting of canned roast beef, canned green beans, canned peaches, and drop biscuits from a just-add-water mix. They drank apple juice.

Megyn listened as Tawny and Sami replayed their day of bunker exploration. Her mind wandered and she smiled to herself when she thought of Gisele's impending fury when she saw the footage of her own words contradicting her phony accusations.

Peace washed over her at the thought of a good night's sleep and the genuine possibility of vindication. She couldn't wait to reunite with her parents and get her life back. She would work with her mother's foundation and continue making the world a better place—only this time in ways that would empower others and be sustainable into the future.

Her attention bounced back to Tawny who was explaining that she didn't know how long they would be able to stay in the bunker. "We found a log book that shows this place is inspected once a month. The prior entries were all done on the first Monday of each month. That means we have two and a half weeks before someone shows up. It looks like they inspect this entire facility; top to bottom. There's a checklist they follow." She held the binder up for them to see.

Everyone moaned.

"I like it here," Megyn said.

"We all do," Sami said. "The good news? We found the inspection rotation list of a number of other abandoned military sites." She laid the list on the table. "We can set up our own rotation schedule."

Tawny pointed to the numbers she'd written next to each site's name and location. "We can move in this order. At least we'll have places to go, and hopefully this will all be over before we have to visit too many of them, if any."

Bret stood, stretched and touched his toes. "Good work girls. This is really useful stuff."

Nathan told the group about the video he'd managed to obtain and their plans for making it available.

The refugees celebrated their day and decided to watch a couple of old Seinfeld shows from the Internet. Megyn sat next to Tawny and Bret was across the room. She watched him from the corner of her eye and wished they were cuddled up holding hands. When she went to bed she was sure she would sleep.

~

Megyn stood in the hallway, tapping on the door and shuffling from one foot to the other. Bret didn't answer so she walked in and shook him by the shoulder. He rolled over, took one look at her face, and popped out of bed. She was numb and shaking and collapsed into his arms. She felt his hand in hers and the warmth of the blanket he wrapped around her shoulders.

"Sit here and I'll pray," she heard him say.

Ten minutes later she was asleep in the bunk across from his.

~

Bret walked into the office and found Nathan in front of the computer. He rotated his neck and shoulders and took a seat.

Nathan glanced over. "Having trouble sleeping?"

"We need a lot of prayer right now." Bret said. "Is there a way I can reach Pastor Sharpe and the prayer chain to get them to fast for the next few days?"

Nathan shook his head. "Not safely. I'm sure they've tapped into his technology by now. How about we drop a few prayer bombs into different Christian groups? The opposition won't be expecting this, so we should be able to get in and out without detection. We can even tell them it's us asking."

Bret got up and patted Nathan's shoulder. "Thanks, bro. I don't know what we'd do without you."

He walked down the hallway to an empty room lined with bunks. He sat on the side of one of the beds and thought of Megyn's soft breathing and her trust in God's promises. He slid off the side, crumbled to the floor, placed his head in his hands, and lay prostrate before the Lord. "I'm just a man; a man seeking to do your will. I'm not perfect . . . but you are. Please let me speak your words, know your heart, and understand your will. Give me your wisdom and knowledge for each situation. Correct me when I'm wrong, and hold me up when I falter.

"Lord, I need your help with my growing feelings for Megyn. I think I know my feelings but I'm concerned about hers. I don't want her to look to me instead of you. I want the relationship to be centered around you and to progress in your timing.

"I need you. I love you. I call upon your name—the name above all names—the mighty and powerful name of Jesus. In your name, every knee will bow, both in heaven and on the earth. I lift you up. I praise you. I thank you. I worship you."

~

Megyn exited Bret's room and headed down the hall. She whispered a quiet thank you to God for answered prayer and a good night's rest. She stopped by the office and found Nathan asleep in his cot. She wondered how late he'd been up. She yawned and headed to the kitchen for coffee. The building blueprints were on the table from the night before, and she looked them over while she waited for the coffee to brew.

Sami shuffled in, checked the pot, and joined her. She sighed. "Sure wish we could stay here."

"Are the other bunkers as well equipped and safe as this one?"

"Not all," Sami said. "Tawny marked the best ones. Apparently the government keeps them in usable condition in case there's an emergency and they have a need to shelter groups of people."

The coffee was ready. Megyn filled their cups and handed one to Sami. "This certainly qualifies as an emergency, and we certainly needed shelter. Let's go see if Nathan's up yet."

When they heard voices from the office area, Megyn grabbed the pot and Sami snagged a couple of mugs. They entered to find Nathan and Bret intently reading the content of two of the monitors.

"I've brought coffee," Megyn said, holding up the pot.

"And I've got cups," Sami said.

Nathan turned and gave Sami a big kiss. "Hi beautiful."

Megyn smiled and poked Nathan. "What's up?"

"Our last three videos on the Council are getting millions of hits, and the symposium from Singapore has gone viral. People are outraged and many feel duped." Nathan smiled, sat back in his chair, and took a sip of coffee. "The Nethers' have countered this video by saying, I'm one of the best technology experts in the world and have taken their words out of context and edited them, making it sound like they are saying things they never said."

Megyn looked over his shoulder at the monitor. "How're people responding?"

"Believe it or not," Nathan said, "a lot of people believe them in spite of the evidence on the video."

Tawny walked in with a mug in her hand. "So here's the party."

Bret tapped the counter.

Everyone grew quiet and waited.

"A lot's happened in the last couple of weeks," Bret said pointing at the monitor. "We're in a heap of trouble. I've got millions of people praying around the globe and it's not enough." He cleared his throat and turned and looked at each of them. "We're not praying as a group. We need to pray together—and fast."

Tawny inched toward the door. "You know I don't believe in God."

"Bret held out his open hands. "I know, but I feel strongly that we need to do this. The others are all believers. I don't want you to feel like we're an exclusive club, or that we're leaving you out. You're a vital part of our group. You're welcome to join us and not say a word, or not be involved at all," he smiled. "It's *your choice*."

Tawny hesitated.

Megyn fidgeted with the mug in her hands. She knew how Tawny felt. Just a few weeks ago, when Bret first asked her to pray, she'd felt uncomfortable too. "I didn't know Bret was going to suggest this, but I agree with him. We're in deep trouble. We need to pray and fast as a group." She put her arm around Tawny. "If you don't want to, you don't have to. You're still one of us."

Sami got on Tawny's other side and put her arm around her. Tawny wiggled a little, but the other two held on, smiling conspiratorially at each other. Tawny's movements increased and the three girls started to topple and couldn't get their balance. They swayed one way and then the other. They laughed as they hit the floor and landed in a heap with Megyn and Sami still holding on.

Nathan and Bret just looked down and shook their heads.

"How about right now?" Bret said. "Tawny?"

"I'll stick around. But don't expect me to pray. I just want to know what's going on."

Megyn looked at the group. "Let's hold hands. I'm scared and need the support."

They stood in a circle with Tawny positioning herself between Megyn and Sami.

"Dear Lord," Megyn began. "We feel overwhelmed with the situation. It seems like we're losing ground with our arguments. No matter how much compelling evidence we show the world, many still choose to believe our opponents' lies."

"We look to you for guidance," Bret interjected. "We look to you for wisdom. We look to you for power to overcome the evil one."

Nathan cleared his throat. "Give us wisdom beyond our abilities. Give us mercy from our adversaries."

"Help us," Sami said. "Please. Help us."

Megyn groaned. "We need a miracle. We need your power. We need you to show yourself to the world. We need you."

"Hallelujah," Bret said. "Amen."

"Amen," they all repeated.

Megyn felt comforted.

CHAPTER FIFTY-SEVEN

Megyn sat alongside Nathan reading comments from all over the world while he completed the next three videos to go on-line at the end of the day. She crinkled her forehead and sat back. "We provide all this real evidence, and still people don't believe us. I thought the stuff from the Singapore event would turn the tide, but people believe what they want to believe."

Nathan got up. "I've finished these." He stretched. "I'm taking a break. Look them over while I'm gone and let me know what you think. I'll be down in the kitchen if you need me."

Megyn waved a silent good-bye and opened the file. Three more fact-packed videos indicting the Council members, and particularly the Nethers. She shook her head. *The content is perfect, but will enough people believe it?*

The top right corner of the screen flashed, and she reached up and touched the news alert icon. Her parents were being escorted out the front doors of the Buckman Medical Instruments headquarters building by local police. She gasped, pushed back her chair, and stood, leaning over the monitor with her clenched fists resting on the desk.

The screen split into two boxes and a reporter proclaimed, "Arthur and Elizabeth Buckman are being taken in for questioning today in connection with the missing millions of V³ money, the death of Vince Jackson, and the whereabouts of their daughter and her comrades." Megyn followed the live feed of her mom and dad stepping into the back seat of a squad car.

The police vehicle drove away and the video was replaced with a live shot of hundreds of protesters picketing the BMI facilities. The camera zoomed in on a couple of signs, and the reporter on scene talked about the ongoing environmental concerns voiced by the Vanguarders. The final shot showed a young man with a bullhorn leading the group and shouting, "Down with greedy corporations." Megyn thought she recognized the face and bent closer to get a better look. It was Paul, Caller four, from season two.

Megyn barely heard Bret enter. She shushed him before he could speak and pointed to the computer. He fell into the chair next to hers and scooted forward to get a better look.

The reporter stepped in for a close-up as the car was shown pulling away. "This is highly unusual. Big corporate business executives with the kind of wealth and high-priced attorneys like the Buckmans have, are never escorted to the police station. They have the money to pay their way out of any situation. We're expecting a statement from their lawyers in the next ten minutes. Please stand by."

The scene switched back to the studio news anchors, filling the time with film and pictures of her parents and herself. They recounted the Vanguard of Volunteer Voices side of the story and never mentioned the videos, or other evidence, Megyn and her friends had worked so hard to generate and disseminate.

She slapped the table. "Don't they see what's going on here? Or do they even care?" She paced the floor and watched the screen. "The Council is taking everything from Vanguarders; their money, their time, and their future. And they're redistributing it to themselves and their cronies. A couple of them really believe they're creating a utopia that will take care of everyone equally. But most of the members are simply after the power it will bring them and their friends. They're already multi-millionaires and billionaires and are getting richer by the day."

Bret scrunched his forehead. "Your parents would never have allowed themselves to be taken in by the police like that if they hadn't wanted to. Their attorneys could have easily worked a way around such a public display." He gestured for her to sit. "Let's wait and see what they have to say."

Megyn continued to stand, leaning with one hand on the table, and watching the attorneys advance to the row of microphones that had been placed in front of the BMI headquarters' sign. She recognized Mitchell McKinsey, her father's lead attorney.

He cleared his throat to quiet the reporters. "I have a short statement to read and will not be answering questions." He examined his notes. "Today, Elizabeth and Arthur Buckman were taken to the Los Angeles police department for questioning on several matters relating to recent events having to do with the Vanguard of Volunteer Voices. They have not been charged with anything and will cooperate completely with authorities." He folded his paper, turned and walked away holding up his hand in a gesture to stave off the barrage of questions from the media.

Bret rubbed his chin. "I wonder what your dad's up to."

Megyn wrinkled her forehead. "Why do you say that?"

"I think he wants a public forum. He's pushing back." He watched the anchors who were giddy with excitement and massaged his wrist. "Maybe we need to do the same thing."

"What are you talking about?"

"Go public. Set up a broadcast, tell our story, and present our evidence." He swung his chair around. "Push back. Like your parents are."

Nathan and Sami came into the room with Tawny following close behind. Megyn pointed them to the breaking news.

"The Buckmans are providing the perfect atmosphere for us to take our case to the people live," Bret said. "We prayed for God to guide us and help us. I think he's guiding us through the actions of Megyn's parents. We should plan a broadcast where we tell our point of view and share our evidence."

Megyn stood next to him. "When Bret first mentioned this a minute ago, I wasn't so sure, but now that I've had a little time to think about it, I agree with him. We can hype this everywhere and generate a much bigger audience than we have currently reached with our short videos. Look at these anchors on TV. They're almost salivating with anticipation. We can get them to do the same thing for us." She placed her hand on the back of Bret's chair. "We can also set up short teasers that will entice viewers to want to watch."

Bret got more excited. "My prayer support team has been encouraging me since I've been with the V³ by quoting God's words to his people through Moses in the Old Testament. I believe this is what God is telling us. He's telling us to 'Be strong and courageous. Do not be afraid or terrified because of them, for the Lord your God goes with you; he will never leave you nor forsake you.'"

Megyn stepped forward. "Amen," she said.

"Amen," everyone laughed.

Nathan smiled. "Broadcasting this live will be a challenge."

Megyn and Bret nodded.

"Do you want to allow for Q and A?"

"If you can do it," Megyn said.

"The more interactive, the better," Bret said.

"This is a big step," Sami said. "We should include this in our prayer time tonight. We don't want to blow this opportunity. We need to ask for God's leading."

Tawny smiled. "I think the whole thing is a great idea."

Nathan rubbed his fingers together. "We'll want to broadcast from several sites at the same time, and we definitely won't want to be traced. Do you have a day in mind?"

Bret looked at Megyn. "Two days?"

"How about a week?" she said. That will give us plenty of time to hype and tease and build audience."

"A week it is," Nathan said.

Megyn clapped her hands together. "Everyone should contribute. Make lists of what you would like to cover, see someone else talk about, or evidence you want shared. We should all be involved."

~

Megyn sat at the kitchen table and thought about what she needed to do over the next week. Nathan had insisted the broadcast be no longer than twenty minutes for presentations with fifteen for questions and answers, and she had agreed. "We need to be concise, our points clear," she repeated to herself.

They would also make a complete set of videotapes available to support their statements. That meant creating six more recordings, bringing their total library of communications to fifteen vignettes and three various sized copies of the Singapore rally. "Viewers will be able to evaluate the facts for themselves," Megyn whispered as she checked her list of things to do.

Bret wandered in and sat down across the table. "Going over your lists?"

She took a deep breath. "This will be the most important day of our lives. It could mean prison, or even death, if we fail."

Without thinking she took his hands in hers, bowed her head, and spoke what was on her heart. "Dear Lord. We place our lives and our days in your hands. We ask that your Holy Spirit move across the continents and bring healing and renewal to all mankind. We want your message to be our message. If what we're planning is not in your will, we ask that you intervene, and that your will be done above all others. Amen."

She released his hands and looked embarrassed. She stammered. "I was thinking about God and feeling I should talk with him." She stared into the distance. "I guess I was kind of overcome with a need to pray."

Bret raised his eyebrows. "I'm going to fast for the next week. Join me?"

"No food?"

"A liquid fast. Liquids only."

She tapped her pen on the paper. "And this will help me grow closer to God?"

He nodded.

"I'm scared to death. I can't make it past lunch without eating." She heaved a big sigh. "Okay. I need him to get me through this."

CHAPTER FIFTY-EIGHT

The burgundy sheet draped the back wall. Four chairs covered with taupe colored sheets were placed in front of it. Nathan rigged lights to create a studio look and set several cameras and microphones around to pick up everything the Callers would say or do.

Megyn watched him move around his stage, fine tuning his handiwork. She smiled. "Nervous?"

He fidgeted with one of the lights. "There's so much at stake." He bent over to adjust a sheet. "Remember. Your entire presentation is timed to the video that will run alongside your comments." He moved back and examined the scene again. "Everyone has to stay on schedule. We start and end exactly on the times I gave you."

She touched his shoulder; her hands shaking. "We'll be fine."

Sami stood in the corner with her arms wrapped around herself. "I can hardly breathe."

Tawny shook her limbs and rotated them in the air. "I feel sick. I can't wait until this is over."

Bret walked in and looked at the clock. "Seven minutes till show time. Let's take our seats and pray one last time before we go live. We truly need God's intervention, and it will help calm our nerves."

Megyn sat down in the lead chair and took a deep breath. She gripped Bret's hand and lowered her head.

Bret looked down the row of chairs. "How about we start at the end and work this way? Sami, Tawny, me, and then Megyn can close." He looked at Tawny. "You okay with this?"

"I feel like the army guy in the fox hole. I'm afraid for my life and ready to seek a higher power." She shivered. "I'll say something."

Nathan yelled from behind the panel of controls. "Watch the clock."

Sami began. "Dear Jesus. Please be with us today. We're afraid and need your intervention. Help us to stay on script and get our messages across." She squeezed Tawny's hand.

Tawny cleared her throat. "Please be with the audience and let them open their minds and listen to the things we're telling them." She started to shake. Sami and Bret put their arms around her shoulders. "Thank you for the friends you've given me." She pressed Bret's arm.

He leaned forward. "We come before you Lord, with hearts full of fear and concern. We don't know what the future will bring, but we know you are in control. We seek your will, your strength, your wisdom, and your peace." He squeezed Megyn's hand.

Nathan hollered, "One minute, folks."

Megyn had fasted all week and suddenly felt a peace that spread throughout her body and surpassed her ability to understand. The atmosphere took on a warm glow and a strong wind swept around the room and surrounded them. Her soul yearned with desire for the presence of God and the warmth grew and spread and filled her with a fire from above.

Nathan pointed his finger and called out, "Five, four, three, two, one, go."

She didn't hear him, or see the video playing across the screen. "Dear Lord. We've strayed so far from you. We've been selfish and arrogant. We've wanted what we've wanted when we've wanted it. We strive to help others, but do we truly seek what you would have for them? No. We think we know better."

"Yes, Lord," Sami whispered.

Megyn continued. "We act before we seek you; the one who planned for us, formed us in your image, and knows us completely."

Bret jumped in. "Yes, Jesus. We look for love, for peace, for independence, and for purpose. We strive and work and demand. And we turn our backs on the true giver of love, and peace, and independence, and purpose."

"Forgive me, Jesus," Tawny moaned.

Nathan's make-shift spotlights suddenly went out, but the room shone brighter than before.

Megyn trembled and fell to her knees. "We come before you with contrite hearts and give ourselves to you completely. We ask you to kindle and grow the fresh wind and fire of your Holy Spirit across the continents and around the globe—in the days, and weeks, and years, to come."

Bret raised his hands towards the heavens. "Holy, holy, holy is the Lord God Almighty. Who was, and is, and is to come."

The girls extended their arms. "Holy, holy, holy is the Lord God Almighty. Who was, and is, and is to come."

They all said. "Holy, holy, holy is the Lord God Almighty. Who was, and is, and is to come."

"Hallelujah," they said as one.

"Come quickly, Lord Jesus," Bret said.

"Yes," Megyn whispered. "Come quickly."

The room fell silent.

The cameras clicked off and the bright light paled slightly.

Megyn was disoriented. She looked around and noticed the other Callers doing the same. She walked to the screen. It showed a list of links to their resources; and new instructions for their viewers were scrolling across the monitor as quickly as Nathan could type them in.

Nathan walked from behind the control panel. He put his hands on his hips and grinned from ear to ear. "Wow!" he said. "I think that's what's referred to as a revival, or an awakening. I never thought I'd be a part of one."

Megyn stared at him. "What are you talking about?"

Nathan punched her shoulder. "You guys prayed through the whole thing."

"We couldn't have," Megyn said. "We only prayed for a couple of minutes."

Nathan shook his head. "Fraid not. God came down in the form of the Holy Spirit, took over, and used up the entire time. You went live with your prayer."

Everyone was silent.

Nathan pointed to the spotlights. "Look, they're out. The room is still bright with his glory. I'm telling you, God showed up today and used you guys to spread his message of true transformation and purpose."

Bret moved to the monitors. "What are people saying?"

Nathan fell into his chair and scrolled through the comments. "Messages from all over the world are rushing in. Many are dazed and confused. Some accuse us of trying to pull a stunt. Others claim to have been overcome and are giving up drugs, alcohol, sex, food, and other vices. They want to know what has happened to them. They want to know more about God."

Megyn watched her friends. They were peaceful and joyful and had a glow about them. They looked like what she imagined someone would look like if they had been in the presence of God.

Nathan pulled up another screen. "The broadcast is already going viral. People are publishing it on their own sites and sending it to their friends."

Bret took over a second computer. He whistled. "A lot of people were touched. Could be in the millions." He grinned. "We've got a ton of work ahead of us."

Megyn leaned back and braced herself on the counter. "We need help to handle this kind of volume."

~

Gisele stood over Mary in the media room. She pounded her fist on the desk and swore. "What are they trying to pull? They're not going to get away with this."

Mary shook her head. "Millions are responding to them. We've suffered a big blow. I don't know how we're going to win these people back."

Gisele shoved a random monitor from its desk and it slid across the floor. "I won't have this. They will pay. Find them." She turned and slammed out of the room.

Mary continued reading the posts. She wiped sweat from her forehead. *The tide is definitely turning against us.*

ABOUT THE AUTHOR

Johnna Howell has worked in leadership roles in global organizations, provided consulting services to Fortune 500 executives, and seen firsthand, the strangle hold that money and power bring to those who give in to their influence. She holds a graduate degree from the University of San Francisco and cherishes the lessons gleaned from over six decades of real life experiences.

In a world searching for purpose and meaning, Johnna has dedicated her retirement years to encouraging today's young people to step up and take a stand—to realize their potential in Christ, his mighty power, and his perfect will for each of our lives.

She, and her husband, live in California's Central Valley with their children and grandchildren nearby. Visit her at www.JohnnaHowell.com

Made in the USA
San Bernardino, CA
15 October 2013